In Paris

R.J. Groves

Copyright © 2018 by R.J. Groves
Edited by Graham Toseland
ISBN: 978 0 6452675 0 1
Groves Publishing
Formats available: eBook, Paperback

This is a work of fiction. Names, characters, businesses, places, events and incidents are products of the author's imagination. Any resemblance to actual persons, living or dead, or actual events is purely coincidental.

About the author

Australian author R.J. Groves has been passionate about writing since she could put pen to paper and can usually be found jotting plots and stories down on anything she can get her hands on. Describing herself as a mum, wife, author, and coffee lover, her other passions include music, cooking, books, adventures, and searching for plot bunnies in even the most mundane activities.

Facebook: facebook.com/rjgauthor
Instagram: instagram.com/r.j.groves_author
Twitter: twitter.com/rjg_author
Website: www.rjgrovesauthor.com

Books by R. J. Groves

The Bridal Shop series
Save the Date
Be My Valentine
Say You'll Be Mine

Jilted Brides series
Finding a Bride
Written in the Sand

Cities of the World series
In Paris
The Irish Maiden

Set Ups series
The Set Up

Mail Order Brides series
The Calm in the Storm

The Warmth in the Winter
The Song in the Silence

Standalones
Writing You
Two Babies Too Many
Second Chance
The Boyfriend Application
Sweeter Things
Home Bound
Stay With Me
Her First Noel
When Dreams Come True
To Fall For You

To MGFA for never giving up on me.

In Paris

R.J. Groves

Prologue

Small footsteps thudded through a secret garden, hidden behind two houses in Leeds.

'Eddie!' A small voice called out. 'Eddie, where are you?'

Olivia found the place near the brook where she and Eddie usually met. Sometimes, they would be there for only a moment. Other times, they would be there for hours. They hardly ever got in trouble for it. His parents never noticed that he was gone, her parents were never home to notice, and Nanny Mel always preferred that Olivia entertained herself.

She sat down on the familiar large rock at the edge of the brook and straightened her blue skirt, tracing her fingers along the pale-yellow lace trimming. Eddie would come—she knew he would.

Before too long, there was a rustle in the bushes behind her and a cheeky face, framed with a mop of dark-brown hair, popped into view. She jumped up to hug her friend.

'Oh, Eddie!' she said.

'Hello, Livvy,' he said as they both returned to the rock.

They talked for what seemed like hours. She told him about her ideas for new tricks to play on Nanny Mel when she wouldn't expect it. Eddie told her of how his dad hadn't been home for weeks and how his mam didn't seem well. She knew that Eddie's dad beat him and his mam whenever he was home—she once made him tell her why he always had fresh bruises whenever his dad was home. At first, she thought that he had another friend who he would go on adventures with, but the bruises looked too big. Besides, they were best friends and spent all of their free time together, so there was never any time for other friends. But that never bothered them—they were okay as long as they had each other.

'I wish I could come on holiday with you,' Eddie said.

Now laying on the rock, they both let out a sigh. Even at twelve years old, they knew what was going on around them—they knew what plans they wanted to follow through with.

'One day, Eddie, we'll go on the longest holiday ever! Just you and me.'

'Where will we go?'

'To Paris.'

***

After being in Scarborough with her parents for three weeks, Olivia couldn't wait to tell Eddie all about her holiday. She stared out of the car window, seeing the familiar trees and buildings as they neared their home. She was so excited to tell Eddie everything, that she didn't notice the removal van outside of his house. As soon as their car had stopped in their driveway, Olivia jumped out and ran to her best friend.

'Eddie! You have to go to Scarborough, Eddie—it was so wonderful! There was so much to see and do and there's a castle there too! Well, some of it—it's really old and damaged but—'

Olivia paused when she realised that Eddie seemed sad. Her eyes followed his mam directing two strong men carrying heavy boxes to the van that was already half-filled—the most recent box labelled *Eddie's things*.

'Eddie,' she said. 'What's happening? Why are they taking your stuff?'

In her heart, she knew the answer but wished it wasn't so.

'We're moving, Livvy,' he said, pulling his crumpled sleeve down to cover a fresh purple bruise on his arm. 'To London.'

'But, why?' She felt hot tears prickling her eyes.

Eddie watched his mam follow the men back inside and he leaned in close to Olivia.

'Dad came back while you were gone, Livvy,' he whispered. 'He was worse than before—hurt Mam bad. She was even in hospital for a few days. Then, he left again. So, Mam said that we're moving before he comes back. Gonna live with my uncle for a while, I think.'

They heard Eddie's mam call for him to help with the boxes and he headed towards the house.

'I'm sorry, Livvy,' he said.

'Will I ever see you again?'

'Of course.'

'Where?' A tear finally fell from her eye.

'In Paris.' He grinned, then turned away for the last time.

Chapter 1

'Olivia? Can you do that for me?'

Olivia snapped out of the haze of daydreams and memories that drifted through her head and looked at her frazzled friend. Vanessa's short, brown hair was standing up in an unbrushed mess as she rushed to find lunchboxes and missing shoes. Olivia hated losing focus on her friend's stressed conversations—she usually ended up agreeing to more than she would prefer.

'Do what?' she asked.

'Liv!' Vanessa moaned. 'Can you please mind the kids after school? My boss is having me chase my tail for that promotion—I won't be able to get to them on time.'

Olivia thought for a moment—she loved her

godchildren and enjoyed spoiling them, but, lately, she'd been minding them for a lot longer than the usual hour or two at a time.

'Liv?' Vanessa was desperate.

'Sorry! Yes, all right, I'll mind them. But promise me that you'll be back for tea—I have plans.'

Vanessa looked relieved and hugged Olivia as though she was a lifesaver.

'I promise!' she said. 'Oh, thank you so much!'

Olivia helped her friend find the last missing shoe, handed her a brush, and hugged her godchildren before telling Vanessa that she had to go.

'I almost forgot,' said Vanessa. 'How's your new man?'

'Antoine?' Olivia blushed. 'He's fine—but he's not really my 'man'.'

'You've been dating for a month, right? I'm pretty sure that means he's your man.'

Olivia said her goodbyes and headed to her favourite patisserie whose name had always changed, but the food and people stayed the same. She had never really thought about where she stood with Antoine—she liked him, and they'd always enjoyed each other's company. They *had* been dating for a month, but there had never been a discussion or anything to indicate that they were actually *in* an exclusive relationship.

Since she left Leeds and moved to Paris, she had never been in a relationship. She had dated—a lot— but for never more than one or two dates. One date only lasted ten minutes before she called it short.

She had met all kinds of men—from nice men, to jerks, to men who couldn't possibly maintain a relationship with anyone. Antoine, on the other hand, was different. She enjoyed their time together and liked his touch. They saw each other most days, but they weren't always dates. Sometimes, they would just be time spent in each other's presence.

'*Bonjour*, Olivia,' the familiar waitress said to her.

'*Bonjour*, Marie—you're looking well. What's the name of this marvellous place now?'

'*Michelle's Fameux Patisserie*,' Marie said with a smile. 'They say this name is for good.'

Olivia ordered an espresso and a slice of berry tart and looked over at her usual table in the corner—Antoine was there in all of his dark-blonde hair, blue-eyed glory. They exchanged smiles and she headed towards him. One day, she would ask him where they stood. But for now, she would enjoy what they had.

***

Scott ran his worn, calloused fingers through his grimy dark-brown hair as he examined the plans of the building they had been working on. *Why weren't the measurements adding up?* He shook his head—Jack had got the figures all wrong and now they were presented with the potential dilemma of a particular room being too large. Before too long, their boss would find out, and he wouldn't be happy. He felt for Jack—he was a hard worker and a good colleague, but often made careless errors that could cost him his job and potentially others too. He racked his brain for a resolution for the issue—how could someone, *anyone*, stuff up a measurement by so much? He rolled up the building plans and walked to where the other builders had gathered around to insult Jack for his mistake.

'*Imbecile*! I'll lose my job over this!' one of the other builders yelled.

'*Calme-toi*, mate,' Scott said, defending his apprentice. 'It's not your fault. No one will lose their jobs—as long as it gets fixed before the boss finds out.'

Scott proceeded to announce his plans on fixing the situation. Since it wasn't yet permanent, it was still fixable—and, *hopefully,* his boss wouldn't notice. He liked Jack—he liked all of his builders—and he didn't want anyone to get in trouble for anything. Ultimately, it came down to him. He trusted that Jack got the figures right. He knew that he should have double-checked them, but he was proud of the confidence that Jack had in himself. Well, he knew better for next time—and hopefully Jack learnt something too.

After what seemed like hours, it all looked as it should and the boss would never need to know about the mishaps of the day. He checked his watch and sighed—time to go home. Just as he expected, the boss came to do his end-of-the-day check and found nothing wrong. Jack had gotten away with it this time, but he had to sharpen up.

Packing up all of his work gear and nodding his goodbyes to his colleagues, Scott paused for a moment to observe the people walking past. Out of all the places he had lived, he loved Paris the most— he knew that he would. He loved the views, the people, the coffee, the environment, everything. The only thing he didn't like was that he was there alone—but, hopefully, that would change soon. After all, he did have a date tonight. Maybe he would connect with this one.

While he was driving home, he thought about how he had managed to get to where he was now. As a child, he never would have thought that he would be the project manager of a building site, or even in Paris. But now, at twenty-seven years old, anything seemed possible. He saw the traffic light ahead turn red and slowed his car down. He didn't mind waiting at traffic lights—it was another chance to watch people just passing by.

When he saw her, his heart skipped a beat. He didn't know why, and he didn't even notice that, for a moment, he stopped breathing, and all time seemed to slow down. She was like a goddess. Her long, golden locks that were pinned to one side bounced against her shoulders as she strutted across the road. Her blue floral dress draped lightly over her slim body, trailing behind her in the breeze. He watched her in awe as she reached the other side of the road and walked up the pavement as though she did it on a regular basis before she disappeared around the corner.

Scott was jostled out of his trance by the loud toot of a car horn and realised that the light was green. Continuing to drive home to get ready for his date, his mind was hazy and filled with thoughts of the beautiful goddess. She hadn't seen him, but he had seen her.

***

Scott looked all around him. He had brought his date to an Italian inspired restaurant that his boss recommended—and it was, indeed, nice. The atmosphere was warm, intimate, and pleasant, and the tables and chairs were close enough to accommodate a lot of people, but not so close that you can hear the conversation of the people next to you. There was a large fish tank with many exotic fish that shone with brilliant colours and swam patterns around the tank. Soothing classical music played quietly in the background and the food was delectable. Yes, he would come here again.

Usually, he didn't take recommendations from his boss, but this time, he was glad that he had. He always thought that his boss seemed a bit suspicious. He was usually a nice guy if he was in a good mood, but, once something went wrong, he could be a real hot-head. That was why he didn't want his boss to find out about the mishaps at work—he had seen the boss unleash his fury on the previous project manager when something went wrong. Scott would have jumped in to try and calm him down if another worker hadn't beaten him to it. Needless to say, neither of them ever returned back to work and Scott was promoted to be the new project manager.

Since that day, Scott and all the other builders stayed extra wary and extra cautious of everything that they did in an attempt to avoid another conflict with the boss. So far, they had remained successful, but today, it came too close—way too close. Jack, having worked there for only a few months, still didn't seem to comprehend how much of a hot-head their boss could be. Apprentice or not, the results would still be the same. Thankfully, Scott got to it first.

He gathered his thoughts and tried to concentrate on his dinner companion, Melissa, who perhaps was a bit more excited than she should have been. Since they sat down at the table, she had not stopped talking. She talked about her family, her cats, her hometown, her cats, her whole life story and, oh, her cats. How had he managed to get into this?

'So, Jack told me that you're the project manager of the building he's working on and that you saved the day.' She fluttered her eyes at Scott while she spoke.

Oh, that's right—she was Jack's cousin. Why had he agreed to come on this date? He nodded his response and she smiled at him and continued talking, twirling her auburn hair between her fingers. Admittedly, she was pretty and pleasing to look at, but he just couldn't stand her—or her cats. He wished the date was over and he wouldn't have to see her again.

Right at that moment, the door of the restaurant opened, and a familiar man walked in, accompanied by a brown-haired, nicely dressed lady. Scott didn't know what he should do in this situation—it had definitely become more awkward than he anticipated his evening would be. If it was a friend of his, he would have no hesitation in calling him over for a chat. But his boss—the very man who recommended the restaurant to him—was a different matter. He preferred to keep his distance from him wherever possible.

Despite trying to hide from view, his boss still saw him and brought his date over.

'Hello, Scott,' he said. 'I see you took my recommendations. What do you think of this place?'

'It's definitely a good one, boss.' Scott now wished he had decided to take Melissa somewhere else.

To Scott's surprise and embarrassment, his boss asked the waiter to join their tables so that they could sit together. Oh, how he hated Jack right now! If Jack hadn't set him up with his cousin, he wouldn't be in this restaurant having a double-date with his boss! He eyed his boss's companion, Jan, and felt sorry for the girl—it appeared that it was either their first or second date and now she, too, had been lured into having to double-date. Now, whatever escape that he could have had from his single date with Melissa seemed to have vanished. He knew he was in for a long night.

Throughout the evening, the conversation seemed to drift between Scott's boss and Melissa, while Scott and Jan remained in an awkward silence, observing what was going on around them. He had to smile when he thought he saw amusement on Jan's face, she was obviously thinking about something else, rather than the topic of politics and cats that the conversation seemed to cover. He, too, allowed his mind to wander again in hopes that the evening would soon come to an end.

His thoughts drifted back to the goddess that he saw on his way home from work, his body aching to see her again. He wanted to run his fingers through her long golden hair and stare into her eyes—he wondered what colour they were, and he imagined that they would be enchanting. He wanted to stroke her cheek and examine every feature of her face before lifting her chin gently to kiss her soft lips. He wanted to feel the shock of her tongue teasing his own as he would lean in to kiss her more passionately, his hands tracing the curves of her body that were hidden by her blue floral dress. He wanted to love her and feel the warmth of her body against his own. He wanted her—he desired her.

The goddess had already taken over his every thought—he just had to meet her.

Chapter 2

Olivia didn't mind picking up Chad and Vanessa's children after school. As a florist and the owner of her store, she had the flexibility to work her own hours. There was also Betty, who worked for her regularly and could mind the store when she had errands to run. She was glad that she hired Betty, especially since her store was open every day of the week. She was a hard worker, a nice girl and made it much, much easier for Olivia to have a life outside of her work. Of course, in return, Betty's hours could be flexible too, they just had to ensure that at least someone was at the store during opening hours. And, as much as her godchildren loved coming back to her store, some days it was just easier to take them back to their home.

Thankfully, for Vanessa's sake, Olivia's plans had been cancelled for the evening. She was supposed to be going on a date with Antoine, but he had said that he couldn't do tonight when they caught up at the café in the morning. They were able to enjoy their morning tea together, but Olivia was still disappointed that he cancelled their date. They did reschedule for another day but for lunch rather than for dinner.

'On Sunday,' he said. 'We can have lunch.'

He never did say his reasons for cancelling and, although she kept telling herself that he didn't have to, she couldn't help wondering why he'd bailed and wondered how much she actually knew him. In the end, it was just as well that he had, because Vanessa was late home—again. Chad was home early, so he would have taken the kids off Olivia's hands, but Olivia decided to stay and help.

She had known Vanessa and Chad since she first moved to Paris to attend University. Her and Vanessa were roommates in the live-in dormitories and stuck together like glue. Olivia had already done courses in floristry and went to University to study Business Management so that she could learn the tricks of the trade in running a business. Vanessa studied Journalism and now worked at the local newspaper. She remembered the moment when Vanessa and Chad met each other. Vanessa had recruited her to operate the camera for an assignment she had to do. She was interviewing students about what they thought is most attractive in a partner and Chad was one of the people she interviewed.

'I could show you,' was his response with a wink. 'But no cameras allowed.'

You could almost see the electricity bouncing between the two of them. After that, they were Vanessa and Chad. Chad and Vanessa. There was nothing that could come between them and, as far as Olivia was concerned, there never would be. But, as infatuated as they were with each other, they made sure that Olivia never felt left out.

Olivia could hear Chad organising dinner in the kitchen while she played pretend with her godchildren. First it was Princes and Princesses, then they were Pirates sailing the seas, and then the floor was lava. She kept an eye on the three youngsters as each of them jumped from the couch to the wooden coffee table and back again. Joey and Max, who were identical twins, would be seven in a couple of weeks and inherited Vanessa's brown hair. Emmy was five and inherited Chad's blonde hair and was usually very shy—except, of course, when Olivia was around.

Vanessa's return home did not go unannounced. As soon as the key clicked in the front door, all three kids forgot that the floor was lava and raced to welcome their mother home with screams of delight and enthusiasm.

'Sorry I'm late!' Vanessa called out while wrestling with the kids.

Before too long, everyone had settled down at the table and were drooling over Chad's spaghetti bolognaise.

'How was work?' Chad asked his wife.

'Exactly the same as it was all week,' she said, shaking her head. 'I'm starting to wonder if that promotion is actually worth it.'

'I bet you're glad it's the weekend, then,' Olivia said, Vanessa nodding her response.

'She's been counting down the days since Monday morning,' Chad said.

A few minutes of laughter and a rousing up for the kids later, they were able to return to their conversation and their meals.

'You didn't have to cancel your date, Liv,' Vanessa said between mouthfuls. 'Chad is quite capable of minding the kids *and* making dinner.'

'I didn't,' Olivia said.

'*He* did.' Chad made sure to emphasise the *he*.

'Again?' Vanessa's eyes grew wide. 'When was the last time he *didn't* cancel a date?'

Olivia shrugged and swallowed hard. 'Maybe our second date?' she said. 'But it doesn't bother me. We still catch up for coffee.'

Vanessa put her fork down and leaned forward so that the kids wouldn't hear their discussion although they were too intrigued in a game of pulling faces and stealing each other's food to make notes.

'Liv,' she said. 'I'm telling you this because I love you. You can't base a relationship solely on coffee conversations.'

'It's worked so far,' Olivia said.

'It's true, Liv,' Chad piped in. 'Coffee dates last only for the length of the coffee. No more, no less.

There's not enough time to get into the deep stuff and really connect.' He put his arm around Vanessa.

Olivia stared at the plate full of food in front of her. It looked so yummy—and it was. Chad made the best spaghetti bolognaise she'd ever had. But she had lost her appetite and she could feel her heart pounding in her chest. She really liked Antoine, but her friends were right. They needed to go on proper, lengthy dates. The ones where you learn everything about each other. Sure, she enjoyed their little coffee dates, but their conversations were so … superficial … and would usually be spent organising a date that he would eventually cancel. She didn't know anything about his family or his upbringing. All that she knew was that he worked at a construction company. Not the actual labouring part, but in the offices. Or, so she gathered anyway since he was always in a suit.

But those eyes! She wouldn't be able to concentrate on holding a conversation when she was gazing into those striking blue eyes and hearing his soothing accent. He was everything that she dreamed a handsome French man would be like. And he was interested in her, it seemed, since they continued to see each other.

'I'm sure he had a good reason for cancelling,' she finally said, more for herself than her friends.

***

There she was, in her blue floral dress with her

golden locks illuminated by the sun. He couldn't quite picture exactly where she was, but she was standing near a fountain. A steady wind moved her hair to one side, exposing her elegant neck, and pressed her dress against her so that the curve of her body and the shape of her legs could be seen. He could almost smell the strong perfume that she wore, mixed with the sweet smell of the cherry blossoms that fell around her. She lifted her hand from her side, the sun glimmering against a silver coin as she tossed it into the fountain. He wondered what her wish might be. He hoped it was the same wish that he would make. He stepped closer and saw her body tense and her back straighten. She knew he was there. She heard him. He thought he heard her heart pounding as he stood behind her. Or perhaps it was his. She turned around.

Scott woke to the sound of someone knocking at his door. He looked around him, observing the ray of sun shining through the slit between the curtains, and the dust motes that danced in the light. It had been two days since he saw the goddess walking across the street, but it seemed she now inhabited every thought and every dream that his mind dared to have.

He heard the knocking again. He groaned as he stood out of his bed and pulled some jeans on. He wished that the dream didn't have to end.

'I'm coming,' he yelled, plucking his shirt off the back of his couch, pulling it over his head, and opening the door.

'Jack?' he said. 'What are you doing here?'

'Don't you answer your phone?' Jack said, walking past Scott, and flopping onto the couch.

'Oh sure, come on in,' Scott muttered under his breath, closing the door, and facing his colleague. 'What do you mean?' he asked.

'Your phone.' Jack pointed at it. 'I've been messaging you for the last two days and you haven't replied. How was it?'

'How was what?' Scott replied, rubbing his head as he started making some coffee.

'The date with Melissa,' Jack said.

Scott stood still. Of course, Jack wanted to know how the date with his cousin went. It all came back to him, the memory of the four of them sitting at the table. The night seemed to go on far longer than Scott intended on staying. If it wasn't for the waitress topping up his glass every time he emptied it, he wasn't sure how he would have gotten through it. Though, that did result in a killer headache that was only now seeming dull. He wasn't even sure what time he did manage to get home, but he did know that he managed to avoid bringing Melissa with him.

'Well?' Jack prompted.

'What did she say?' Scott asked, not sure if he should tell him the truth.

'She said that she had fun.'

'Did she tell you that the boss joined us with a date of his own?' Scott raised his eyebrow.

'*Our* boss?' Jack's eyes widened.

'At our table.'

'Wasn't that—'

'Awkward?' Scott said. 'Yes, it was. But serves me right for taking my friend's cousin to a restaurant that my boss recommended.'

Jack stared at his hands folded in front of him. He opened his mouth and closed it as though he wanted to say something but decided against it.

'What?' Scott handed Jack a coffee and took a sip of his own.

'Do you plan on seeing her again?'

Scott stared at his friend. He looked like a child that just found out he wasn't going to get his way.

'We're two very different people,' he said slowly, easing himself into the seat across from Jack.

'They say opposites attract.' Jack's eyebrows lifted, full of hope.

Scott let out a sigh and shook his head. 'Jack,' he said. 'I don't want to lie to you. Melissa is pretty, but she's not my type. I mean, she talked about her cats—a lot.'

'You don't like cats?' Jack raised his eyebrow again, this time in surprise, like it had never occurred to him that anybody wouldn't like cats.

'I despise them,' Scott said with a smile.

Jack bent his head to stare into his coffee, silent for a moment, then his body started to shake. Scott leaned forward in his chair, surprised that his acquaintance could be so disappointed about his decision. Then, he heard a chuckle that soon turned into rambunctious laughter, filling the room that was silent only a moment ago.

'What's so funny?' Scott asked, downing the rest of his coffee. He was going to need another one, it seemed.

'You should have seen your face,' Jack said between breaths. Scott stared at him for a moment in puzzlement then stood to get more coffee. 'You seriously thought that I would be disappointed,' Jack's laughter subsided slightly, 'that you didn't want to see my obnoxious cousin again.'

'I'm sure she's a nice girl,' Scott said, allowing a smirk to flash across his face. 'And I think the boss has his eyes set on her after last night.'

Once more, the room filled with laughter and Scott was glad that he managed to get out of a very awkward situation. From now on, he would refuse any dates that were set up. And, he would certainly not take restaurant recommendations from his boss ever again.

Chapter 3

Scott watched as the goddess closed the book she was reading and checked her watch. She had been sitting right by the window at the table in the corner for at least an hour and had ordered nothing more than a cup of coffee. Scott looked down at the cup in his hand. This was his third—or maybe fourth—refill. He was ready to leave after his first cup but found that he was practically glued to his seat once he saw her walk in.

Her hair was as golden and bouncy as he remembered in his dreams, but it wasn't pinned to one side. Today, she had her hair completely out and it framed her porcelain face perfectly. He still hadn't seen all of her face, but he could see her side profile. The way the tip of her small, delicate nose caught the sunlight and how her pink lips shimmered in the light. She wore tight-fitting jeans and a loose t-shirt with a scooped neckline, enough to let his imagination run wild.

She placed some money on the table, paused for a moment, glancing out the window once more and rose to her feet. Scott downed the rest of his coffee, plucked some money from his wallet and placed it on the table. He watched as she left *Michelle's Fameux Patisserie*. He rose to his feet and followed.

***

Her friends had been right—she was sure of it now. They had to have the conversation, she knew that too. In fact, she was ready to have that conversation today. Planned it, even, and had stayed awake for most of the night wondering what he would say. She was going to be confident. She was going to take charge of the situation. She was even going to look over the fact that she never once dreamed of having the conversation with anyone before. She liked Antoine, but she wanted them to be on the same page. She'd be damned if he didn't even bother to show up.

Olivia was furious. She felt the hot blood rushing through her veins and she wanted to let out her frustrations on him. He's the one that said to meet him there for lunch on Sunday. And she was there. She was there ten minutes early like she always was and waited like a lovesick school girl pining for her crush. Her cheeks reddened, and she felt flustered. Well, she wasn't going to wait anymore. She laid some money on the table, picked up her bag and stormed out of the café before stopping briefly outside to decide which way she would find him.

She didn't know. She didn't know where he lived, or where he worked, or even what he was doing. She laughed to herself. She must look like an idiot, standing outside of a café trying to decide which way she would go. Who is at home or at work for Sunday lunch anyway? This is Paris, after all, and it's a beautiful day. Granted, she usually worked on a Sunday, but she was a florist and business has always been good on the weekend. She didn't even know where to start or what she would say to him if she did manage to hunt him down.

'Excuse me!'

Olivia snapped out of her thoughts and spun quickly on her heels to see who was calling her, tripped on a crack in the pavement, and bumped into a hard wall she was certain wasn't there before. She was also sure that walls didn't have arms to help her regain her balance. She tore her gaze away from the solid wall and looked up into two striking, hazel eyes.

She studied the man in front of her.

His short hair was a deep brown, framing a very manly face and his defined jawline was shadowed with two-day stubble. He looked the very opposite of Antoine. One could easily tell that this man was hardworking. His build was strong, Antoine's was lean. He looked rugged, though his clothes were neat. Antoine always wore a suit. But there was something about this stranger that she found alluring and attractive. She felt his arms tensing under her hands.

'I am so sorry!' She blurted out the apology while tearing herself away from this incredible creature and took a step back, stumbling on the crack again. But the stranger caught her, again.

'You're not very good at this, are you?' He laughed.

'Excuse me?' Olivia shook off the stranger's hands and crossed her arms. 'If you hadn't been so close to me I wouldn't have bumped into you in the first place.'

'If I hadn't been so close to you,' he said with a smirk, 'you would have landed face-first on the pavement.'

Olivia pursed her lips and stared at the pavement where she would have landed.

'You're welcome.'

Olivia shot him a look. This man was not only an incredible creature, but a rude one at that.

'For what?'

'For cushioning your fall.' He extended his hand towards her. 'And for returning your book.'

Olivia stared at the book he held in his hand and let her arms fall to her sides. Now it started to make sense. After all, why would he be so close to her if she hadn't forgotten her book? The last book her mother gave her before the accident. She let out another laugh.

'Thank you,' she said. 'I can't say it enough. You don't know how important this book is to me … uh?'

'Scott,' he said, extending his arm again, this time to shake her hand. She took it.

'Scott.' She let his name roll over her tongue. 'Well, thank you, Scott.'

Their hands lingered together and Olivia couldn't tear her gaze away from his intriguing eyes and playful smile.

'And you?' He gave her hand a squeeze before letting it go.

'Me … what?' she said, fluttering her eyes to the book she now held in her hands. She didn't know why she was disappointed when he let go of her.

Scott laughed again. A glorious laugh that made Olivia's insides churn in a way she hadn't known before.

'Your name.' His smile broadened and his eyes gleamed.

'Oh … errm.' For a moment, caught in his gaze again, she just couldn't recall it. 'Olivia.'

'Olivia? What a pretty name.'

Oh God. Olivia's face reddened and she looked away again. She tried desperately to recompose herself to little avail.

Eventually she managed, 'Thank you.' She smiled at him again.

'Are you waiting for someone?' Scott said, looking down the street behind them.

She could smell his scent—his sweet, masculine scent. It was a mixture of cologne and something very uniquely him. She felt her insides squirm and her thoughts swimming all over the place.

'No,' Olivia said quickly—maybe too quickly. 'Well, I was, but I'm not now. I mean, he didn't come—' *Stop talking.* '—although I waited, you know?' *STOP TALKING.* 'Oh, God knows, I waited. I waited for over an hour and he didn't bother so much as to even call me or send a message to cancel—again!'

By then, it was too late.

***

Scott stood, wide-eyed, in front of Olivia, studying her face as she regained her composure. Who would have known that his goddess was so spirited? Her sky-blue eyes had a fire in them, her face that was pale before was now tinged pink where it should be, and her curls blew to one side with the wind, stray strands crossing over her cheeks, her lips.

His hand reached out to tuck the stray hairs behind her ear, his thumb brushing gently across her tinged cheek. He held her gaze and fought with all his might to not close the gap between them and kiss her. It wasn't the time, he knew it. But it didn't stop him from wanting to. He let his thumb linger against her cheek before dropping his arms to his side. They stood in silence for a moment longer before she finally broke their gaze.

'I'm sorry,' she whispered. 'I said too much. I ... I have to go.'

'No,' Scott said quietly.

'Thank you, Scott.' Olivia took a step back, holding up the book. She smiled at him before turning to walk away.

'Will I see you again?' The words came out of his mouth before he could stop them.

Olivia turned back to face him and pointed to the café that they stood in front of.

'I come here often,' she said, smiling. 'If we happen to bump into each other,' she blushed at her unintended pun, 'then yes, I'm sure you'll see me again.'

And with that, she was gone.

Scott stayed standing, staring, where he had just met the goddess he had been dreaming about. He caught himself whispering her name and suddenly realised what he had done. He felt the blood drain from his face. What on earth possessed him to touch her like that? To want to kiss her so badly when they had only just met? She was stressed and upset, and he almost took advantage of that. He scolded himself, cursing under his breath for possibly blowing whatever chance he might have had with Olivia. He gathered his thoughts and started walking back to his car.

He smiled at the thought of the fire in her eyes and the pink tinge in her cheeks and her lips, the touch of her skin underneath his thumb and her hair through his fingertips.

'Olivia,' he allowed himself to whisper again.

What he would love to do to the bastard that

stood her up. Then again, maybe it worked out for
the best.

Chapter 4

'He touched your face?' Vanessa's expression was unmistakable—her friend was just as surprised as she was.

Olivia nodded, allowing a quick smile to brush across her face before shunning the thought. Scott touched her face. The stranger she just met ... had touched her face.

'Are you sure?' Vanessa was still in disbelief.

Oh, she had no doubt that the strong handsome man with dark locks and intense hazel eyes had, indeed, touched her face. She still felt the trace of his thumb from her cheek to her ear. An electric shock still pulsed there. A very pleasant electric shock. Olivia blushed.

'Well, I know I didn't imagine it,' she said with a

smile.

'Huh,' Vanessa said.

They started their second lap around the oval. Chad was kicking a football with the kids and chasing them around, so Olivia and Vanessa were able to walk in peace. They smiled as Emmy let out another squeal of delight as her father chased after her.

'The nerve!' Vanessa finally said. 'Why on earth would he think he can touch your face when you just met?'

Olivia shrugged. 'He did catch me when I tripped,' she smiled again. 'I mean, he was touching me before we met.'

Vanessa's eyes widened.

'And that,' Olivia blushed again, 'came out very wrong.'

The two friends laughed uncontrollably, stopping their walk to catch their breath.

'So,' Vanessa said between breaths. 'Do you think you'll see him again?'

Olivia sobered. 'I don't know. Maybe. I didn't get his number.'

'But you'd *like* to see him again.' Vanessa was nothing if not persistant, looping an arm through Olivia's.

'Who wouldn't?' Olivia shrugged, smiling. 'He was handsome—'

'Handsome?' Vanessa said.

'And gorgeous—'

Vanessa interrupted again. '*Handsome*?'

'And incredibly, undeniably sexy.' Olivia finally

managed to get her words out.

'Who says *handsome* anymore?' Vanessa's eyes were flashing. She was obviously enjoying this.

'I think *handsome* is a very becoming word to describe a man that quite obviously inspired the pure existence of the word,' Olivia said, correcting her friend. 'In fact, I think that it should be used more often. *Handsome* is making a comeback!'

Olivia and Vanessa continued walking and laughing, stopping only to intercept the football from going past the oval perimeter.

Yes, Olivia thought. *Scott is handsome. And, he touched my face.* The thought made her blush and her stomach explode with butterflies. Since meeting Scott only a few hours ago, those feelings were becoming all too familiar.

But what about Antoine? Surely, he made her feel this way too. Maybe not in the eye-fluttering, heart-thumping way that Scott made her feel. Antoine did make her smile, but the very thought of Scott made her blush and her stomach fill with butterflies, and the memory of his touch gave her that euphoric feeling that she craved more of.

If only she knew for certain that she would see him again. Why didn't she give him her number? Or why didn't she get his? At least she would know they could talk again. *'I come here often'*—what was she thinking? Who would go to a café to meet someone who may or may not even be there? She might not even be alone when—if—they bump into each other again. Paris is a big place—surely the chances of him coming to the café when she's there were slim. Surely, he wouldn't spend his every waking moment waiting at *Michelle's Fameux Patisserie* for her to get her daily coffee.

God, she wished he would.

***

Scott hit the snooze button and stared up at his ceiling. The alarm was nothing but welcome today, especially since he hardly slept all night. And the few moments he did sleep, he dreamt of her. Mind you, they were very pleasant dreams. And he could still feel the softness of her curves and see the fiery passion in her eyes. The touch of her lips on his ...

Scott groaned and rolled over in his bed. He had lain awake all night thinking of Olivia—the goddess who was making his thoughts scrambled and his actions irrational. He waited for his alarm to go off all night but, now that it had, he didn't want to get out of bed. Truth be told, he didn't want to stop thinking about her. That is, if he had any control over his thoughts anymore. He just hoped he could be more functional while thinking about her.

He still wasn't sure if he should be mad at the man who stood her up for hurting her, or if he should thank him for giving him a chance to meet her. *'I come here often'*—he hoped she meant it. He wanted to be at the café from the moment they opened until the moment they put the 'closed' sign on the door, just so he might see her again. He hated that the café wasn't visible from his work. At least then he could keep an eye on it all day and rush over once he saw her. But he would just have to rely on chance and hope that she would be there when he was able to make it. Maybe she would be spending her days there, waiting, just in case he came.

God, he wished she would.

***

'Morning, Betty,' Olivia said as her employee walked into the shop.

Betty looked at her watch and then around at the shop. Extravagant bouquets of flowers were neatly displayed around the room—even more than usual—and she looked to where the voice came from.

'*Bonjour, mademoiselle.*' She eyed the shop warily. 'You're here early. And you're clearly sorted for the day.'

It wasn't uncommon for Betty to arrive before Olivia did. In fact, she was usually there first.

'I couldn't sleep.' Olivia shrugged.

Olivia had spent the night tossing and turning, unable to sort her mind out. It seemed that Scott had taken over her every thought and it, quite literally, sent her brain into complete shambles. Having resigned to the fact that she wouldn't be getting any sleep, she decided to get to work early and make a start on things in hopes that it might take her mind of Scott. And it did. For very brief moments, at least, until her mind began to fantasise what being with

Scott might be like.

While she arranged the bouquets, she wondered if he was the kind of man to buy flowers for a woman.

She wondered if he would ever cancel plans.

She checked the time herself—just after seven in the morning—and sighed. Her lack of sleep was catching up on her and she was feeling in desperate need of a strong coffee. *Michelle's Fameux Patisserie* was just around the corner from her florist shop, but it wasn't open for another fifteen minutes. Maybe they would let her in early. And maybe Scott would be there, too.

***

'If anyone asks,' Jack said, puffed out from having run over to Scott to speak to him first. 'You're still dating Melissa.'

'What?' Scott couldn't believe his ears. 'I'm *not* dating Melissa!'

Nor did he want anyone to think that he was dating someone—just in case it ever got back to Olivia, of course. But also, because the events of his date with Melissa had already reached all of his co-workers, courtesy of Jack. And now there was another rumour to deal with, courtesy of Jack.

Damn you, Jack.

'Why on earth would I say that I still am?'

'Well,' Jack fiddled with his hard hat, 'I kind of told the boss that you are.'

'Jack!' Scott ran his fingers through his hair. It was way too early to deal with this, especially since he'd had no sleep.

'He was asking after her!' Jack threw his arms in the air. 'I don't want him dating my cousin.'

'So, you told him that *I'm* with her?' Scott was running out of patience. What he would do for some coffee right now. 'You couldn't think of anyone else to have the honour?'

'It's more believable if it's you. After all, he's already seen you on a date with her.' Jack shrugged. 'I didn't know what else to say.'

Scott shook his head and loosened his arms. It was no good even trying to argue. What was done, was done. And he could certainly understand Jack's reasoning. However inconvenient it was for him.

'I'm not going on any more dates with her,' he said after a moment, pointing his finger at Jack.

'You don't have to.' Jack smiled, relieved. 'Just say that you are if the boss asks.'

Scott stormed off to start sorting out the plans and his tools. Surely his day could only get better from here. While he studied the work plans, he heard one of the other workers meowing in his direction. He sighed, shaking his head. It was going to be a long day.

Chapter 5

It was Wednesday, and Olivia still hadn't bumped into Scott at the café, even though she had increased her visits in hopes that she might see him. It was all in vain, anyway. Either they kept missing each other or he just wasn't that interested in her. She was kicking herself for not getting his number, but maybe even that would have backfired on her.

She still spent her nights tossing and turning before falling into a restless sleep from exhaustion. If only she could know for sure how this incredible creature that filled her dreams felt about the moment they had—about her. Maybe she was just reading too much into it. Maybe she *did* imagine his touch on her cheek and his hand lingering as he shook hers. And maybe she imagined having spent so long in his arms after he caught her.

She pinned her hair to the side and took one last look in the mirror. Thinking about Scott simply wouldn't do when she was on her way to see Antoine. She already felt bad thinking about him when she didn't even know what her and Antoine really had.

After not showing up for their scheduled lunch on Sunday, Antoine called Olivia two days later to reschedule, claiming that he got caught up with work. Perhaps some people are still busy with work on a Sunday, but he had told her he was so determined to avoid working weekends. She had to believe him, though. She couldn't think of any other way to find out how true his alibi really is.

He wanted to reschedule for another day at the café, but Olivia had insisted on meeting somewhere else, explaining that they always meet at the café. She didn't want to say that she didn't want Scott to see her sitting with someone else if he happened to come into the café. Knowing her luck, that's when he would come in. But it was her secret. One that she intended on keeping.

Antoine finally decided that Olivia should come over to his place and he would cook her dinner. Olivia agreed. At least he couldn't cancel so easily this time. And he certainly wouldn't be able to stand her up. Maybe she would be able to get some answers.

***

Antoine made a very nice dinner for Olivia that night. She couldn't remember what he called it, but it was something with chicken, melted brie and vegetables. She was also pretty sure that she could taste some kind of white wine through the sauce. Whatever it was, it was nice, and it made her relax a little more given how she was feeling when she knocked on the door.

She knew they had to have the conversation, but she struggled to find the right moment. All through the meal and the delicious dessert—a lavender crème brûlèe—to finish, the conversation was light and superficial. As it usually was. It wasn't until he poured her another glass of wine and they sat down on the couch that she found the courage.

'Antoine.' She placed her glass on the coffee table, turning to face him. 'I have to ask you something. It might sound a bit childish and I feel silly asking it, but I have to know.'

'Go ahead, sweetheart,' he said, putting his own glass down and positioning himself so they were both facing each other, his left arm draping over the back of the couch and his fingers playing with the end of her curls. His other hand was resting on her leg.

She struggled to find the words to say. The courage that she had finally built up was dissolving and her thoughts were wandering to his fingertips drawing circles on her knee.

'Are we together?' His circling fingertips froze.

'What do you think?' he replied, raising an eyebrow. 'I don't see anyone else here.'

He shuffled a little closer to her, the hand playing with her curls now caressed the back of her neck and his right hand wandered to her hip.

'I mean to say, are we d—dating?' Her mind was going blank. Damn him for distracting her.

'I'd say this is a date, wouldn't you?' He shrugged, moving closer again.

She could feel his warm breath lingering on her forehead where he planted a kiss, before leaving a trail of kisses over her temple, her cheeks, her chin, her nose.

'Yes,' she whispered, her heart stopping in her chest.

He lifted the hand from her hip to nudge her chin up slightly, so their lips met. First softly, gently. Then he parted her lips more forcefully and darted his tongue into her mouth. She didn't notice his hand return to her leg, but she did notice it moving up her thigh and causing tiny vibrations through her stockings as the rough of his fingers caughts on the delicate fibres.

Olivia pulled back, swiping his hand from her thigh, and rose to her feet. She felt frazzled, confused. What were they doing? Well, she knew what *he* was trying to do, but it just confused her more. Surely, she should have expected it. He did just say that they were dating, that they were together. She shouldn't be confused.

'Olivia, sweetheart?'

She heard him say the words but it sounded so distant. She needed to get out of there and get some fresh air. To go for a walk. She scoffed at herself. Her boyfriend was obviously wanting to make love with her and she wanted to go for a walk—by herself. She wasn't ready for this.

'I have to go,' she murmured, grabbing her purse. She walked briskly. She heard him say something, but she didn't register what it was. All she knew was that she had to go.

***

It had been a long few days. Not only had his co-workers given him a tough time about Jack's rumour, but Scott still hadn't seen Olivia again, despite his frequent visits to the café. He hoped that she really did mean it when she said that she went there often. Hopefully she hadn't changed her mind. What he would give to see her again. He thought it might get easier after the first night, but he was still spending his nights lying awake thinking about her until he fell asleep from exhaustion.

She still filled his thoughts with the mystery that is Olivia. But he was finding that he was becoming more functional while thinking of her, which was a bonus. He wondered what she was doing, what she was thinking, where she was. He had so many questions he wanted to ask her.

He wanted to know everything about her.

He should have got her number.

Scott resolved to taking a long walk through a park not far from where he lived every night before bed, hoping that it would help him get to sleep. Tonight, especially, he felt like he needed it. He felt as though he acted like a fool in front of Olivia. It could have been his one and only chance with her and he didn't even get her number. Let alone schedule a specific time to see her. Damn him for not thinking clearly.

He thought he was usually pretty smooth with women, but Olivia was different. She made his thoughts scramble and his body rebel against him. She made him think about her consistently and fantasise in his dreams. She turned him from being a switched-on guy with no distractions to being preoccupied and thinking—doing—things that he wouldn't usually do. She made him into a fool, and she probably didn't even care.

Scott scolded himself for falling for her womanly charms. How had he let his guard down? He decided that he would control himself if he ever did see her again.

He walked briskly through the front gate of the big park, it was dimly lit with scattered lights along the path. He turned right to walk the loop, hearing the rumble of thunder from an incoming storm. Perhaps he had better turn back to avoid getting caught in a downpour. He kept walking. He could feel the tension in the air—the storm was close. He heard the rumble again. He turned to go back and froze.

She was there.

God, she was a picture, standing still, staring at the lake that ran through the park. Her golden locks were being tossed around with the wind that was picking up. She wore a simple black dress, angled at the hem to expose one knee but not the other. It fit snugly around her waist, her bust.

He heard another rumble, louder this time. Her body didn't falter at the sound. She seemed as oblivious of the thunder as she was of him watching her. Her calm allure, drew him in. His body was betraying him, but he walked towards her anyway until he stood next to her.

'I hope you're not planning on going for a swim,' he said, wishing he could have thought of something better to say.

He thought he saw her jump a little before a smile crossed her face.

'Just clearing my head,' she said calmly, turning to face him. 'We meet again.'

She was as beautiful as he remembered—even more so. Her lips were perfect, turned into a smile that seemed happy to see him, but her eyes—her beautiful sky-blue eyes—were darker, troubled, distracted. It tore at his heart and it took all of his power to not pull her into his arms.

'Scott?' The smile was gone, replaced by a look of concern.

He had been gawking at her like a fool. He shook his head to sort out his thoughts.

'Sorry,' he said. 'I was hoping I'd bump into you again.' The smile was back, and he watched Olivia as her cheeks tinged pink and she turned to stare back at the lake for a moment. 'Though I thought it would be at the café, not in a park late at night.'

'Me too,' she whispered. She looked like she wanted to say more, but she didn't. Another rumble.

'What are you doing here, Olivia?' Scott said, turning her to face him. 'It's dangerous to be in the park by yourself late at night, especially—'

'Especially since I'm a girl?' The fire was back in her eyes. 'In case a stranger comes to talk to me?'

He felt his chest tearing. She really had no idea how she underestimated him. He gritted his teeth.

'Anything could happen, Olivia,' He felt a rain drop on his cheek and saw one sliding down her nose. He wanted to wipe it away.

'Should I be worried that you're the stranger?'

'That's not fair.'

'What are you going to do to me, Scott?'

She started to walk away, leaving him standing, amazed at how the discussion escalated. He shook his head and urged himself to follow after her. He couldn't blow it again. Not this time.

'Olivia!'

Another crack of thunder, this time preceding a downpour of rain. He grabbed her arm to stop her from slipping in her high heels, and guided her to the gazebo to get out of the rain. It hurt that she shook his hand off her and walked to the bench to sit down. But why should he expect anything else? They *were* strangers, after all.

'I didn't mean it like that,' he said, sitting down

beside her.

She laughed. He raised an eyebrow, shifting on the bench to look at her.

'You think that I shouldn't be here by myself because I'm a girl,' she said, shaking her head. 'How can you not mean it like that? I can look after myself, you know.'

'I have no doubt about that,' he said, gently turning her face to look at him.

'Then why did you say it?' she replied quietly, her composure softening as she stared into his eyes.

'*You* said it,' he said to remind her, his tone smooth. 'I was going to say that it's because you're so damn beautiful. No man would be able to keep their hands off you.'

'Oh,' she sighed, dropping her gaze to her hands.

Scott was sure that he could see her cheeks redden. He saw her shiver as another clap of thunder drowned out the sound of rain falling on the roof of the gazebo. He shrugged out of his jacket and put it around her. She tugged it tightly across her body and smiled her thanks at him.

'What about you?' she said finally.

'What about me?' Scott raised an eyebrow.

'Should I be worried about you?' she said, gazing up into his eyes again.

He stared deeply into her eyes, holding her gaze as intently as he could. He now understood what she was trying to say. He knew what he wanted in that moment and he knew what he had to say to gain her trust. He just wished they could be the same thing.

'I would respect your wishes,' he said finally.

Her smile widened, and her eyes glistened, all signs of their misunderstanding behind them. He wished that she would give him any hint of wanting him to kiss her, because, damn it, he wanted to so badly. He wanted to brush her hair, now dangling in wet, tousled curls, from her face and feel the warmth of her breath mingling with his. He wanted to fulfil her every desire and make her feel cared for, loved, special. But he would respect her wishes. He wouldn't dare go against that. He'd be damned if he did.

Chapter 6

Olivia stared at the slip of paper in front of her that held Scott's number and remembered last night. Out of all the opportunities that she could have bumped into him again at the café, they met in the park. Late at night. The one that she had rarely gone to before but did because it was on her way home from Antoine's.

She shuddered at the thought of her date with Antoine. How did she manage to find herself in that predicament, anyway? Of course, she didn't even think that he might have some ulterior motives for inviting her to his place. She was so hung up on needing to know what he considered they were and didn't want him to bail on their date again. Having their date at his place seemed to be the only guarantee he wouldn't cancel, but she didn't think about the position it put her in.

They are together, they are dating. She was relieved that she finally had an answer, but it's as though the answer wasn't sufficient. Isn't that what she wanted—to know that they were in a relationship? So why did she feel so uneasy about it?

Antoine called her in the morning. She didn't answer. She didn't feel like talking to him after the way he tried to come onto her. She still felt like she needed to clear her head and sort out her thoughts. He cancelled dates on her and made it difficult for her to contact him, so now it's her time. She wouldn't talk to him until she was ready.

But, Scott. She continued to stare at the number, holding her phone in her hand. She wanted to call him and talk to him—get to know him. He intrigued her and there was just something about him that made her feel relaxed and comfortable. He made her feel like they already knew each other, but they didn't. She had never met a Scott Henders before in her life. She would remember meeting him if she had—*that* she was certain about. He was a stranger to her, yet he made her feel more herself than Antoine had ever done.

'More coffee?'

Olivia snapped out of her thoughts and looked up at Marie, who was swapping her empty mug for a full one. For a while, she had forgotten where she was. But it didn't seem to bother Marie. She must be used to Olivia coming to the café and getting lost in her thoughts.

'Thank you, Marie,' she said, smiling.

'You should call him,' Marie said, giving Olivia a knowing smile.

'Who?' Olivia felt her heart stop.

'Oh, don't give me that,' Marie continued. 'I know the look—I've seen it a million times in here. You've been staring at his number there with the phone in your hand for the last hour.'

Olivia's eyes widened. Had she really been staring for an hour?

'Surely not,' Olivia looked at her watch. 'Huh, it really has been an hour.'

Marie left Olivia to process the news. She should call him. God, if he made her act like this then she may as well, right?

She couldn't do it.

She didn't want to come across as being eager. Besides, he had her number. He should call first. She hadn't realised that she had typed his number on her phone and had her finger hovering over the call button. But she hesitated. She didn't know what to say to him. Her thoughts wandered back to the night before.

She chuckled for finding herself caught in the storm with him. But it was nice, sitting under the gazebo together. He noticed that she was cold and gave her his jacket to wear. She was sure that no one had ever done that for her before. Besides, she was usually prepared with her own jacket but in her moment of fleeing Antoine and sorting out her frazzled mind, she hadn't felt the cold—or realised she didn't have a jacket—until she was soaked to the bone and sitting next to Scott.

She had been rude to him and took offense at what she thought he was going to say. She had never been one to assume like that. She supposed Antoine's impropriety had made her act that way. But Scott only reacted with kindness and sincerity. He was even better than she remembered from their first meeting. Even better than in her fantasies.

I would respect your wishes—did he mean that? Already he was making her second-guess everything with Antoine. Or maybe Antoine had done that himself. In that moment, Olivia wanted Scott to kiss her. No one had ever made her feel so safe, so respected. Scott was a considerate man and she found that attractive. He made her forget about what had happened only moments before. In fact, he made her forget everything. She just wanted to stay there, with him, listening to the storm going on around them and getting to know him.

But their moment was short-lived, because the storm didn't last long and, when the rain stopped, he insisted on walking her to her car before it poured again. If only Antoine was half the gentleman that Scott was.

Olivia jumped when her phone started ringing in her hand. She answered it without looking.

'Hello?' she said.

'Hey,' the voice said. Her heart stopped. 'It's Scott.'

He called her. He actually called her. She was at a loss for words. She must be imagining it. Surely he wasn't thinking of her at the same time as she was thinking about him.

'Hello?' Scott said again.

'Hi,' Olivia managed to force out. She thought she heard him laugh a little. There was a moment of silence.

'So, I have searched my whole house,' he continued. 'And I still can't find my jacket. Any idea where it might be?'

'Why would I know where your jacket is?' She sounded confused, even to herself.

'Well,' he said slowly. 'You had it last.'

Olivia froze. His jacket! Of course. She had it. She meant to give it back to him when he walked her to her car.

'I am so sorry.'

'You killed my jacket?' he said. Did she catch a hint of teasing in his voice?

'No, I have your jacket,' she said quickly.

'What's the ransom?' He was laughing now.

'Ransom?' Olivia pressed her fingers to her forehead.

This guy was too quick for her. How could she think clearly when she was kicking herself for forgetting to give him his jacket back? And he walked home! She let him walk home in the cold without a jacket while she drove, nice and warm, in her car. She was a horrible person. Hopefully he didn't have to walk far.

'Well, it *is* my favourite jacket,' he said. 'So, what's the price?'

Was he flirting now? She couldn't tell.

'I … I don't know,' she muttered.

'What about a movie? We could have dinner afterwards?'

'I'm not sure about that.'

Why not? Why couldn't she agree to it?

'Coffee?'

'Scott,' she said. She had to tell him she was with Antoine. She knew she did. But she couldn't bring herself to do it.

'Come on, Olivia,' he begged. 'It's my favourite jacket!'

She laughed. She could tell that he was only pretending to beg. But it was true—she had his jacket and he had to have it back.

'Coffee sounds good,' she said, smiling.

'Great!' He sounded excited. 'Tomorrow then, at our café? I can get there at five in the afternoon.'

'I'll be there,' she said. 'With your jacket.'

They said their goodbyes and hung up. Olivia stared at her phone. *Our café*. He considered the café to be theirs. She felt a gawky smile crossing her face and she realised that she'd had butterflies in her stomach for the whole conversation. Surely coffee would be okay?

***

Scott stared at the phone in his hand. He couldn't

believe that Olivia had agreed to have coffee with him. He commended himself for thinking of using the jacket as an excuse. Truth is, it *was* his favourite jacket—even more so now. And he certainly missed it walking back home last night when the rain picked up again. He hadn't realised how cold he was until after she left. He felt like an ice block by the time he got home. But he would never tell her that.

He spent all morning at work trying to figure out what to say when he rung her. He didn't want to put it off, but he also didn't want to sound too eager. Turns out the jacket proved to be a good excuse.

'Hey, Scott,' Jack said as Scott was walking back over to where they were building. 'You don't need to worry about telling the boss you're with Melissa now.'

'That's a relief. Why is that?'

'One of the guys overheard him talking on the phone about trying to snag a 'blonde beauty'.' Jack shrugged. 'So, I guess he's moved on.'

'Just as well,' Scott said as they reached the others.

He didn't say that he pitied the blonde beauty. Nor did he say that he thought the boss's habits were pathetic and disgusting. Who was he to say anything? He no longer had to lie about dating Melissa and he was having coffee with his goddess tomorrow. Nothing could bring him down now.

Chapter 7

Scott sat on the bench outside of *Michelle's Fameux Patisserie*, waiting for Olivia. When he arrived, the waitress was pulling in the tables from the front. He asked if they were closing early and she said they had to due to unforeseen circumstances. It was just his luck that they would be closed when Olivia arrived, but he managed to convince the waitress to make two coffees to go before she turned the sign to 'closed'. The least he could do was make sure he had coffee for Olivia, even if they couldn't have it at the café.

He could smell the two coffees balancing on the bench beside him and examined the elegant bouquet of flowers in his hands—complete with lilies, carnations, sprigs of cherry blossoms and baby's breath. He wanted to get her the biggest and most expensive bouquet that he could find at the florist but settled for the smaller, more elegant bouquet. In fact, he thought the flowers might be a risk so soon.

But he couldn't help himself when he walked past the florist shop. It was as though he blacked out when he looked in the window and regained consciousness outside the shop with the bouquet in his hands. He hoped she would like it. He had to figure out a way to explain it if it turned against him.

'Oh, don't tell me they're closed!'

Scott looked up at the goddess walking towards him and smiled. She seemed to get more beautiful each time he saw her. He didn't know how on earth he was going to keep his promise.

'I was just as surprised,' he said, standing to greet her. 'But I got some coffee before they did.'

'Your jacket, kind sir,' Olivia said, stopping with only a short gap between them, the jacket in her outstretched hand and a playful smile across her face. 'And don't worry, it hasn't been harmed.'

He took the jacket from her and made a scene of hugging it and assuring it that it was back in safe hands. He couldn't help but notice her joyous, addictive laugh which made him present the bouquet to her with as much ease as he hoped there would be.

'These are for you,' he said, smiling. 'For the safe return of my jacket.'

'I thought coffee was the ransom,' she said, blushing as she took the bouquet and smelt the flowers.

Scott committed the scene to memory. He was sure that he hadn't seen anything more perfect than watching Olivia smell the flowers, her eyes closed and her cheeks tinged pink. Her hair was pinned in a bun, but loose, rebellious curls had escaped and were framing her face.

'I could have sworn that flowers were, too.' He pulled a face that made him look as though he was thinking hard.

'Well, thank you.' She smiled at him, holding the bouquet to her chest. 'So, what's the plan now that the café is closed?'

'We could get some dinner.' Scott raised both eyebrows in hope she would say yes.

'I don't think I'm dressed for that, Scott,' Olivia said, pointing down the length of her plain purple dress.

Scott had no doubt that she would get into the fanciest of restaurants dressed as she was, but he didn't want to push it. *Baby steps*, he reminded himself.

'Sure you are!' He handed her one of the coffees. 'I know a great street vendor on the way to the Seine—the best hotdog you'll ever have.'

He smiled when his desired result was achieved. Olivia was in fits of laughter as the two started to walk down the street towards the Seine. The conversation was light and seemed to imitate a crash-course on getting to know each other. He found out that Olivia was—thankfully—a dog person, had no siblings, moved to Paris seven years ago to study at University, and very much loved her coffee.

***

It took them no longer than fifteen minutes to walk to the street vendor. Olivia couldn't believe it when Scott stopped and ordered two hotdogs with everything on it and handed one to Olivia.

'You know,' Olivia said, examining the food she held. 'I thought you were joking about the hotdogs.'

'Oh, I never joke about food,' Scott said, taking a bite.

So, that was something else to add to the list of things she knew about Scott. She also discovered that he hates cats, loves dogs, has a sister, moved to Paris only three years ago, and works as the project manager of a building site. Well, that explained why he was so strong, masculine, and looked to be a very hard-working man.

Olivia watched as Scott took yet another bite of his hotdog. Already, he'd eaten half of it and she hadn't even taken a bite of hers. She sighed, then took a bite, pleasantly surprised at the flavours rolling around in her mouth.

'This is incredible!' she muttered, still chewing.

Scott smiled at Olivia before finishing off his hotdog. She truly couldn't believe how delicious any kind of food from a street vendor could be, especially since she'd had a bad experience with each of the few times she'd been game enough to try food off the street.

By the time both of them had finished their food and coffees, they reached the Seine and found a bench to sit on where they could enjoy watching the steady flow of the river. They could hear some shouts of excitement from the other side of the river—a stag night, they decided—and could see the lights of the Eiffel Tower in the distance. Olivia stared down at the bouquet that she still held in her hands, eyeing the round, golden sticker that held the paper together and smiling when she found it familiar.

'You never said where you lived before Paris,' Olivia said when the ruckus from the party started to sound more distant.

'Australia,' he said, staring at the water.

'Well, that explains your accent.' Olivia nudged him.

'I don't have an accent!' Scott said, breaking his gaze from the water and smiling at her. The nudge seemed to work in getting his attention.

'You do too!' she said with a chuckle.

'I was in Australia for eight years.' He leaned back, crossing his feet in front of him. 'Before that, I was in London.'

'That's a big move,' Olivia edged slightly closer on the bench. 'Why did you do it?'

'I moved with my family.' He shrugged. 'My parents were originally from Australia and they wanted to move back. I got my trade there and worked for a few years before moving here.'

'Don't you miss them?' she asked quietly.

Olivia pulled her jacket around herself and wondered if Scott noticed that she'd brought her own this time. It was becoming cold and the breeze by the river wasn't helping. He must have noticed because he stood and offered his hand to help her up. She took it, but let go once she was on her feet. Side by side, they started to walk back towards the café.

'Of course,' he said finally. 'I mean, we still keep in contact by any means possible, but I had to move—for me.'

'Why here, though?' Olivia raised an eyebrow.

'Why not?' Scott stretched his arms out beside him. 'It's Paris.'

Olivia froze for a moment, old memories coming back to her before disappearing as fast as they appeared. She shook her head and started to walk again, catching up to Scott and hoping he didn't notice her lag behind. There was no point dwelling on the past. She gave up on that many years ago.

***

He tried not to show that he noticed. Surely she wouldn't have wanted him to. Judging by the look on her face when she froze, she didn't even want to think about whatever it was that bothered her. Scott hoped that it wasn't something that he said that made unwelcome memories or thoughts disturb the nice time she seemed to be having. Maybe she saw something that he didn't. Or maybe she realised that she'd forgotten to do something. He had to change the subject.

'So, you never told me where you work?' Surely that would get him some bonus points.

'Where did you say you bought these flowers from?' she replied, smelling the flowers again. She seemingly hadn't heard his question. Perhaps she was too deep in thought that she didn't register it.

'I didn't,' he said. She raised an eyebrow. 'I walked past a nice little florist shop not far from the café. They were so pretty that I couldn't resist getting them for you.'

She smiled again, her eyes glistening.

'Well,' she said. 'There's your answer.'

'My answer?' Scott shook his head slightly. How could such a beautiful woman be so confusing?

'Where I work.' She shrugged.

Scott stared at her for a moment, his brows furrowed, trying to work out her riddle. What did the flowers have to do with where she worked? His eyes widened when it finally all made sense to him.

'The florist,' he whispered, looking back out to the river. Of course she worked at the florist that he just bought flowers from.

'Actually, I own it,' she said casually.

So, she didn't just work there, she *owned* it. She was the business owner of the florist that he just bought flowers from. For her. *Aww, heck!*

'But you—' he said slowly.

She finished the thought for him. 'I wasn't there, no.' Her smile was the widest he had ever seen. 'I left early today. You would have met Betty—she works for me.'

'Well,' Scott sighed, shoving his hands in his pockets, 'this isn't awkward at all.'

'Oh, no—it's not!' Olivia said, turning to face him, and stopping him by the arm. 'See, I'm biased—I think my flowers are the best. I don't like anyone else's.' She let go of his arm and started to walk again. 'So, really, I like this bouquet even more than I could have if they were from any other florist. In fact, this specific one has been my favourite all day. So, thank you.'

Scott felt more at ease, allowing his hands to fall back to his side. He supposed it all made sense, in a quirky kind of way. He still wondered how on earth he managed to buy flowers from the florist owned by the beautiful lady he was buying them for. And that it subsequently made her like them more than if they were from another florist. He couldn't complain about that.

'I'll remember that,' he said, smiling. She gave him a look of confusion. 'I'll make sure I only get you flowers from your shop,' he continued. 'But what if you're there when I'm getting them?'

His tone was almost joking. Almost. But he was as serious as serious could be about his question. He liked to keep flowers a surprise, not something expected. He didn't just buy them for anyone. If she wasn't going to appreciate other flowers as much as the ones from her shop, how was he going to buy them in the future without her knowing?

'Well,' she seemed to really consider his question. 'I could go out the back if I ever see you. Or, you could get them when I'm not there.'

It was a challenge—he was sure of it. And he didn't fail to notice that she never told him not to buy her flowers. He felt his steps lighten and his smile brighten. Perhaps it wasn't going to be so hard after all.

Chapter 8

Olivia focussed on the book in front of her, tracing the gold leaf lettering on the cover. It was the same book that Scott returned to her outside the café when they met. She still hadn't made it past the same page she was stuck on that day. She pulled her dressing gown tighter around her, and stood to close the open window that was allowing the cool, variable breeze to sweep through her lounge room. She went to the kitchen to pour herself another coffee before settling down on the couch.

It was Sunday—a week had gone since meeting Scott. And in that week, she had gone from confused and hopeful about Antoine, to distraught about how their date went, to even more confused about everything. She still couldn't wrap her head around the idea that she and Antoine were together, especially if she wasn't sure how she actually felt about him. She thought that she was sure about her feelings, that she wanted to be with him. That is, until their date on Wednesday and definitely before she met Scott.

She rubbed her head, sipping her coffee. This was why she decided to take the day off work—to try and gain some kind of organisation with her thoughts and attempt to work out what she was feeling and why. She wasn't used to being so confused about everything. It wasn't her.

She knew she liked Antoine. Well, thought she liked him. Sure, she was angry at him and frustrated with his frequent cancellations, but she was sure that she did have feelings for him. On the other hand, she couldn't resist Scott's charms—his humour, his smile, his deep hazel eyes, the feel of his muscles tensing beneath her hands.

Olivia felt her face flush. She couldn't deny it— there was something there. But she didn't want it to be. She was with Antoine now and was before she met Scott. It was improper to be thinking of another man when she had a boyfriend. But she couldn't help it. She had to find a way to get her mind off Scott, as difficult as it is to just put thoughts of such an incredible man aside. A very attractive man.

She shook her head and picked up her phone, searching through her contact list to find her mother's rehabilitation centre, hesitating before calling. Her thoughts wondered back to the day of the accident, tears welling in her eyes as she remembered what the doctors had said to her.

'Your mother has brain damage,' the doctor said. 'It's very unlikely that she will be the same person when she wakes up.'

She remembered them handing her a bundle of pamphlets on dementia, outlining what to expect, symptoms, causes, everything to know about it. But she couldn't take it in. Not when her mother had almost died because of an irresponsible driver. The doctors were right—her mother was a completely different person when she woke up. She didn't know who Olivia was until Olivia brought her photos of her childhood. Slowly, her mother grew to remember Olivia, or what Olivia had told her about the memories they shared. At least now she remembered who she was whenever she visited, thanks to her carers.

She blinked back the tears, trying to remain strong for her mother, urging herself to make the call that she knew wouldn't be any different to previous calls.

'Hello?' she heard the attendant say.

'Hi, it's Olivia Harley here,' she said. 'I'm just checking on how my mother is going today?'

She heard the attendant sigh, which she knew meant that there hadn't been any improvement.

'Mrs. Harley is having … one of those days,' she said. 'She seemed to be improving slightly, but woke up this morning back to where we started. I'm sorry Olivia, but it seems she's taking one step forward, two steps back.'

'Should I visit?'

'I think it would do more harm than good today.' The attendant sounded genuinely upset. 'Sorry, Olivia.'

'Thank you.' Olivia ended the call, tears welling up in her eyes again. She, knew that it was only going to be a matter of time.

***

'I just don't know, Vanessa,' Olivia said. She was walking towards the café to meet up with Scott for a coffee, fitting in a quick phone call to her friend while she walked.

'So, tell me again,' Vanessa replied. 'You asked Antoine if you were dating and he said you were, then you kissed, he got a bit too touchy-feely and you ditched?'

'Well, it seems I don't need to tell you again,' Olivia replied, biting her lip while she walked. Usually Vanessa could figure out anything of this nature and offer advice. Maybe this time was a little bit different.

'Why didn't you stay?' Vanessa's voice reached a pitch higher than her usual tone.

'Wait, is Chad there?' Olivia paused on the street.

She heard silence on the other end of the phone before her friend responded.

'Why would Chad be here?'

'Hi, Olivia—ouch!' She heard Chad's voice trailing

through the phone and what sounded like Vanessa hitting him on the arm.

Olivia sighed, beginning to walk again. She knew that Chad was filled in on what happened with Olivia—after all, Vanessa shared everything with him. The fact that he would know didn't bother her so much, it was just when she was in a rush and trying to steal some advice from her friend.

'I don't know why I didn't stay.' She tried to ignore the obvious distractions on the other end of the call. 'I guess I just wasn't really convinced.'

'Convinced that you're together?' Vanessa replied.

'Did he actually say that you were together, or did he answer you with another question?' Chad's voice was louder now as though they had the call on speaker phone.

'A question, I guess.' Olivia slowed her pace.

'Uh-oh,' Chad said.

'What?' Olivia said, feeling her heart skip a beat.

'Honey,' Vanessa said, cautiously. 'His answer doesn't sound definite. It just sounds like he was saying what you wanted to hear.'

'Oh.' Olivia felt her face flush.

Of course, it made sense why she wasn't fully convinced. She felt like a fool for believing what Antoine said. Maybe he truly did mean it—she hoped he did. But she saw him, searching for answers, thinking that she got them, only to find out that it really didn't get her anywhere.

'Well, I'm here now,' Olivia said, seeing the café a

few shops up from her.

'Say hi to Scott for us!' Vanessa said before hanging up.

Olivia scoffed, she definitely wouldn't be passing that on to Scott. If she did, he would know that she had talked about him.

***

Scott sat in the same seat that he watched Olivia from the day he met her, waiting for her to meet him for coffee. It had been a week. A whole week since they met. A week and two days since he first saw her. It felt like a lifetime. It's as though every other woman seemed sub-standard compared to her beauty and the impact that she had already made on him. He felt like a teenager with his first crush, feeling like this about a woman he barely knew.

Olivia had taunted him in his dreams, teasing him, flirting, seducing. She visited his thoughts often—all the time, in fact. And each time she did, he felt himself falling deeper. He knew that he shouldn't. He tried to push aside his feelings, willing himself to keep an open mind. To control himself. He made a promise to her and he wanted to keep it. But his mind and his dreams ran wild, breaking his promise from all angles.

He couldn't be falling for her already, they hardly know each other. Sure, he was trying to change that. Besides, she made her intentions clear every time she turned down his offers to have dinner together.

He just had to suppress his fantasies and thoughts and focus on developing a friendship. At the very least, he had to have a friendship with her. He would hate it if it was never more, but it would kill him if he never saw her again.

Olivia walked through the door, pulling apart his decision, inch by inch, with a simple smile. He could never stop trying to be more with her. It was impossible. But he made a promise.

'I was hoping you would come.' He flashed his brilliant smile as she sat across from him.

'Well, I wasn't going to be a no-show.' She matched his smile.

As soon as she was settled in her chair, the waitress brought the two coffees over that Scott ordered when he arrived. Olivia shrugged out of her heavy black jacket, revealing a deep-fuchsia, off-the-shoulder shirt. His eyes followed her neat, golden curls falling onto her bare shoulders, then traced the curve of her neck, down to where her collarbones met. He caught a glimmer of a golden necklace, the pendant hiding behind the top of her shirt.

He wanted to kiss her. He wanted to trace the same line with his lips instead of his eyes. He couldn't keep his promise. One day, he would break, regardless of how hard he urged himself not to. He wouldn't be able to resist her. But, damn it, he had to try.

'You look nice.' He blurted it out, wishing that it didn't sound so forced.

The truth is, it wasn't forced. Not in the way it

sounded, at least. But in the way that it forced through his internal battle of trying not to flirt with her, escaping his lips before he could stop it. He knew that it would always be a losing battle. She would just have to cope with his compliments and flirting.

'Thank you,' Olivia said, blushing. 'So do you.'

Scott released the breath of air he was holding on to, relieved that she didn't seem to object. But he couldn't help but notice that she seemed distant, distracted. The look was becoming too familiar on her pretty face.

'Is everything okay?'

'Oh, it's nothing.' She shook her head and plastered a smile on her face. Her eyes didn't hide anything. 'Just a rough day.'

'You should take some time off every now and then, you know,' Scott said, hoping to receive a true smile. 'Especially since business owners usually don't get any time off.'

'Today *is* my day off.' She laughed. Her laughter was quiet, just for the two of them, but it seemed to surround them completely.

'And you've had a rough day? Maybe you shouldn't take time off.' Then he continued, hoping to make things better for her. 'Do you want to talk about it?'

***

Olivia stared into the eyes of the handsome dark-haired man sitting across from her. She couldn't believe that he picked up that something was wrong. After all, they hadn't known each other for long, so he shouldn't be able to determine her moods yet. But he did. It made her stomach feel warm.

She couldn't tell him everything. She couldn't tell him that she took the day off to process her thoughts. Thoughts about Antoine. Thoughts about him. They were what bothered her the most. Those thoughts were the reasons why she couldn't think straight anymore and forcing her into a predicament that she didn't care much to be in.

She remembered her phone call earlier in the day. Sure, that made her feel out of sorts, but it was also something that, unfortunately, she had grown used to. She had stopped expecting that her mother was going to make a miraculous recovery between her visits and calls. It only made her disappointed and more upset. If she had no expectations, it wouldn't be so hard. If it was only that simple.

'I just heard some bad news today, that's all,' she said finally, staring into the dark liquid steaming in her cup.

'What happened?' Scott said, his voice low. She felt more than saw his hand rest on her arm and his head move closer to her over the table to allow a deeper conversation.

'I called my mother's dementia ward,' she said, almost a whisper. 'She's having a difficult day. She's been having a lot of those lately.'

Olivia gripped her cup tighter, focussing all of her

energy on the cup and willing her threatening tears to stay behind her eyelids.

'Olivia.' She could feel the concern in his voice. 'Do you mind me asking what happened? Surely, it's not from age.'

'An accident,' Olivia whispered. 'She was riding her bike and a car hit her. She was lucky to survive, but she's had dementia ever since. Some days are all right, and I can visit her, but visits on days like today only make her worse.'

'I'm so sorry.' His eyes focussed on her arm underneath his hand.

'I've learnt to accept it.' Olivia shook her head to urge the tears away.

She looked into the hazel eyes, filled with concern. Even now, they were enchanting, tempting. She moved her gaze over his lips and his chiselled jaw, both tightened as if to prevent him from saying something. His shirt fit him loosely, but she could still tell that he was muscular, firm. She could feel the hairs raising on her arm from the gentle, smooth touching of his fingers on her arm. She wished there wasn't a table between them. She wished they were alone. She blamed her emotions for making her feel like this.

Olivia forced herself to pull away from him, standing to her feet, his hand dropping to the table.

'Excuse me,' she whispered.

Chapter 9

Scott stared across the table where Olivia had been sitting before going to the bathroom. He knew that she would be back, she left her jacket and her purse. He figured she just needed a moment to herself. He thought about what she had just told him—about her mother. For her to open up about that, she must trust him. At least a little. He was sure there was something else that worried her. But maybe his intuition was wrong. He didn't want to press her.

His mind filled with memories of his own. He knew what it was like to lose someone. But it was a shock for him, it was quick. Olivia had lost her mother and continued to lose her every day. It was a slow, torturous journey—one that would cause her more pain than he could ever imagine. He couldn't know what that was like.

He wasn't sure how long he was staring at the empty seat across from him, but the only thing that snapped him out of his intense gaze was a shadow falling across the table. He looked up, hoping it was Olivia.

'Hello, Scott.'

Damn.

'Afternoon, boss,' Scott said.

He returned his gaze to the table in hopes that his boss wouldn't want to join tables again. He felt a stab of disappointment when his boss took the empty seat in front of him, despite Olivia's jacket and purse shouting out that the seat wasn't available.

'Having some coffee?' His boss stated the obvious.

'Sure am,' Scott said coldly. 'And you?'

'Looking for someone,' he replied, scanning the café. 'I thought she would be here, but it seems not.'

'That's too bad,' Scott said, keeping his face expressionless and his gaze directed at the table.

'You have company.' He nodded at the half-empty cup in front of him and the purse beside it.

'Yes,' Scott said, looking at his boss. 'If you don't mind, you're actually in her seat.'

'Melissa?'

'Someone else.'

'I see. I'm leaving now, anyway,' his boss said, standing up and straightening his suit. 'Enjoy the rest of your date.'

***

Olivia stared at herself in the mirror, dabbing at her eyes with a tissue. It had been hard telling Scott about her mother. Heck, she rarely told anyone about it. Chad and Vanessa knew, but she mostly kept it to herself. But for some reason, Scott managed to batter down her walls of self-preservation and made her feel like she could share her deepest secrets with him. Well, maybe not her *deepest* secrets, especially any that involved him.

Apart from the blush in her cheeks from her previous thought, she decided that she looked presentable and controlled enough to go back out to Scott. She would try to keep the conversation off her and try to learn more about him. She straightened her shirt and starting walking back towards the table, freezing when she saw a familiar suit and head of dark-blonde hair talking to Scott.

She felt like she couldn't move. Why was he here, talking to Scott? Surely, they didn't know each other. She urged herself to move forward, towards the two men that inhabited her every thought. She had almost made it to the table when the man in the suit rose to his feet and turned to face her.

'What are you doing here, Antoine?' The words sounded harsher than she intended.

'Looking for you, actually,' he replied, straightening his suit.

'Wait, you two know each other?' Scott said.

'Since you wouldn't answer any of my calls, I had

to come looking for you the hard way.' He ignored Scott's question.

'There's a reason for that.' Olivia pushed past Antoine to pick up her jacket and purse.

Antoine's glare turned to her things that she just picked up, then to Scott, then back to Olivia.

'You're here together?' he said, his jaw tensing.

'We're having coffee,' Olivia said quickly. 'That's what friends do, Antoine. They have coffee. But this outing has now been spoilt, so we're going. Scott?'

She looked at Scott, feeling a longing in her chest. He looked baffled, disappointed, like he couldn't wait to get out of this situation. She wanted to reassure him. He didn't answer—Antoine didn't give him a chance to.

'He is *not* going with you,' Antoine said, his face reddening. 'You're with me, Olivia. Or have you forgotten that already? You came to me, damn it! You wanted to know if we were together and then you ran out of my house like a scared rabbit—I haven't even heard from you since Wednesday!'

Olivia glared at Antoine, shot an apologetic glance towards Scott, turned on her feet, and left.

***

Scott couldn't believe the scene that was unfolding before his eyes. He felt helpless, shocked. He didn't know what he should say—what he should do. He should have guessed that Olivia had a boyfriend, but she never told him. It angered him that it was his boss out of all the people in Paris. It never even occurred to him as a possibility. He hated Antoine for ruining their time together. He tried to process the heated conversation that he was witnessing as quick as he could.

Something happened between Olivia and Antoine on Wednesday—the night that he saw her in the park. He felt his body hardening. He should have guessed then. She was distracted and upset—she must have just left Antoine's place. She refused to have dinner with him every time he asked because she had a boyfriend. All this time, it was because of *him*.

He watched as Olivia walked out the door. He wanted to follow her—desired to follow her. But he couldn't move. He couldn't gain control of his body, no matter how much he willed himself to follow her. She wasn't his. She never was.

'The 'blonde beauty',' he said, remembering what Jack said to him a few days before.

'What?' Antoine said, turning his glare towards him.

Scott swallowed the rest of his coffee and stood to face his adversary. For some reason, he wasn't as intimidating now as he had originally seemed.

'You sick bastard,' he said, shaking his head and taking enjoyment in seeing his boss quiver. 'It's only a matter of time before she sees it, too.'

'She's not yours, Scott,' Antoine said, his eyes narrowing. 'But you can have your fill when I'm finished with her.'

Scott tensed, and before he knew it—before he could stop himself—his clenched fist connected with Antoine's jaw, wiping any hint of that smug grin off his face. He watched Antoine stumble backwards, his hand covering the throbbing spot where Scott punched him. He could hear nothing but silence and felt every eye on the café watching them. A quick glance around the room confirmed his suspicion. He picked up his jacket and started to leave.

'Oh, and by the way,' Scott said, pausing to look at Antoine again, 'consider that my resignation.'

With that, he left.

Chapter 10

Olivia fumbled with the paperwork in front of her, trying her best to immerse herself in her work instead of focussing on the incident at the café just moments before. She could still feel her body shaking and her heart pounding. The last person she wanted to see was Antoine but there he was, in all of his glory, looking for her when she was having coffee with Scott. She relived the anger and fear mingling together the moment she saw him at their table, talking to Scott.

Maybe that's what worried her more—that he was talking to Scott. Had he been watching them having coffee together, waiting for her to leave the table so that he could swoop in and threaten Scott? Surely, they couldn't have known each other before now. She felt her hands pressing harder against the workbench at the thought. *Oh, God, what if they did?*

The thought had never occurred to her before. What if Scott and Antoine did actually know each other? What if they were friends? Would the unwelcome scene at the café be the end of their friendship? She hoped desperately that they weren't close—that they were acquaintances at the most. She wondered how they would know each other when they were both from two completely different worlds. It would be best if it was just a coincidence.

But now, she didn't know where she stood with either of them. Obviously, Antoine still wanted her, but she was still mad at him. She was even more mad at him now than she was before. Before the café, she was starting to calm down enough to answer one of his calls or see him. But after he caused a scene like that in front of Scott, every inch of her being was defiant and set on avoiding him more.

And Scott—she didn't want that to end. She felt like she wouldn't be able to survive without having Scott in her life, despite only knowing him for a week. It felt like they had known each other forever. She wished that they did. Maybe then it wouldn't be so hard to know what he was thinking right now, or how he was feeling. She liked him. She felt like they had a connection from the moment she bumped into him. But it scared her. Scott seemed like an incredible man and she didn't want to ruin their growing friendship by acting on her irrational feelings.

She decided that she would just have to be content with being friends with him—if he would ever talk to her again. But she wanted more.

***

Scott rubbed his knuckles, feeling the pulsing and ache in his hand after punching Antoine. He shook his head, keeping his eyes on the pavement ahead of him. It wasn't like him to act out like that and just punch someone—especially in a nice cafe that he would really like to return to. He just felt so confused and dumbfound. There was so much more to Olivia than he knew, so much more than he thought existed.

He reminded himself that he had only known Olivia for a week and that it was only natural that he wouldn't know everything about her. But she had a boyfriend. She told him about her mother, but she failed to mention that she was in a relationship. With someone else. With his boss. His *former* boss.

'Damn it!' he said, quickening his pace.

She was out of his league. He didn't know what he was thinking, chasing a girl who was obviously interested in men who had money and titles to their names. Why would she be interested in him—a builder? She clearly liked her men to be clean, professional. He worked a hard, dirty job and would only wear suits for funerals, weddings, or formal events.

He turned a corner, his pace slowing.

He couldn't let her go. He didn't want to just be friends with her. You don't fantasise about your *friends*, imagining undressing them slowly, inch by inch, and showering them with kisses. *Friends* don't inhabit your mind every moment—awake or asleep—and make you feel like this. But he made a promise—a damn promise—and God help him for making promises that he knows he won't be able to keep.

He stopped and faced the door to Olivia's florist shop. The displays were gone, the sign was turned to 'closed' and the lights were turned off—except for the light in the back room casting a shadow of a slender woman against the back wall. He knocked on the door.

Nothing.

He knocked again, louder this time.

Still nothing.

He contemplated knocking once more but decided against it. Perhaps it was for the better. He turned his back to the door and watched the cars whizzing past that were completely unaware of what was going on around them. He was just about to leave when he heard the lock click and the door open.

'Scott?'

He closed his eyes and swallowed all of his thoughts that he had just been having. Her voice— the way she said his name—had a way of giving him hope when his mind had already decided that he had to let her go. He couldn't stay away. He was addicted to her and he had barely even had a taste. He turned to face the goddess he knew he had to fight for.

'Can I come in?' he asked.

***

Olivia stared at Scott, surprised that he had dropped past her shop—that he knew she would be here. When he hadn't moved by the time she left the café, she was certain that she wouldn't be seeing him soon. But here he was, standing at the door, asking to come inside.

She pulled the door open wide and stood aside to let him through. She didn't know what to say, or what he was going to say. But he wanted to talk to her. Why else would he be here? She closed the door and led the way to the back room, shifted the paperwork aside, and turned to face Scott.

He looked around the room, taking in everything around him, before bringing his gaze to meet Olivia's. He opened his mouth as if to say something, then closed it. She watched his Adam's apple move up and down as he swallowed. Even that looked enticing.

'You have a boyfriend,' he said finally, only a little more than a whisper.

'Scott,' she said, taking a step towards him. He shook his head.

'You have a *boyfriend*,' he said again, lifting his hands to emphasise his point.

'I was going to tell you,' Olivia said quietly, placing her hands on the workbench.

'When?' Scott asked. His voice was louder now, and he started pacing. 'When were you going to tell me, Olivia? Sometime before our first kiss? Or were you going to wait until I was on bended knee?'

He stopped his pacing and faced her. His eyes were filled with fire and felt like they were boring into her soul. She blinked back tears, speechless.

'You didn't tell me.' His voice broke, quieter now, the fire in his eyes dying out. 'You told me about your mother and your history, but you didn't tell me you had a boyfriend.'

'I didn't want to lose you,' she whispered, a tear escaping. 'Scott, believe me, please. I wanted to wait for the right time—I wanted to know you! I didn't want to lose our friendship because of a minor detail.'

'A minor detail?' he threw his hands in the air. 'Olivia, you are in a relationship. That is not a *minor* detail!'

'I'm sorry, Scott.' She stepped closer to him. 'Please believe me.'

They stood in silence for a moment, staring at each other. Scott looked tense, unnerved, like he was fighting a battle. More than anything, Olivia wanted to close the gap between them and kiss him, hoping that it would wash away the bad feelings. But she couldn't. Scott was right—her being in a relationship was not just a minor detail. But she had hoped it wouldn't come between them, especially since she wasn't so sure about Antoine anymore.

'Fine,' he said eventually. He sighed and brought

his right hand to his face to rub his forehead.

'Your hand,' Olivia said, closing the distance, and grabbing his hand from his face, analysing it.

'What about it?' Scott said, his face turning pale when he glanced at what Olivia was looking at. He tried to pull his hand away. 'It's nothing.'

Olivia didn't let go, but pulled him over towards the light to look at it better. She pressed her fingers against his knuckles, staring at Scott when he let out an 'ouch!' and pulled it away.

'You're hurt.'

'It's nothing,'

'It's swollen,' she said, grabbing his hand again. 'What happened?'

'You don't want to know.' He pulled his hand free of her vice-like grip.

'Tell me, Scott, please.'

Scott stared at her, hesitating for a moment, then averted his gaze to the floor.

'I, uhh.' He sighed. 'I punched your boyfriend.'

'You what?' Olivia said, her pitch rising.

'I punched Antoine.' He shrugged.

Olivia felt like her heart stopped. She couldn't stop the thoughts from swirling around in her mind. Everything confused her. She thought that the discussion would have ended when she left the café. Clearly, she was very wrong about that. And now, she finds out that the man that she has developing, uncontrollable feelings for, punched her boyfriend.

'Why the hell did you do that?' she yelled, unable to control herself.

'Hear me out.' He lifted his hands in surrender.

She glared at Scott, not wanting to continue the conversation, but nodded for him to continue. After all, he did let her explain about the excluded information that caused all this mess in the first place.

'He asked for it.'

'Scott!'

'Be careful of him, Olivia,' he said, stepping closer to her. 'He's not the man you think he is.'

'Neither are you, by the sounds of it.'

Scott took a step back, his mouth gaping and his eyes wide open. He swallowed, nodded, and turned to leave.

'Scott, wait,' Olivia said, grabbing his arm. 'I'm sorry.'

Scott turned to face her again, his jaw clenched.

'He's my boss, Olivia,' Scott said, his face inches from hers. 'Well, *was* my boss, until I resigned ten minutes ago. I know the kind of man he is, Olivia, and he's not who you think he is.'

Olivia's hands fell to her side. She wasn't sure if she should be hurt, or feeling defiant because Scott was challenging her relationship with Antoine, or thankful. She was worried about Scott, since he didn't have a job anymore and that she was the reason why.

'What kind of man is he?' She wasn't sure if she wanted to know the answer.

'Let's just say,' he hesitated, 'that you're not the only one he's dating.'

Olivia stood in shock as she watched Scott leave her shop, unable to move, and unable to breathe.

Chapter 11

Olivia tapped her fingers on the workbench, staring at the man walking slowly through her shop. He seemed to be examining every single flower on every single bouquet that she had on display. Never mind that he was now on his third round through the shop. He had started bringing a bouquet to the register on his first round, then changed his mind and started looking at every bouquet again. Olivia sighed. She had never seen someone so indecisive before.

'Can I help you come to a decision?' she asked from the register.

'I don't think so,' he said, placing a bouquet of roses and lilies back in its bucket. 'I think I have to look at them all again.'

Olivia resumed tapping her fingers. It was Tuesday morning, two days after her conversation with Scott and the dispute with Antoine. She hadn't talked to either of them since then. She had noticed a missed call from Antoine, but she didn't feel like talking to him. She needed time. Time to sort out her feelings, to rationalise and attempt to work out what Scott meant.

'You're not the only one he's dating.'

She couldn't stop thinking about that. She had to know an answer, but she was scared of what the truth might be. But it troubled her, especially since Chad and Vanessa had also told her that it didn't sound like Antoine considered them exclusive. Olivia had fallen for his charms, convinced that he was hers and she was his. Maybe she couldn't see the signs. Or maybe he was just a really good actor.

But then, if Antoine is Scott's boss—*was*, she corrected herself—how would Scott know about his habits? Antoine never came across as one who would share his personal life with his work acquaintances, particularly with people who worked *for* him. Maybe Scott said it out of jealousy. But even though he practically said that he had feelings for Olivia, she wasn't so sure if they remained. The look in his eyes when he talked to her in her shop and the fact that he hadn't called her since then said it all.

She watched the man start his fourth round through the shop and sighed. She couldn't deal with this today. She had to attempt to bring some kind of organisation into her head and she knew that, before the day was finished, she had to talk to Antoine.

'Betty, I'm going home,' she called out. 'Do you need anything?'

Betty walked out from the back room.

'I'm fine,' she said. 'Will you be coming back, or should I lock up?'

'Lock up, please,' Olivia said, gathering her things to leave.

***

Scott leaned up against the wall, watching intently as hundreds of people filed from the airplane into the airport. He still couldn't get Olivia out of his head after their discussion at her shop. He knew that he probably shouldn't have knocked on the door when he did. He should have just left it and called her later. But he knew that she would have found out that he punched her boyfriend and, knowing the bastard that Antoine is, she would have been even more upset at him than she is now. She had to hear it from him. He had to tell her before the story became warped with Antoine's interpretation of it.

But he still hadn't heard from her. He wanted to give her some time to process what he said. She would know that he would be there if she needed it, if she called him. He had hoped that it would be sooner rather than later. He'd even foolishly given her his address in hopes that she might visit if she couldn't get in contact with him. But still, nothing.

'Well, if it isn't Scott Henders!' a familiar voice

said.

He smiled, turning around to greet his old friend.

'Alex Carter! It's about time you came for a visit,' he said, shaking his hand.

'Thanks for picking me up, mate,' Alex said with a smile.

Alex had been born and bred in Australia. They worked together on many building sites, Scott as a builder and Alex as a painter. They spent a lot of time collaborating on the projects and soon found themselves building a friendship outside of work. With moving to Paris and dedicating a lot of his focus on his job, Scott didn't have many long-lasting good friends. But his friendship with Alex seemed indestructible and, despite the distance and time differences between them, they still kept in contact.

They waited together for Alex's suitcase, then grabbed a coffee from the café in the airport.

'How's Mum and Dad?' Scott asked.

'They're going well,' Alex said after sipping his coffee. 'Suzie sent a care package home with me last week. I think she believes that I still can't cook.'

Scott smiled to hear that his parents were doing well. He always considered Alex to be like a younger brother to him. Alex lost his mother when he was a child and was raised by his father who also lined him up with his painting apprenticeship. His father passed away the year Scott left Australia to move to Paris. Since Alex had spent a lot of time with Scott's family when they worked together, he continued to visit them regularly after Scott moved. For that, Scott was appreciative.

'Can you?' Scott teased.

'If you count baked beans on toast as cooking, then yes.' Alex smiled back.

The two friends bantered for a while, catching up on everything that had been happening back in Australia. As much as Scott loved Paris, it made him homesick.

'So, how long are you staying for?' Scott asked as they climbed into his car.

Alex shrugged. 'Don't know, yet.'

'But didn't you take leave?'

'Didn't have to,' Alex said, staring ahead.

'Why are you here, Alex?'

Scott watched his friend grow tense, avoiding eye contact with him. Something was going on and he knew it. Finally, Alex turned to face Scott.

'The company foreclosed,' he said simply. 'Apparently, the boss was doing some shady, underhand business. So, I figured, what better time to come to Paris?'

'You don't have a job anymore?'

'Was hoping I could get one with you,' Alex said, smiling. 'It could be like the old times.'

'Well, I suppose we could look for work together,' Scott said, his face solemn.

'You don't have a job?' Alex was wide-eyed.

'I resigned on Sunday.' Scott wished he could avoid this topic for a later conversation.

He started the car and began to drive towards the hotel that Alex had booked. They had too much to catch up on, but Alex wasn't giving up.

'Why?'

'Because I punched my boss.' Scott glanced over at the shocked look on his friend.

'Do I want to know why?'

'Because we had a disagreement.'

'About?'

Scott looked over at his friend, surprised that he still hadn't given up. But, then again, it was like Alex to want details like this. Scott smiled—he had missed his friend.

'A woman,' Scott said.

Alex didn't say anything, just looked out the window at the city around them. Scott knew that Alex loved to travel, but he had never been to Paris before. He looked like he was in awe. He wouldn't be surprised if Alex did decide to stay.

'When will I meet her?' Alex said, finally.

'I'm not sure you will,' Scott said, matter-of-factly.

'You're not together?' Alex raised an eyebrow.

Scott shook his head.

'And you punched your boss?'

Scott nodded.

'You're going to have to give me something here, Scott,' Alex said, his face full of concern. 'Because it's not making much sense.'

'He's a jerk.' He sighed. 'And she's dating him.'

Damn it. Admitting it to Alex felt like it hit home again. He didn't know what she saw in Antoine, but he knew what she didn't see. He just wished it didn't have to pan out the way it did.

'You like her.' Alex observed his friend's face for a reaction.

'I blew it.'

***

After checking Alex in at the hotel, Scott took him on a walking tour of Paris. He showed him the café that he goes—*went*—to with Olivia, where he worked, the Seine, and the hotdog vendor. They continued to talk and catch up, just like they used to, and decided on going to the next closest bar for dinner and some drinks.

Walking down the street, Scott slowed down as they came closer to Olivia's florist. Would she see them walking past? Should they turn back and go the long way around to get to the bar? He stopped walking right before he passed in front of the window.

'What's wrong?' Alex turned to Scott.

'This is her shop,' Scott said quietly.

'She works here?'

'She owns it.' Scott corrected him.

'Let's go in,' Alex said, a mischievous grin on his face.

Scott froze.

'We can't go in!' he said, trying to keep his voice to a whisper as a man walked out, carrying three different bouquets.

'Well, you stay here, then,' Alex said, opening the

door and walking in.

Damn it.

Scott waited outside of Olivia's florist shop, receiving a number of different looks from people passing by. He felt like he must have waited for over ten minutes, but he didn't want to look through the window just in case Olivia saw him. What was Alex doing in there?

As carefully as he could, he peeked through the window, hoping that no one would see him. Alex was standing at the register, a small bouquet in his hands, talking to someone, judging by the way he nodded his head and moved his arms, but he couldn't see who he was talking to. He moved away from the window again. A few more minutes passed before Alex walked through the door, a smile on his face.

'Well?' Scott asked him, still not daring to walk past the window.

'Hmm? Oh,' Alex said, looking wistfully at the bouquet in his hands. 'Well, she is definitely pretty— if you don't want her, I'll gladly take her.'

'Get in line, Alex,' Scott said, frowning. 'She has a boyfriend.'

'I hope not,' Alex said, his smile teasing. 'Because she agreed to go on a date with me tomorrow night.'

Scott's heart sank. Surely his friend was joking but, somehow, he wasn't so sure. He felt his heart stop when Alex presented the business card with a name and number scrawled on the back of it. He grabbed the card off Alex and studied the writing carefully.

'Betty?' Scott said, relieved that it wasn't Olivia's name scrawled on the card.

'That's not the girl?' Alex scrunched his eyebrows. 'She was the only one in there, I thought it must have been her.'

Scott peered through the window again and saw the brown-haired woman adjusting some flowers in a bouquet.

'Olivia owns the shop,' Scott said. 'That's Betty, her employee.'

'I see,' Alex said, a smile on his face again. 'Just as well, since I'm going on a date with Betty tomorrow.'

They laughed and continued on towards the bar, Alex giving the bouquet that he bought to the first pretty lady they passed on the street.

Chapter 12

Olivia stared at the solid, threatening door, her fist lingering inches away from it. She knew that it was time. She had to deal with the issues with Antoine before she went insane from not knowing. She took a big breath to steady her nerves and knocked.

She waited a moment, debating whether or not she knocked loud enough and if she should knock again. She tapped her fingers on her leg, feeling her stomach churning, and every inch of her trying to convince her to just stay mad at him a while longer. She knew that she should have had another glass of wine before coming over, that the second one just wasn't enough.

She lifted her hand again to knock, but the door flew open and Antoine was standing there, clearly surprised to see her. His hair was a mess and looked damp—as though he had just had a shower—he smelt clean, too, and he wore pyjama bottoms and no shirt.

'Olivia,' he said, definitely surprised.

His mouth opened and closed a few times as if trying to say something but finding himself speechless. Olivia smiled at herself, pleased that she could manage to get such a reaction from him. She pushed past him into his flat, took another breath and turned to face him.

'Are we exclusive?' she asked.

'What?' Antoine said, looking somewhat nervous. 'We've talked about this, Olivia.'

'We really haven't. I asked you if we were dating and together and you implied that we were, but you didn't say it, Antoine. You tried to seduce me, instead. Probably to avoid this whole conversation altogether.'

'This isn't a good time.' He plucked a shirt off the back of the couch to put on.

'It's a damn good time, Antoine.' Olivia's voice was becoming more frantic. 'I wanted answers and you just made me more confused and not knowing what to think of us. You cancelled almost every date we set and then you got upset when I didn't return your calls. Well, guess what? I needed time! I needed to try to figure out the mess that you left me with.'

'Are you drunk, Olivia?' Antoine said, moving closer to her so that he stood inches from her.

'No,' Olivia retorted. 'But I wish I was, because

that seems to be the only way I can deal with y—'

Antoine's mouth had closed over hers, interrupting her rant, and his arms were holding her tight. She didn't want the kiss, she was mad. But it felt good. Though, maybe she *was* drunk. He finally let her go.

'Does that answer your question?' He rested his forehead against hers.

Olivia didn't say anything. She didn't know what to say or what she should do. She looked behind him, trying to avoid eye contact with him. She saw two empty dinnerplates, a candle, and two wine glasses on the table. She couldn't even move.

'Now, go home, Olivia, and get some rest.' He was oblivious to what she saw. 'I'll call you tomorrow.'

Olivia could feel the fury building inside of her. She could see a line of red lipstick along the rim of one of the glasses.

'Why don't I stay?' she heard herself say.

Antoine's eyes widened.

'Not tonight,' he said quickly. 'I have to work early in the morning.'

'Oh, but you're the boss,' she said. 'You can start whenever you want to.'

'Not tomorrow. There's an early delivery.'

Olivia thought she could see alarm in his eyes. *Good*, she thought. She wanted him to squirm.

'What's the matter, Antoine? Do you already have company for tonight?'

She heard a thump coming from his bedroom and

beelined towards the sound.

'Olivia!' he said, rushing to get in front of her.

Olivia pushed past him and opened the door to his bedroom, just in time to find a woman with dyed-blonde hair sitting on the edge of his *unmade* bed, clutching the sheet to her chest to hide her nakedness. She turned to Antoine, more sure of how she was feeling than she had been in a while, and slapped him. He gritted his teeth and stared at Olivia as if waiting for the brewing storm. She could see the red handprint beginning to form on his cheek where she slapped him.

'You're a liar,' Olivia said, pointing her finger at him. 'A dirty, sleazy liar.'

'Olivia—' he said, as if about to explain.

She interrupted his excuses. 'No. Do you know what you are?' She felt her body shake with fury. 'You are a slimy, pig-nosed, no-good, jerk-faced, arrogant, ventripotent ASS! That's what you are! And you almost had me believing you like a fool!'

Olivia started marching herself over to the door, somewhat in disbelief as to what she had just experienced.

'Olivia!' Antoine was whined, following her to the door.

'Don't ever talk to me again!' she yelled at him, slamming the door in his face.

***

'I'll see you tomorrow,' Scott called out as the cab

pulled away from the curb.

He watched as Alex stuck his head out the window and waved to him, headed back to the hotel. Scott turned towards his house and smiled at the fun evening that he'd had with his old friend. Since Scott drove to the hotel to pick up Alex before their tour of Paris, he wasn't intending on having much to drink at the bar. But the two friends got so caught up with their conversations that he had more than he planned to. He didn't feel overly drunk, but he knew he was a bit tipsy and definitely unfit to drive. He laughed, remembering one of the conversations they had, as he entered his building and started walking up the stairs to his flat.

If Alex was trying to help him feel better about blowing it with Olivia and losing his job, then he had succeeded. For the few hours that they were at the bar, Scott felt like he was back in Australia, laughing and joking about everything with his friend as though nothing that was happening was actually going on. For a while, he felt like he could get over Olivia. But that might be the drink talking.

He started fumbling with his keys as he rounded the corner of the stairwell to start on the last set of stairs before his floor, but froze when he looked up.

'Olivia?'

He wasn't entirely sure if he actually said her name or not, or if she was even there—sitting at the top of the stairs, a bottle of wine in her hands, and her face red from crying. He wondered if he had actually had more to drink than he thought he had.

'You were right,' she said, her voice choked with tears.

He urged himself up the stairs towards her, taking two steps at a time, and felt himself sobering. He sat down next to her and pulled her into his arms, fresh tears flowing from her eyes.

'You were right,' she said again. 'About Antoine.'

Scott didn't need to ask about what happened. He could guess. He held her closer, her head resting against his chest, and he rubbed her back and stroked her hair. He planted a soft, gentle kiss on her forehead and she leaned further against him, her sobbing lessening slightly. He hated Antoine for making Olivia hurt like this. But he couldn't help but smile to himself. He thought that he had blown it with Olivia, but here she was, at his flat door, in his arms. She could have gone to anyone, but she came to him. And it made him feel good.

***

'I am a free woman!'

Scott watched as Olivia waved her wine glass around in a drunken state. After he comforted her in the stairway for a while, they relocated into his flat to avoid drawing too much attention from his nosy neighbours, which didn't take much convincing. Olivia was all too willing to waltz into his flat and try to sit on his couch. It made quite the scene, though, when she had missed the couch completely and landed on the floor in front of it. But that is where she stayed put, leaning her back against the couch, while Scott fetched her a wine glass at her request and returned to grab a beer from the fridge for himself.

'I can do whatever I want,' Olivia continued. 'I can talk to whoever I want and go wherever I want to go.' She polished off the wine in her glass and filled it again. 'I slapped the son of a bitch—and it felt good. I can see why you punched him.'

Scott winced at the reminder of his uncontrolled outburst. Even after having some drinks, he didn't feel the need to punch anyone. Antoine must have really hit a nerve to get that reaction from him. He wandered slowly towards Olivia, wondering where he should sit. He didn't want to sit on the floor next to her because that would be too close. It would be too hard to control himself. Sitting opposite from her would be the same because he would have a full, front-on view of the goddess on his lounge-room floor whose breasts were coming dangerously close to popping out of her dress. He settled himself on the couch, right up against the armrest and as far from her as the couch would allow. He had to keep himself controlled and together.

'Why did you come here, Olivia?'

'Because I wanted to see you.' She turned to face him.

Scott clenched his jaw. He knew that sitting opposite from her would have probably been the safest spot for him to sit, but his mind had somehow convinced him otherwise. She was leaning with one arm up on the couch and her legs folded beneath her. She held the wine glass delicately in her other hand and the strap of her dress had fallen off her shoulder. If the strap fell even an inch more, he wouldn't be able to control himself.

Damn it.

'And Vanessa has Chad, the kids would be in bed.' She shrugged, the strap creeping down her arm even more. 'And, well, you're the only other person who knew about Antoine.'

Scott swallowed, trying to tear his gaze from her bare shoulder and her delicate neckline.

'I thought you wouldn't mind,' she said, pouting.

Scott succeeded in moving his gaze from her shoulder, but only to stare at her pouted lips. They sent his mind reeling. Her delicious, perfect, seductive lips. He wondered if they would taste like the wine she was drinking or if the taste was uniquely her—sweet, delectable, irresistible.

'Oh, you don't want me to leave do you?'

She put the empty wine glass down on his coffee table. She managed to pull herself up onto the couch beside him, her eyes were pleading, and her hand was on his leg. He could smell her sweet perfume— she *was* irresistible.

'Scott?' she whispered.

The way she said his name drove him wild with desire. He wanted her. He *needed* her.

'Definitely not,' he said, feeling himself moving closer to her—ever so slightly.

She smiled. Her gorgeous, incredible smile that

pushed him over the edge. Before he knew it, their lips had met. His hand was touching the delicate skin below her ear and his other arm was around her waist, pulling her closer towards him. She did taste delicious—sweeter than the wine she was drinking. The taste was so uniquely her, and her lips were soft against his. But she was just as eager, leaning closer against him and moving her mouth willingly against his. She was addictive. And she wanted him. That's all he needed to know.

It was the best damn kiss he had ever had.

Chapter 13

It was inevitable. Scott was there, the timing was right, and she wanted him. Olivia couldn't help herself. She could feel his lips pressing eagerly against hers, only leaving her lips to kiss her nose, her cheeks, her neck. She could feel his desire for her, matching the longing that she had for more of him. Their attraction was undeniable. And, in this moment, nothing could come between them. She could feel the heat of his body against hers, the sting of his tongue teasing hers. She could feel the warmth of his hands as they caressed every inch of her body ...

Olivia's eyes shot open. Her heart was racing, and her body was shaking. She blinked at the ceiling and groaned at the throbbing ache in her head and queasiness in her stomach. She looked around the room, blinded by the light glaring through the window, trying to make sense of where she was and what she had done.

She was in a big comfortable bed—Scott's bed—alone. The blanket was skewed, and the bed was unkempt. The tastes in her mouth confused her. She could taste the bitterness of alcohol lingering in her breath, but there was a sweetness that lingered and a tingling in her lips—the tingling that comes after a kiss. A very thorough kiss.

'Oh, no,' Olivia shot upright.

She clutched the sheet to her chest just as the woman in Antoine's bedroom had done. She felt the blood drain from her face at the situation she found herself in. Her clothes formed a dishevelled heap on the floor near the bed. She was completely naked. In Scott's bed.

'No, no, no, no!' she said frantically. 'Oh, God, no!'

She slid off the bed, pulling the sheet around her as she rushed to gather her clothes and took them to the bathroom to change. She saw the shower first, and considered having one to wash away the dirtiness that she felt. She didn't want to wake up in a man's bed unable to remember what happened. She wasn't that kind of woman. And she certainly hoped that the man would still be lying next to her when she woke up. Scott was nowhere to be seen.

She decided to skip the shower and have one at home. But when she turned, she couldn't help but stare at the person looking back at her in the mirror. This wasn't her. The person in the mirror clutched desperately at the sheet around her as if to make her feel like she wasn't completely naked in a house that wasn't her own. Her hair was untidy, and her makeup was smudged. She didn't know who the woman in the mirror was, but it sure as hell wasn't her.

Olivia scolded the woman in the mirror for being so irresponsible and bent over the sink to wash her face. It didn't make her feel as clean as a shower would, but it made her feel a bit more presentable and eased her headache a little. She fumbled through her hair to find where her hair tie was hiding and pulled it into a bun—the only hairstyle that could hide unbrushed hair. She let the sheet fall from her body only to put her clothes on. She looked back at the mirror. The woman was still a stranger to her, but at least she looked like Olivia.

Content that she looked presentable enough to be seen in public, she poked her head out of the door into the lounge room, just to make sure that she was alone. She was. She sighed. It hurt that Scott hadn't at least stayed in his flat to see her off, but it also made her escape easier. Maybe he thought this was for the better.

She found her shoes and her purse and took one last look around the place, gaining a better appreciation of Scott's tidiness than she could have had last night. She thought that he was a decent guy. Last night, she was drunk. Possibly more drunk than she had ever been in her life. She couldn't remember what state he was in but, drunk or not, he took advantage of her. And she knew that, because of that, they couldn't be together, regardless of how much she liked being with him.

Olivia closed the door to Scott's flat and started the descent down the stairway as quick as she could manage, feeling as though she had left her heart and herself behind.

***

Scott locked his car and began walking towards his flat. He hated leaving Olivia by herself this morning, but she looked too peaceful to wake. He figured she would still be asleep by the time he got back from picking up his car from the hotel. He imagined that she would wake up with an even worse headache than he had, considering she seemed to drink so much more than him. So, he dropped past the café on his way home to pick up some coffee.

Hopefully, she would be asleep, and he could wake her, perhaps re-enact their kiss and he would let her freshen up while he cooked her breakfast. He had to do this right. He wanted to make her feel special and worth every single thing that he gave her. He just hoped that she felt the same way.

He reached to open the door to his building, but found it already swinging open with Olivia pushing her way through it. She froze when she saw him there, blocking her exit.

'Scott,' she said.

'I've got coffee.' He held up the coffee tray with two cups in it.

Her gaze avoided his eyes as if she didn't even want to look at him.

'I was just—'

'Leaving?'

Olivia nodded, her eyes looked saddened, worried. Frustrated.

'I was going to make you breakfast,' he said, breaking their silence. 'Or we can go out, if you would rather.'

'I can't,' she said, squeezing around him to leave. 'I have to go, I have things to do.'

He started walking beside her along the street. She was being evasive, and she didn't have to be. He didn't know what he could do or say to make her stay.

'Do you need a lift?' he asked. If she wanted to go, he could take her. At least that would give them more time together.

'No, thank you, Scott,' she said, flagging down a cab and crawling into the back seat. 'You've done enough.'

She closed the car door and she was gone. Scott watched the cab driving away, disappearing out of sight when it turned a corner. She was gone. He turned and started walking back to his flat.

'Damn it!' he yelled, tossing the coffees into the bin on the street.

Damn it.

***

Olivia had her shower. Twice. But it still didn't wash away the thought of what she may have done. Scott was trying to make her feel better. He got coffee for her and was going to make her breakfast. And she couldn't even look at him in the eyes for fear that she would cave. He confused her. Every damn thing about him confused her.

She thought that their attraction was mutual, undeniable, and they could have, maybe, one day, worked it out. But then, last night happened, and she didn't know what to think anymore. He made her someone that she didn't recognise. He made her feel things that she had never felt before. She didn't know what to make of that.

All she wanted to do was sit at home by herself, preferably sleeping so that she wouldn't have to think about it. But even her dreams seemed to defy her. She blushed at the memory of the dream that woke her up that morning. Her dreams were definitely not a safe place at the moment. So, she had come into work, trying to do what she does best—arranging flowers. But she couldn't hide anything from Betty.

She told Betty about her break up with Antoine. She pretended that he was the reason why she was so out of it this morning. Truth be told, she was more relieved about the break up than she was upset about it. It was Scott that distracted her, that saddened her. But she didn't tell Betty about her rendezvous with Scott in her drunken state.

'Well, you're a free woman now,' Betty said, poking some roses into a bouquet of baby's breath. 'And Antoine clearly wasn't worth the paper his name was written on.'

'I'm not sure being a free woman is very becoming of me,' Olivia mumbled, more to herself than to Betty.

She knew that, after crying about Antoine for a while last night, she was happy that she was now a free woman. She cringed at the misty memory of freely expressing that thought to Scott last night. It seems he took it too literally.

'Nonsense,' Betty chimed. 'I know! You need a date!'

'Oh, I do *not* need a date right now,' Olivia said quickly.

'It'll make you feel better,' Betty said excitedly, now facing Olivia. 'I've got it. I'm going on a date tonight, so come with us.'

'And be the third wheel? I don't think so.' Olivia shook her head, knowing too well what Betty was hinting towards. But she knew deep down that she wouldn't get out of this arrangement—even if she told her about Scott. That would just make Betty more persistent.

'I'll tell him to bring a friend,' Betty smiled. 'He's a very attractive man. And very attractive men tend to have very attractive friends.'

'What if he doesn't want to bring a friend?' Olivia

asked, trying desperately to get out of it.

'Oh, he will,' Betty chided. 'Because if he doesn't, I won't be going on the date.'

Olivia smiled at Betty. The last thing she wanted to do tonight was go on a double-date—her date being someone that she hadn't met before. Then again, maybe Betty was right. Maybe she did need to go on dates—no strings attached—to get over what happened with Antoine. And then with Scott. It was worth a try.

'All right,' Olivia sighed. 'I'll go.'

***

Scott didn't tell Alex about his night with Olivia, especially after Alex was already under the impression that he blew it with her. He didn't need to know that he blew it again. But keeping it from his friend was hard. He knew that Alex would be able to tell that something was up. And he was right—Alex did end up asking him why he was so out of it. All Scott could say was that he just had a hard night getting to sleep. Everyone suffers from those nights on occasion. Alex didn't need to know why.

He tried to keep the morning light and entertaining for Alex. After all, Alex didn't come to Paris to be encumbered with all of Scott's problems and get caught up in heaps of drama. Besides, he only had to worry about the day with him because Alex was going on a date with Betty tonight and, if all goes well, he wouldn't have to be the only one entertaining him each day. In fact, he could take solace in knowing that Alex would be in very capable hands. That was until Alex got a phone call that seemed to be making him rather frustrated.

Scott sipped his coffee while he watched his friend through the door to the balcony. Alex was rubbing his forehead with his hand and paced back and forth before finally putting the phone back in his pocket and walking inside.

'Everything all right?' Scott said.

Alex shook his head, his eyes apologetic.

'I need a favour,' he said. 'Betty's refusing to go on the date tonight unless she can bring a friend so that it's less awkward with the whole not knowing who I am thing.'

'Wouldn't that make it more awkward?'

Alex shrugged, looking at Scott, attempting to make his intent clear. Scott froze when he realised what Alex was trying to say.

'No,' he said simply.

'Come on, Scott.'

'No,' he repeated, 'I am *not* coming on the date with you.'

'I have to bring someone, I'm begging you.' Alex clasped his hands together in front of his chest. 'Otherwise Betty will cancel.'

'Let her cancel, then,' Scott said.

'Seriously?'

'Or take someone else with you.'

'I don't know anyone else here, Scott!' Alex said. 'Come on, it'll help you get over Olivia.'

Scott doubted it would, but it seemed that he didn't have much of a choice. Alex had been looking forward to his date with Betty and was feeling quite proud of himself for managing to get a date on his second day in Paris. From what he had gathered from their catching up, Alex needed this. What would a few hours of talking to a stranger matter, anyway? Especially if it meant so much more to Alex than it did to Scott. He cringed at the memory of his date with Melissa.

'You owe me—big time,' he said, pointing at his friend.

Chapter 14

Scott and Alex stood at the bar in the restaurant, sipping on a beer each while they waited for their dates to show up. Scott didn't want to be on this date, but he decided it wouldn't be too bad when Alex told him that it was at a restaurant that had a bar attached to it. At least a few beers would help him through the night like it did on his date with Melissa. He wondered if his date would be like Melissa. He hoped not. He didn't think he could deal with a passionate cat-lover in his current state. He checked his watch.

'They're late,' he said, leaning against the bar.

'Girls are always late, Scott,' Alex said, shaking his head. 'That's why you pick them up first.'

'So, why didn't we?'

'That's not the way of the double-date,' Alex said, scanning the growing crowd. 'On single dates, you pick the girl up because you expect to be invited in when you drop her off. On double-dates, you meet wherever it is that you're going. It's less awkward that way.'

'When did you become an expert on dating?' Scott nudged his friend.

Alex avoided his question and started craning his neck to see the door. Their dates were still not in sight.

'What's my date's name, anyway?' Scott asked.

'Betty didn't say,' Alex replied.

'So, she's an unnamed mystery woman,' Scott replied, taking another sip of his beer.

He had a feeling he might be needing more of it.

'I'm going to check outside—they might be looking for us,' Alex said, heading towards the door before Scott could reply.

Through the crowd, he caught a glimpse of a beautiful golden-haired goddess and quickly turned to face the bar. *Olivia was here*. Scott wondered what she was doing here and if she had seen him. He hoped that she hadn't. He didn't want her to see him here with another woman—that would put him in the same boat as Antoine. He downed the rest of his beer and ordered another.

Who was she here with? Never mind the thought of her seeing him here with another woman—he didn't want to see her with another man. Surely, she wasn't here with Antoine. But who else could she be with? At least he didn't know the person he was on a date with. She wouldn't be here with someone that she didn't know, he was sure of it.

He picked his fresh glass of beer up almost as soon as the bartender put it down and gulped half of it. If he hadn't already blown it twice with her, he was just about to blow it again if she saw him there. Maybe he could sneak out and tell Alex that he felt like he was coming down with something. That might work. He was just about to set his plan into motion when his friend started speaking again.

'I found them,' Alex said.

It was too late. Scott turned around to face Alex and Betty and his date for the evening.

'Ladies, this is—'

'Olivia—' Scott said.

'Scott,' Olivia said at the same time.

Alex and Betty both looked at each other in disbelief while Scott and Olivia stared at each other.

'What are you doing here?' Olivia asked, directing her question at Scott.

She didn't sound very happy. Maybe this was his chance, after all.

'Waiting for you, apparently.' Scott was trying to lift the tone.

'*You* are my date?' Olivia asked, flustered.

'You two already know each other?' Betty asked with a smile.

'Betty, can I talk to you for a moment?' Olivia said, grabbing Betty by the arm and pulling her away.

Alex turned to Scott, his voice at a level that only

Scott could hear.

'Olivia?' he said. '*The* Olivia?'

Scott nodded.

'Tell me,' Alex said. 'Did anything else happen—apart from you punching her boyfriend? Because she looks a lot more annoyed at you than that.'

'They broke up last night.' Scott shrugged.

'Because of you?'

'No,' Scott said. 'Yes. I don't really know. But there's more.'

Alex nodded for Scott to continue. As much as he had tried to keep it from Alex, he had to tell him now. Otherwise, they may as well leave—if the girls hadn't already.

'She was at my house when I got home last night,' he said, holding his hand up to stop Alex from interrupting again. 'Yes, after we were at the bar. Well, she was drunk, and she stayed the night.'

'Did anything happen?' Alex asked, his eyes wide.

Scott hesitated before nodding.

***

'Olivia, what is going on?' Betty said, pulling her arm free of Olivia's grip.

'We have to go,' Olivia said.

'What? No, we're not going anywhere,' Betty said. 'How do you know Scott?'

'We … ahh. We had a bit of a thing.'

Betty raised an eyebrow at Olivia and crossed her arms, urging her to continue.

'I may have slept with him.' Olivia couldn't meet her friend's gaze.

'Like, months ago?' Betty asked, her eyes widening.

'Last night,' Olivia said, biting her lip.

'Oh.' Betty furrowed her brows. 'Oh! But didn't you—'

'Yes.'

'And you—?'

'Yes.'

'Was it good?'

'Betty!'

'We can't leave!' Betty threw her hands out. 'They know we're here now, so it would be rude if we left.'

Olivia crossed her arms. She knew that she wouldn't be able to sit through this date acting like nothing had happened with Scott. But Betty was relying on her.

'So, my vote is that we find our table. Ready?' Alex said as he and Scott came to stand next to them.

'Yes, we're ready,' Betty said, smiling at her date, and looping her arm in his.

'Well, let's go,' Alex said.

Olivia watched Alex and Betty walking ahead before turning to face Scott.

'Olivia—' He started to speak but she held her hand up to stop him from continuing.

'I am only staying because Betty begged me to,' she said. '*Not* because I want to be here.'

She started walking towards the table, Scott

following behind her. It was going to be a long night.

***

'You lived in Australia?' Betty directed her question to Scott.

Alex had just finished telling Betty how he and Scott had met. Betty had been holding on to every word. Olivia had to admit, Alex was a good story-teller. But she couldn't bring herself to be involved with the conversation. Instead, she alternated between avoiding looking at Scott and straight-up staring at him. He didn't look nearly as uncomfortable as she felt. He had to have set this up.

'For eight years, yes.' Scott sipped from his glass.

'And before that?' Betty asked.

'London.'

'And before that?'

'Let's just say,' Scott said, his lips turned into a cheeky grin. 'I moved around a lot.'

'Interesting, don't you think so, Olivia?' Betty said staring straight at her.

Olivia glanced at the three sets of eyes waiting for her reply. Betty clearly didn't need her help in making conversation—not that she would have been much help now, anyway. And if she didn't know otherwise, Betty was obviously trying to mend the tension between her and Scott. It wasn't going to work.

'Oh, yes. A definite travel bug.' She refused to let herself look at Scott.

'What's that supposed to mean?' Betty asked, her demeanour changing as she leaned towards Olivia.

'It means that he gets itchy feet—loves to move around,' Olivia said, shrugging, before begrudgingly directing her gaze to Scott. 'You've been in Paris for, what? Three years? Where's your next adventure going to be?'

'Olivia,' Betty said, sounding a note of caution.

'Don't worry, Betty,' Olivia said, looking back to her friend. 'It won't be long until Scott's had enough of Paris and moves to the other side of the world again. You might be okay with dating someone who won't stick around, but I'm not.'

***

So, that's what this is about, Scott thought. Silence surrounded the four of them—everyone else in the restaurant was completely oblivious of the tension that hung in the air. *She thinks I'm going to leave.*

'I'm not going anywhere, Olivia,' he said, gripping his glass.

'And why should I believe you?' Olivia said, her glare cold as ice. 'Why did you leave Australia, anyway, Scott? Did you leave a woman there?'

Scott knew that he didn't leave a woman behind in Australia. But he wasn't going to tell her that he came to Paris *for* a woman.

'What?' Scott couldn't believe the accusations being thrown at him. 'I didn't run away, Olivia. I came because I always wanted to move to Paris. Not that I have to explain that to you, since you couldn't get away from me any quicker.'

He hadn't meant to say that—not in front of Alex and Betty. Even though he was sure that they knew to an extent. But the shocked looks on their faces showed that at least Betty didn't know how it ended. Scott wasn't concerned about Alex and Betty right now. He *was* concerned about Olivia's outburst and the daggers that she was staring at him right now. He wondered what had possessed her to act like this.

No one had to think of something clever to say to diffuse the situation. Olivia, hurt crossing her face, gathered her things, stood, and started to leave, telling Betty to stay and enjoy her night.

***

Scott knocked on the door. Then knocked again. He tapped his fingers on the doorframe, waiting for Olivia to appear at the door. She wouldn't be happy to see him—she made that clear at the restaurant. But he had to talk to her and Betty was all too willing to give him Olivia's address. He heard footsteps coming closer to the door and the handle click.

The door opened, Olivia standing there with a surprised look that quickly turned to a cold glare. Then, she slammed the door in his face. Scott sighed, disappointed that this was going to be harder than he hoped. He banged his fist on the door.

'Olivia, please!'

'Go away, Scott.'

'Come on! Please.' He rested his forehead against the door. 'We have to talk.'

There was silence on the other side.

'Olivia?' He slapped his hand against the door.

'I don't want to talk!' she yelled back.

'Please? I'm sorry.'

He heard a door open, but it wasn't Olivia's.

'*Tais-toi!*' her neighbour yelled. 'She doesn't want to see you!'

'Sorry,' he said, waving at the elderly man.

The elderly man slammed his door, muttering something that he couldn't make out.

'I'm not leaving.' He returned his attention back to Olivia's door.

'You set it up!' she yelled at him through the letterbox.

'What?'

'The date, you idiot,' she yelled back. 'You set it up.'

'No, I didn't! Olivia, open up!' he yelled, banging on the door again.

He had to get in there. He heard her neighbour's door open again, the elderly man yelling profanities at him. But he focussed on the door in front of him.

'Please, Olivia?'

There was silence again, and he almost gave up. He tapped his fingers on the door again, then took a step back. He started to turn when he heard the door click open and Olivia stood in the doorway.

'Your neighbour is going to kill me,' Scott said, nodding towards the elderly man who was waving his fist at him.

Olivia looked at her neighbour, then back at Scott. She turned, walking back into her flat but leaving the door open. Scott followed her, closing the door behind him.

'I didn't set up the date,' he said. 'I was just doing a favour for Alex so that he could go on the date with Betty. He didn't even know that you were the one coming with her. I had no idea. Please, Olivia, believe me.'

Scott had closed the gap between him and Olivia. He couldn't stand the distance from her. He placed his hands on her arms, willing her to look at him.

'Promise?' she whispered, finally bringing her gaze up to meet his eyes.

'I had nothing to do with it.' He smiled, hoping that all was right in the world again.

She dropped her gaze again and shrugged free of his grasp.

'Then, what about last night and this morning? You were nowhere to be found when I woke up,' she said, putting space between them.

'I had to pick up my car!' Scott explained. 'I caught a cab home last night and I had to get my car back before it got towed. Trust me, I didn't want to leave you by yourself, but I was coming back.'

'You took advantage of me, Scott!' she yelled, throwing a cushion at him. 'I was drunk and upset and you took advantage of that!'

Another cushion came flying at Scott's head. He caught it and held onto it. He might need it for protection. *That damn kiss.*

'Took advantage of you?' he yelled, blocking a flying coaster with the cushion. '*You* came onto *me*, Olivia. You started that kiss!'

'It was more than a *kiss*!'

'Well, it was a rather heated kiss,' Scott said, pleased at the memory. 'But I'm certain there wasn't more than that.'

Olivia froze, a vase in her hand.

'We only kissed?' she asked quietly.

'You don't remember?' Scott was relieved the vase hadn't come flying at him. 'Wait, what did you think happened?'

Olivia looked at the vase in her hand and didn't answer. She looked as though she was still considering throwing it. Scott closed the distance between them, prying the vase from her hand and putting it back on the coffee table.

'Olivia?' he said, urging her to answer.

'We didn't do anything else?' she whispered.

'No,' Scott said. 'Though, I wanted to. But I'm not that kind of guy, Olivia. I would never take advantage of you like that.'

'But I was naked.'

'What?' Scott said, surprised. He had to make sure he heard that correctly.

'When I woke up,' she said, studying his face. 'I was in your bed, and my clothes were on the floor.'

'All of them?' Scott asked, unable to move.

Olivia nodded.

'Are you sure?' he asked again.

'I think I would know,' she laughed. Her face grew serious. 'You didn't know?'

Scott shook his head. Olivia was in his bed with no clothes on. On one hand, he was glad that he didn't know because he was sure that he wouldn't have been able to resist. But then, who wouldn't want to know about a beautiful girl being naked in their bed?

'What happened, Scott?' Olivia asked, her eyes pleading.

'Well, we were talking.' He started to explain, struggling to find words to say with an image of a naked Olivia in his mind. 'Then we, ahh, kissed, and you said that you wanted to go to the bathroom. You were gone for ages, by the way. I went to check on you and found you asleep on my bed. So, I tucked you in. But you definitely had clothes on.'

'Where did you sleep?' She raised an eyebrow.

'On the couch. I didn't want my alarm to disturb you,' he shrugged. 'I don't know how you lost your clothes during the night, but I promise you that I had nothing to do with it.'

'Thank you,' Olivia whispered, looking up into Scott's eyes. 'For not taking advantage of me.'

He rested his forehead against hers, refusing to break eye contact.

'You're welcome,' he whispered back, allowing her to entwine her fingers between his. 'So, we're okay, then?'

'We're okay,' she replied, nodding. 'We are definitely okay.'

Chapter 15

'Please, please, please!' Vanessa begged on the phone. '*Please*, tell me that you're coming to the twins' birthday party on the weekend!'

'I've told you every day since you started planning it. I will be there,' Olivia said, mouthing an apology to Scott.

'Promise me, Olivia! Because I desperately need you there.'

'I'll be there,' Olivia said again. 'Just text me what you need me to bring and I'll be there early.'

'You are a lifesaver! Thank you!' Vanessa said excitedly, ending the call.

Olivia tucked her phone into her bag and focussed on Scott while they walked through the park, coffees in hand.

'I am so sorry,' she said. 'My friend is having her twins' seventh birthday party on Saturday and she's desperate for me to be there.'

'Sounds like you will have your hands full,' Scott said, nudging her. 'Any chance you'll be able to sneak out in time for dinner?'

'I doubt it.' Olivia shook her head. 'The party's in the afternoon and we usually have some drinks after the kids are in bed.'

'What about breakfast?'

Olivia shook her head again.

'I'll be there all day helping set up,' she said, sipping her coffee.

'What about Sunday?' he asked, his eyes pleading.

'I can't,' Olivia replied, stopping to look at Scott. 'I'm sorry, Scott. I'm doing the flowers for a wedding and they want me there for the whole time.'

'Tomorrow?'

'Prepping for the wedding.'

Now that Scott and Olivia were back on good terms, they seemed to be having a hard time organising catch ups. Olivia found it very disappointing because she wanted to spend more time with him. She always seemed to have time to organise things with Antoine, even though he always cancelled on her. So, why was it so hard now? Sure, she was going to be busy over the next few days, but it shouldn't be so hard considering Scott's time was rather flexible at the moment.

Since reconciling after last night's double-date,

they stayed up talking for hours until Scott decided that it was time to go home. Olivia wished that he could have stayed, and they could have a repeat of the night before. Maybe they could have kissed again—and maybe she could have woken up in her own bed with her pyjamas on. But she knew they had to take it slow, and he clearly did as well, since the only kiss she got last night was a peck on her forehead when he left.

'Well, it was nice knowing you,' Scott said, sighing.

'I'm sorry,' Olivia said, grabbing Scott's arm. 'How's your job hunting going?'

'I've applied for some jobs,' Scott said, sounding optimistic. 'I haven't heard from them yet, but I'm sure I'll find something. I've been meaning to ask—what does Betty think of Alex?'

'She seems quite taken by him,' she said, smiling. 'In fact, she's taking tomorrow off work to spend the day with him. They're going to do the tourist thing and see everything that Paris is famous for.'

'Alex was saying something along those lines,' Scott replied.

'Tomorrow!' Olivia said excitedly.

Scott turned to Olivia, his face questioning as if trying to understand what she was saying.

'Come to the shop tomorrow and help me with the preparations.' She tugged on his arm. 'If you want to.'

'Are you sure?'

'Of course!' Olivia said, jumping a little with her

excitement. 'Betty won't be there, and I'll need an extra hand. Oh, it will be fun! And I'll pay you, so you don't need to be worried about free labour.'

She watched Scott as he studied her face. He looked amused, perhaps at her sudden excitement. Sure, they would be busy with the work, but it would give them a chance to talk some more and they might even be able to squeeze in a coffee.

'All right,' he said, smiling. 'But you don't need to worry about paying me. For you, I'll work for free.'

She smiled as he nudged her again. They continued walking through the park, Olivia unable to control her excitement, butterflies floating in her stomach. She couldn't believe that they were going to spend the whole day together and he could see what she did in more detail.

***

'Olivia?' Scott called out the next day as he entered her shop.

He was surprised about Olivia's suggestion that he help her. Though, he had nothing else to do and it meant spending the day with her and watching her do what she loves. He wasn't sure how much help he would be, but she clearly had faith in him. In saying that, he never thought he would see the day where he would be arranging flowers in a florist shop.

'Out the back!' she shouted.

He walked towards the back room and poked his head through the door.

'Morning, boss!' He couldn't resist the tease. 'I'm not one to be a teacher's pet, but I brought a coffee for you.'

The smile on Olivia's face made everything worthwhile for him. She looked so radiant with her loose curls framing her face and her simple grey dress caressing her curves. She had an apron on, the ribbon tied in a bow at the small of her back. Her cheeks were tinged pink and her eyes flashed with excitement. She accepted the coffee in exchange for an apron.

'I don't have to wear this, do I?' he said, shaking the apron out to view its entirety.

'It's your uniform.' She shrugged.

He pulled it over his head and tied it around his waist. He looked down at the apron, assessing how it must look.

'Well, it certainly doesn't look as good on me as it does on you,' he said, smiling when he saw her blush. 'But it will have to do.'

He watched as Olivia tilted her head to the side, eyeing the apron he was wearing as if also assessing it.

'It would look much better if you weren't wearing a shirt,' she teased.

He grinned. He was glad that they had made up and were able to joke with each other. Though, he still wasn't sure on what they were. They seemed to be able to flirt and tease each other, but she still refused his offers for dinner or anything date-like. He wanted to kiss her so much after the double-date, and again at the park yesterday. But he didn't want to push her. As much as he didn't want to, he had to take it slow. He would rather do that than lose her for trying to rush things. But he'd be damned if she didn't make it hard to go slow.

'Oh, now,' he said, teasing her back. 'It's my first day and you're already coming on to me! What if your other workers see? They might get jealous because you're playing favourites.'

Olivia's reaction was exactly what Scott was hoping for. She laughed hysterically until her eyes were watery, but it only made Scott want to take her in his arms and kiss her even more. But they had work to do. Maybe, if they finished quickly enough, she might let him take her on that date.

'Oh! Before I forget,' Olivia said, fiddling with a camera that she had on the bench. 'We need to document your first day.'

Scott smiled at Olivia and congratulated her in his mind for being so smooth about getting a photo. She held the camera at arm's length and stood next to Scott. He put his arm around her and held her close, allured by her sweet perfume. She took the photo and turned the camera to look at the picture.

'How is it?' Scott asked, allowing his arm to linger around her.

'It's perfect.'

***

Olivia watched as Scott steadily fashioned a large

bouquet out of pink roses, carnations, ferns, and sprigs of blossoms. She admired how he was able to choose combinations with such ease.

Maybe because he's a builder, she thought, deciding that he had an eye for colours and floristry.

His focus intrigued her. He looked like he was actually enjoying working with her in her shop. And the way he dealt with her customers—she was sure that they had had a more productive day than usual. Even though he denied it, she was certain that he had done work of this kind before.

'How am I doing?' he said, glancing up from his project.

'I'm thinking of replacing Betty with you,' she admitted.

Scott looked up, surprise on his face. He wore that cheeky grin—the one that made her melt. Olivia looked down, furrowing her brow at the mangled daisy in her hand. She hadn't realised that she had been twisting the flower while watching Scott.

'Really? I'm not that good.' He returned his gaze to the fiddly task at hand.

'You're right,' Olivia teased. 'You're a natural.'

Scott looked back at Olivia and held her gaze for a moment. It felt so right for him to be here with her, in her shop, working together. She wished that it wasn't just for the day. She even wondered if she could afford to employ him as well as Betty. She crunched the numbers in her mind only to be disappointed. She didn't think that she could afford them both. Besides, he probably wouldn't want to work in such a feminine profession.

'You're lying,' he said, squinting at her. His lips were still turned in a grin.

Olivia shook her head.

'Have you seen what you're doing? I'm afraid that you'll start your own florist and put me out of business!'

'I wouldn't dare,' he said, his eyes appreciative of the compliment.

***

Scott started on another arrangement for the wedding while Olivia closed shop out the front. It had been a busy day and he hoped that he had helped Olivia as much as he could. She thought that he was a natural. He smiled at that thought. He honestly had no idea what he was doing. He simply gathered a collection of flowers and twigs and tied them all together, hoping that they would look nice. He didn't think they were anywhere near as nice as Olivia's, but he liked that she had faith in him.

The day had kept them so busy that they still hadn't finished the arrangements for the wedding and Olivia was saying that she would stay late to finish them. Of course, Scott didn't want to leave her alone, so he insisted that he stayed to help her. She didn't refuse.

It was almost time for dinner and Scott didn't have any plans. From the way Olivia was planning on working late at the shop, he gathered that she didn't either.

'What are your plans for dinner?'

She looked up from her bouquet, her eyes weary but still beautiful.

'I hadn't thought about it,' she said, refocussing on her project.

'Let's go out.' He tied the ribbon around his bouquet.

'There's too much to do, Scott,' she said, shaking her head. 'We haven't finished the flowers for the wedding and I still have to make enough bouquets for tomorrow morning. We basically sold out today.'

'Come on, Olivia,' Scott pleaded, rising from his seat, and moving closer to her. 'You have to eat. We've almost finished the wedding flowers. I'll come in early with you tomorrow before the party and help you make enough bouquets for tomorrow and we can finish the wedding flowers on Sunday morning.'

Olivia tied her ribbon into a bow and turned to face Scott. She looked like she didn't know what to say. She looked like she definitely needed a break and to enjoy a nice meal. Preferably with him. He placed his hands on her arms, just beneath her shoulders.

'Please?'

Olivia studied his face. He held her gaze, seeking an answer.

'Okay,' she said. 'But I'm not letting you pay.'

'You have to let me pay.' He smiled at the thought of finally getting to have dinner with the beautiful Olivia.

'No, you don't have a job. I can pay for myself,' she said stubbornly.

'I have savings.' He shrugged. 'Besides, I will never let you pay.'

Her smile tilted to the side. 'Not even if you were a homeless man on the street?'

'Not even if the clothes on my back where the only things I had to my name.'

***

There she was, sitting across from him in a quaint restaurant down the street from her florist shop. She looked refreshed to be having a break from their busy day. He was glad that she had finally agreed to have dinner with him. He was certain that it wouldn't be considered a date, as dates require notice and preparation. But he couldn't help but hope. For him, this was a date. And he wouldn't want to be on it with anyone other than the goddess sitting across from him, delicately eating the chicken dish in front of her.

She glanced up from her dish and smiled at him. He smiled back, still unable to believe that he had spent the whole day with her and was now having dinner with her. It felt good. It felt right. He noticed a little dot of sauce on the corner of her mouth. He wanted to reach over and wipe it away with his thumb. Or his lips.

'So,' she started, wiping her mouth with a napkin.

'What did you think of your first day?'

Disappointed that she wiped the sauce away before he could, he leaned forward in his chair and rotated his glass between his hands.

'I liked it,' he said. 'And I'm surprised that it's still hard work. You must have the energy of a superhero to do that every day.'

She blushed at the compliment.

'You get used to it,' she said, moving some green beans around her plate with her fork.

Scott watched her intently, fascinated by everything that she did. She had moved the beans around her plate, making it look like she was eating them. Though, he hadn't seen her put any in her mouth.

'You don't like beans?' he asked.

'I'm more a peas kind of girl,' she said, glancing up at him and resting her fork on the side of her plate.

He reached over and picked up her plate, putting it on top of his empty one. He picked up the fork, stabbed the green beans and put them in his mouth.

'I take it you like beans,' she smiled.

'I eat everything.' He shrugged, putting the fork down on her now-empty plate.

The waiter came and cleared the table for them and offered to bring out the dessert menu. They both declined, full from the main meal and appetisers. Like he promised, Scott payed for the meal and he was more than happy to do so. They started walking back to Olivia's shop and Scott noticed Olivia shiver a little. He put his arm around her.

'How's your mum doing?' he asked, pulling her closer.

'The usual,' Olivia said. 'I haven't been able to see her lately. She's been having more rough days than good ones and it's heartbreaking to see how she has deteriorated.'

'I'm sorry,' he said, kissing her on the top of her head.

'You would have liked her,' she continued. 'She wasn't very involved when I was a kid, but we grew close after my father died. Until the accident, at least.'

'Did your father look after you more as a child?' Scott asked.

Olivia shook her head, looking up at him with a smile.

'I had a nanny,' she said.

'You had a nanny?'

'She was great.' Olivia laughed to herself. 'But I was always so mean to her. I used to play tricks on her with my friend, but she never told my parents.'

Scott furrowed his brow, deep in thought. Memories of his childhood flashed through his mind. He shook his head to shake them away. They were too far gone.

'I guess every kid goes through that stage,' he said.

'I suppose they do.'

They reached the shop and returned to the back

room to work on the flowers. They seemed to lose track of time and stayed longer than they planned. On the plus side, the wedding flowers were finished, and they managed to make enough bouquets for the morning.

Chapter 16

'Come on!' Olivia yelled, turning the key in the ignition.

Her car hissed and clicked to no avail, refusing to start. Of all the days for her car to fail her, it had to be on the one day she had to be somewhere—the twins' birthday party. She banged her hand on the steering wheel as if trying to knock some sense into the car. She kept trying the key before finally pulling the lever to pop the bonnet open.

Olivia climbed out of the car and propped the bonnet up, examining everything under the bonnet and becoming acutely aware that she had no idea what anything was under there and how to tell what was wrong with it.

She rubbed her forehead with her hands, trying

to figure out what to do. She knew that she would
have to get it fixed, but that would take time. She
didn't have time. She had to get over to her shop as
soon as possible to pick up the things that Vanessa
needed her to bring. She was supposed to bring
them back with her last night, but by the time her
and Scott left the shop, she had forgotten to pack
them in the car.

'Damn it! The wedding!' she yelled again, kicking
the car tyre.

She cried out in pain and hopped on one foot,
realising that kicking the tyre while she wore open-
toed heels was a very bad idea. She waited until the
throbbing pain subsided before checking her toes,
relieved that they weren't bleeding.

The wedding. She wouldn't be able to deliver the
flowers without a car and she definitely didn't have
the time to source another one before the wedding.
She wouldn't even have time to get the car fixed
today. She closed the bonnet and started unloading
the car, knowing what she had to do and hoping that
it would work out okay.

***

'So, because Betty took the day off yesterday, you
worked as a florist for the day?'

Scott nodded, knowing that he was asking for all
the teasing by telling Alex about his day with Olivia.
But he didn't care. Alex could tease him as much as
he wanted, but Scott would not have taken back

being a florist for the day. After all, he got to work with his goddess and, in all honesty, he was disappointed that it was only for the day. He had hoped that, by suggesting that he helps her with the bouquets early that morning and the wedding flowers the next morning, he had ensured that he would get to see her each day. Instead, they felt rejuvenated after their dinner and finished them all off the night before.

Damn it, he thought, disappointed that his plan backfired. That was the only way he could think of to get to see her in her busy schedule and it wasn't going to happen now. So, he made plans with Alex. He leaned back in the couch at the hotel, accepting the coffee that Alex brought him.

'So, I gather you guys made up?' Alex took a seat opposite Scott.

'Yes,' Scott said. 'Her vase would be happy about that.'

'The vase?' Alex looked puzzled.

Scott hesitated, realising that he hadn't told Alex about the cushions, coaster, and almost the vase getting thrown at him while he tried to make up with Olivia. He figured it wouldn't matter. Alex wouldn't tell anyone—he would just tease Scott even more about it.

'The vase that almost got thrown at me.' He shrugged, waiting for the teasing to escalate.

'She threw a vase at you?' Alex' eyes widened.

'Almost,' Scott said. 'Though, two cushions and a coaster weren't so lucky.'

Alex burst out laughing, unable to control himself. Scott couldn't resist a smile before joining in with Alex's contagious laughter.

'Well, it seems you have a feisty one,' Alex said, calming down from his fit of laughter. 'I'm happy for you.'

As if right on cue, Scott's phone started ringing. He put his cup on the coffee table and picked up the phone.

'Hello?'

'I need you.'

'Olivia?' He whacked Alex's hand away from the phone, standing to get away from him.

'Well, I need your car,' she corrected herself. 'And you come with the car.'

'What happened?'

'My car won't start,' she whimpered. 'And I have to pick up some things from the shop and get to the party. Vanessa and Chad are already busy, and I didn't know who else to call.'

'Are you at home?' He grabbed his wallet and keys.

'Yes.'

'I'll be right there.'

He ended the call and apologised to Alex about having to run out on him.

'Olivia's car has broken down.'

'So, you're running to her rescue?' Alex grinned as he teased his friend.

'I suppose I am.' Scott smiled.

They said their goodbyes and Scott left to pick

Olivia up. It seemed that he would get to see her, after all.

***

'Thank you, thank you, thank you!' Olivia said, throwing herself into his arms. 'You're a lifesaver.'

'Hardly,' he said, holding her in an embrace before she pulled away. 'But I'm happy to help.'

'Well, you're definitely saving my butt,' she said, handing him the birthday cake. 'So, thank you.'

He held her gaze for a moment and they exchanged a smile, Olivia breaking the gaze to pick up bags of chips and lollies.

'So, what did you leave at the shop?' Scott was securing the cake in the back seat of his car.

'Decorations,' Olivia shrugged, scanning around them to make sure they had everything.

'What are they supplying for their party?' Scott asked, loading the cooler of drinks into the car.

It seemed to him that Olivia was bringing everything they would need for the party. He gathered he was wrong when he noticed that Olivia was smiling at him, her eyes flashing.

'I forgot that you've never been to one of Vanessa's parties,' she said. 'She really goes all out. Trust me, this was the least I could do to help.'

'I'd like to see it,' he said.

'Maybe you will.' Olivia scooted into the passenger seat.

He climbed into the driver's seat and checked the

back seat to make sure the cake wouldn't be able to move. He admired the handiwork. It was a large, rectangular cake made to look like a treasure map with all the details made of icing, including the treasure chest. He turned to meet Olivia's gaze.

'Did you make that?' he asked.

She nodded, smiling.

'Incredible,' he said, starting his car.

He couldn't believe how truly amazing Olivia was. Not only was she a fantastic florist and the most beautiful woman he had ever laid eyes on, she was also an amazing baker and decorator. He drove her to her shop and helped her load balloons and streamers into the car, still certain that there couldn't be much else to use at a party.

'What's wrong with your car?' Scott asked as Olivia directed him towards Chad and Vanessa's place.

'I don't know.' She shrugged. 'But it can't be serviced until Monday because the garage is closed on weekends.'

'Don't you have a wedding tomorrow?' he asked.

'Yes,' she replied solemnly.

'What are you going to do?'

'I have no idea.'

They rode in silence for a moment, Olivia talking only to give him more directions. Scott broke the silence.

'I can help you,' he said, deciding that his car would hold all of the wedding flowers if it could hold this much for a birthday party. 'I'll be your chauffer until you can get your car fixed.

'I can't ask you to do that.' She turned to face him, her expression sincere.

'You're not asking,' he said. 'I'm offering.'

'Thank you,' she said, smiling.

'Is that a yes?' he asked.

'Yes.'

***

'Where have you been?' Vanessa asked frantically, rushing over to take the cake from Olivia's hands. 'Wait, that's not your car.'

Chad followed, not far behind her, to help unload the car. He stopped level with Vanessa when Scott emerged from behind the car with the balloons and decorations.

'My car wouldn't start,' Olivia began. 'So, Scott—'

'Scott?' Vanessa asked, leaning towards Olivia so that only she could hear. '*That's* Scott?'

Olivia nodded.

'He *is* hot,' Vanessa said.

'I heard that,' Chad said, leaning towards them.

Vanessa grabbed Chad's arm and turned to look at him.

'Did we know Scott was coming?'

Chad shook his head. They both turned back to Olivia.

'He was dropping me off,' she explained. 'He's not staying.'

'He has to stay!' Vanessa shrieked.

'Who has to stay?' Scott joined the conversation.

'You,' Vanessa said.

'I'm sure Scott already has plans,' Olivia said. 'I've already taken too much time out of his day.'

She didn't want to make Scott feel obliged to stay at a kid's party. As much as she would love him to stay, she knew that they wouldn't get to spend much time together. She also didn't want him to find out that she had talked about him to Chad and Vanessa, which she was certain that he would if he stayed.

'Are you good with kids?' Vanessa said, ignoring Olivia.

'I wouldn't know,' Scott shrugged. 'I haven't been around anyone with kids for a long time.'

'Well, you have now,' Vanessa said. 'Our entertainer cancelled at the last minute saying that they double booked so Chad was going to do it—you can help him.'

Chad took the balloons and decorations from Scott and followed Vanessa back to the house, leaving Scott and Olivia both stunned.

'Entertainer?' Scott turned to face Olivia.

'I'm sorry,' she said quickly. 'You don't have to stay, I tried to get you out of it.'

'And what was with that?' he asked. 'You don't want me here?'

Scott started walking back to the car to unload the cooler. Olivia followed to gather the bags of chips and lollies.

'I'm sorry, Scott,' she said. 'Of course I do, but you don't know anyone else here and I'm going to be busy helping with the party.'

'So, you thought I wouldn't want to stay?'

Scott put the cooler on the ground and turned to face Olivia, holding her by the arms. She dropped her gaze to the ground.

'I didn't want you to be uncomfortable,' she whispered.

He willed her to look at him, nudging underneath her chin with his hand.

'I wouldn't want to be anywhere else,' he said, lowering his hands to hold hers. 'Besides, you said there will be drinks after the party, didn't you?'

Olivia nodded, looking up to meet his gaze. He was smiling at her and his eyes were sincere. Surely, he had no idea what he was doing to her, how he was controlling her feelings and easing his way into her world. That his every touch sent a warm shiver down her spine and sent her insides churning. And that the very look in his eyes would make any woman willingly succumb to him.

'Well, I'm sure I'll get to see you then,' he whispered.

She felt him tug her a little closer, their bodies almost touching, his face inches from hers. She didn't want to break their gaze. She revelled in the warmth of his hands around hers and the thought of him kissing her again. He nudged his face a little closer, their lips almost touching. She could feel her heart racing, pushing against her chest, urging her to lift her chin just a little bit to meet his lips with hers.

'Liv, Vanessa's asking where—oh, God!'

Olivia jumped at Chad's voice, Scott releasing her hands to unload the rest of the car. She felt a pang of disappointment, wishing that Chad hadn't walked in on them when he did. Scott smiled at her, handing her a bag, and allowing his hand to brush against hers. Chad was covering his eyes with one hand and waving the other one in front of him.

'Is it safe? I didn't mean to interrupt.'

'Where's Vanessa?'

'In the house, Liv,' he said, still holding his hand over his eyes.

Olivia headed towards the house, conscious of her hands still burning from Scott's touch and her lips tingling from his sweet breath. She tried to shake some sense into herself, trying to forget about their missed kiss. She couldn't forget.

Chapter 17

'You can open your eyes now, Chad. She's gone,' Scott said, pulling the remainder of the bags out of the car and closing the boot.

Chad lowered his hand from his face and looked around, relieved that Olivia had made her way to the house.

'I'm sorry, man,' he said. 'I honestly didn't mean to interrupt.'

'It was nothing indecent,' Scott said, trying to reassure him. 'So, you didn't have to cover your eyes.'

'Just a reflex,' Chad said, grabbing the other end of the cooler. 'I figured it would preserve her dignity.'

'Again, nothing indecent. It's not like you caught us in a compromising position.' Scott shrugged and tried to shake the ache that he was feeling down below.

Chad halted mid-step, making Scott almost lose his balance. He sighed, figuring that he wasn't, yet, on joking terms with Chad. But then, he didn't know how close Olivia was with Chad. He knew that Vanessa was her best friend and figured that Chad, being Vanessa's husband, must at least be her friend as well.

'I'm teasing,' Scott added, unsure if that would help his cause.

'I'm not sure how much you know,' Chad said, starting to walk again. 'But Olivia is like a sister to me. I wouldn't like to see her in a *compromising position* and I would like to keep it that way. What *were* you doing, anyway?'

Scott smiled, wondering if they had just broken the ice. Chad obviously felt somewhat protective of Olivia. He supposed that she considered Chad as a brother as well, especially since she didn't have any siblings. Though, despite Chad's protectiveness, he seemed open enough to get to know Scott and he could definitely see Chad becoming a good friend to him. Maybe Olivia had talked about him to her friends. He wondered what she would have said.

'Well, Chad,' Scott started. 'You walked in just in time to make sure nothing happened.'

'Way to make me feel better about walking in on you,' he said, smiling at Scott. 'I didn't know you were actually together now.'

'We're not,' Scott said solemnly. 'I mean, I want

to be, but I don't want to push her.'

'Have you actually asked her out?'

'I've asked her to dinner.'

'And?'

'And she refused.' Scott shrugged. 'But she's happy to get coffee together and call me when she needs a lift or a hand in her shop.'

'You helped her in her shop?' Chad sounded surprised.

'Yesterday,' Scott explained. 'Betty couldn't work, and she needed some help with wedding arrangements for tomorrow.'

'Scott, Olivia doesn't let anyone help her in her shop,' Chad said, slowing the pace a little. 'It took a lot of convincing just to get her to hire Betty. She doesn't even let us help out when she needs it.'

'I didn't know that,' Scott said, realisation setting in.

'She clearly wants you in her life,' Chad said. 'Just give her some time—she'll come around.'

'How much time?'

'As much as she needs.' Chad shrugged. 'You seem a good enough guy, Scott—you have my approval. And from what I've heard, she likes you. But you didn't hear that from me.'

They got to the door of the house before Scott could respond to Chad's comment. *She likes you*. Now he just had to wait for her.

***

'Vanessa?' Olivia called out as she closed the door behind her.

'In the kitchen!'

Olivia trailed her way through the house to get to the kitchen, her hands still burning from Scott's touch, her lips still aching for his. She eventually found Vanessa putting a tray of pastries and sausage rolls in the oven.

'Where were you?'

'I was, ahh, helping Scott unload the car,' Olivia said.

Vanessa's eyes dropped to the bag that Olivia was holding.

'So, it took that long to bring one bag to the house?'

'I got ... distracted.' Olivia shrugged, putting the bag on the bench.

'So, Scott, huh?' Vanessa smiled at Olivia. 'You didn't tell me you were bringing him.'

'I wasn't planning on it,' Olivia said, searching for a bowl for the chips. 'My car wasn't working this morning and he was happy to drive me.'

'Convenient,' Vanessa laughed. 'Was he with you when your car wasn't working?'

'No,' Olivia said slowly. 'I called him.'

'And he dropped what he was doing to come to your rescue?'

'I suppose he did.'

'Suppose? There's no supposing about it, Olivia,' Vanessa said, handing a bowl to Olivia. 'Have you spent much time with him since the double-date?'

Olivia rubbed her forehead, trying to remember when she told Vanessa about that date and coming up at a loss.

'We've had coffee,' Olivia said. 'And he spent yesterday helping me in the shop.'

Vanessa dropped the baking tray she just pulled out of the cupboard. Her sole focus on Olivia.

'He helped you in the shop?'

'It's no big deal,' Olivia said.

'Liv, you never let *anyone* help you in the shop,' Vanessa said, walking over to Olivia. 'Remember how hard it was to convince you to hire Betty?'

Olivia remained quiet. She knew that having Scott help her in the shop was a big deal. She should have known that Vanessa would know it, too.

'You really like him, don't you, Liv?'

'I don't know how he feels!' Olivia said, sitting herself on the kitchen stool and putting her head in her hands. 'One minute, we're friends, and the next, I don't know what we are. We keep having these moments and I think he's going to kiss me and then something changes, and he'll do no more than kiss me on my forehead—my *forehead*, Vanessa!'

'Oh, Liv,' Vanessa said, moving to embrace her. 'That's still really sweet.'

'And then I thought he was finally going to kiss me and Chad walked in on us.'

'Chad? When?' Vanessa's eyes grew wide.

'Just before, when you sent him to find me.'

'I'm sorry, Liv.'

'I mean, he wouldn't have seen us before he

actually did, but now Scott will probably think better of it,' Olivia said, swallowing hard to hold her tears back. What was he doing to her?

'Don't be ridiculous,' Vanessa said. 'I'm sure he wants you as much as you want him. Maybe he's been hurt before and he doesn't want to lose what you both already have. Just give him time—he'll come around.'

'I hope so,' Olivia said, wiping her eyes.

Vanessa pulled her into another embrace, pulling away only when she heard the front door open and two manly voices headed towards the kitchen. Olivia took a few quick breaths to try and compose herself. She didn't want Scott to see her in such a state here—she was sure that he would know it was about him. She hoped that he wouldn't notice.

'You have a jumping castle for the party?' Scott said as they entered the kitchen.

'Like I said, Vanessa goes all out,' Chad explained, smiling at his wife.

They put the cooler on the ground and Chad scanned the kitchen suspiciously, surprised that there wasn't as much happening in there as there had been all morning.

'Everything okay?' Chad glanced at Olivia before refocussing on Vanessa.

'Everything's fine,' Vanessa said, returning to her post behind the bench.

'Liv?' Chad said.

Olivia glanced up at Chad, then to Scott, holding his gaze for a moment. Scott was focussed on Olivia, as if trying to read her expressions. His eyes were mellow with concern and his brow was furrowed. She knew that she wouldn't be fooling him, but she had to try.

'It's fine,' she shrugged.

Chad's eyes continued to move between Olivia and Vanessa. Scott's was fastened on Olivia, holding her gaze for as long as he could. Olivia dropped her gaze to the bowl she held in her hands and returned to her task of filling it with chips.

'So, I guess we'll keep setting up outside, then,' Chad said, nudging Scott to follow him.

Olivia glanced back to Scott and flashed him a smile, hoping that it would ease his concern. He smiled back, hesitantly, before following Chad back outside.

***

Scott continued watching her as she found her way through the party. Olivia was making sure that each of the children had their costumes sorted. The boys were dressed as pirates, complete with foam swords, hats, and a patch over one eye. The girls were dressed as fairy princesses, wearing pretty dresses, tiaras, fairy wings and fairy wands.

He still couldn't wrap his head around how extravagant this party actually was. There was a jumping castle, game sections, and more food than he ever thought would be present at a children's party. Chad was acting as the entertainer for now, while Scott manned the face-painting table. There were tables of food for the parents who stayed and none of them looked like they planned on leaving their spots.

Occasionally, he saw Olivia standing near the table talking to the parents and even caught them looking in his direction a few times. Even though he could see her moving around the party, he was still waiting for Olivia to come over to his stall. He knew that he and Chad had walked in on a serious discussion earlier. Olivia and Vanessa had both said that everything was fine, but Olivia's eyes were glazed when she said it. He hoped to get a chance to talk to her before the party, but their paths didn't cross and, before he knew it, everyone was there and the party had started.

He sighed, hoping that he wouldn't have to wait too long before he got a chance to talk to Olivia.

'So, can you do that?'

Scott snapped out of his thoughts and focussed on the blonde-haired little girl sitting in front of him who had been talking without him noticing.

'What?'

The little girl sighed, exasperated, before repeating what she wanted.

'I want a butterfly on one cheek and a sparkly heart on the other and a pirate scar on my chin,' she started, demanding his attention. 'Because the bigger girls have a sparkly heart on their faces and pirates have scars. I like pirates, you know? I want to look like a sparkly fairy-pirate-princess.'

'Why do you want a butterfly?' Scott asked, dipping the paint brush in the pink paint to start on the heart.

'Because I like butterflies.' She shrugged.

They sat quietly while Scott painted the little girl's face, adding an extra scar at her request. She squealed in delight when he held up a little mirror for her to see his artwork.

'I bet I can get a pirate patch from Aunt Livvy,' she said, jumping to her feet.

'Who's Aunt Livvy?' Scott asked, puzzled.

The little girl pointed towards the goddess who had just handed out another foam sword to a new arrival.

'O-liv-ia,' she said slowly, smiling when she said it right. 'But I call her Aunt Livvy because it's easier. I'm the only one who does. She makes flowers. You would like her—' she paused for a moment, then waved at Scott. 'Bye!'

Scott watched the little girl bounce off towards Olivia. He watched her reaction when Olivia raved about her face-painting and smiled when he saw the little girl bat her eyelids until Olivia gave her a patch. She knelt down closer to the girl and the girl whispered in her ear and pointed over to Scott. Olivia glanced towards Scott and waved to him. He waved back and continued watching as Olivia whispered something in the little girl's ear and sent her on her way before she wandered over to the face-painting stall.

'So, I see you have met Emmy.' Olivia took a seat

next to Scott.

'Well, she didn't tell me her name or who she belongs to.' Scott shrugged, smiling.

'She's Chad and Vanessa's youngest.'

'She said I would like her Aunt Livvy,' Scott said, scanning the guests at the party before leaning closer to Olivia. 'I think she might be right.'

Olivia blushed, studying her hands in her lap.

'She's the only one that calls me that,' Olivia said. 'I haven't been called Livvy since I was a kid.'

She handed him the paint brush and presented her cheek to him. He studied the curve of her chin and the angle of her jaw. Her skin was fair and delicate. He wanted to feel the softness of her cheek and her neck against his lips. He broke out of his desire when the children erupted into a chorus of cheers at the mention of a sword fight. He cleared his throat.

'What do you want?' he asked, taking the paint brush from her hand.

'Surprise me.'

He smiled, dipping the paint brush in the red paint and brought it to her cheek. He could feel the softness of her skin beneath his fingers as he painted soft, rounded strokes.

'Do you like it?' He broke their silence.

'Like what?'

'Being called Livvy,' he said softly.

'I used to,' she said. 'I only really had one friend that called me Livvy, so, the name sort of ended there. Then Emmy started talking and she just got it in her head that that was my name.'

'What happened to your friend?'

'He moved.' She shrugged. 'And we fell out of contact. I haven't heard from him since.'

Scott dabbed the brush in some glitter and brought it back to her cheek, using it for highlights on his artwork.

'It's really silly,' Olivia chuckled, her eyes distant as if caught in a memory. 'We used to say that we would meet in Paris—'

Scott's fingers fumbled, dropping the paint brush on the floor.

'—but it was just a silly childhood dream,' she said. 'Are you finished?'

Scott nodded and held the mirror up for her. She smiled and touched her cheek just below the red rose that Scott painted on her face. Admittedly, it was the best rose that Scott had ever painted on someone's face. He was proud of his handiwork and hoped that she loved it as much as he loved it on her cheek.

'Scott, it's beautiful,' she whispered, turning to face him.

'It's very fitting, then.'

Olivia picked up the paint brush and wiped it on a cloth, instructing Scott to turn his cheek to her so that she could paint some pirate scars on his face.

'This is a pirate party, after all,' she said. 'And I think a pirate scar might suit you well.'

He sat silently while she dabbed the brush in paint and made short strokes across his cheek. He could feel the softness of her hand as it rested against his chin and revelled in the soft resonance of her voice as she talked about Chad and Vanessa's kids. He could smell her sweet perfume and could almost feel her breath against his skin. He felt his hairs rise on end as her smooth leg brushed against his.

She dipped the brush in red paint which made Scott smile—she was clearly very detailed with her pirate scars to include blood. He just hoped it wouldn't scare the kids. Her closeness felt like it went quicker than it began. Olivia put the brush down, leaned towards him and kissed him softly on the cheek.

'I have to go help Vanessa,' she said, sounding more like she had to convince herself more than him.

Before he could say or do anything, she stood to her feet and headed towards the house. Scott watched her leave until she was out of sight, still feeling the tingling of her kiss against his cheek. Smiling, he picked up the mirror to look at the artwork on his face. He was impressed with the pirate scars on his cheek, but his focus was more on the red paint skilfully placed. It wasn't blood. Rather, it was in the shape of lips, as though he had been kissed on the cheek by someone wearing heavy red lipstick. The very same spot where Olivia's lips lingered in his memory.

Chapter 18

'Well, I am exhausted,' Vanessa said, dropping herself onto the couch next to Olivia.

The day was finally coming to an end. Olivia and Vanessa had finally finished cleaning up inside after the party while Scott and Chad were finishing packing up everything outside. Chad and Vanessa's kids were all in bed while the four adults cracked open the beer bottles to enjoy a drink.

The twins' party had been exciting for everyone. Olivia found herself so swept up in conversations and helping Vanessa that she had barely spoken to Scott since she painted his face. But she always managed to position herself so that she could see him as often as she could.

She smiled as the memories of the day flashed

through her mind. After manning the face-painting stall, Chad managed to convince Scott to help him entertain the kids which ended in each of the kids walking the plank and landing on the jumping castle. How Chad and Scott managed to connive such a plan left Olivia wondering, but it looked like the most fun any of the kids had had in a while.

Her thoughts moved from the plank walking to the looks that Emmy had been giving Scott all day. Emmy was only five, but she followed Scott like a shadow, staring at him with her big round eyes and reaching for his hand whenever she could. If Emmy were much older, Olivia would have some competition.

'The party was great, Vanessa.' Olivia nodded. 'The best by far.'

'I couldn't have done it without you and Scott,' Vanessa said, shaking her head. 'Seriously, Scott saved the day. And he's great with kids—a total bonus.'

Olivia had no doubt in her mind that this was so. Scott had said that he hadn't spent much time around people who had children before, but he was a natural. In fact, *he* looked like he was having as much fun as the kids.

'He is.' Olivia kept on nodding.

Olivia and Vanessa talked for a while, waiting for the boys to finish outside and join them. They heard the phone ring and heard Chad's voice as he answered it.

'Ness,' Chad said, poking his head into the lounge

room. 'It's for you.'

'Tell them no,' Vanessa said, thrusting her hands in the air. 'Tell them that I'm too exhausted to get off my—'

'It's your boss.'

Vanessa threw her head back against the couch in a sign of defeat.

'Fine.' Vanessa pulled herself off the couch, mumbling as she left the room to answer the call.

Chad kissed her cheek as she passed and focussed on Olivia.

'Your boyfriend is outside,' he said, sitting himself down on the recliner chair in the corner. 'He wants to talk to you.'

Olivia stood and started walking out of the room.

'He's not my boyfriend,' she mumbled.

But she wished he was.

***

Scott took a sip of his beer as he leaned against the railing of the patio. He had washed the face paint off his face, but he could still feel Olivia's touch and the softness of her lips against his cheek. If only she knew how just a touch or even her smile made him feel. She was unique to him. A mystery. And he was already falling for her, though he knew it was too soon.

There was something about what Olivia said about her childhood friend. Something that sent his mind into a frenzy.

It was just a silly childhood dream.

Her words rung in his ears. Had she given up on her childhood dream? Had she truly given up on all hope that she might see her childhood friend again or was she just trying to convince herself to let it go? The thought of Olivia possibly seeing her friend again after so long made Scott's stomach churn. He wouldn't be able to compete with someone who had been so close to her.

But, truth be told, he had come to Paris chasing a childhood dream of his own. He desperately hoped it would come true, but then he met Olivia. Now, he had no idea what he would do if he found the woman he came to Paris to look for. A part of him didn't want to give up on his childhood dream, but the rest of him wanted—needed—Olivia.

But that's not what he wanted to talk to her about. He had something to tell her and she probably wouldn't like it. He hadn't thought anything of it before now, but Chad said that he shouldn't wait anymore to tell her. He had made the arrangements before he met Olivia, but time had gone so quickly since meeting her that it had, in a way, snuck up on him. Then, he just couldn't figure out how he should tell her. But he had to. Tonight.

He took another sip of his beer, waiting for her to come outside.

***

'You wanted to talk to me?' Olivia said, joining Scott

on the patio.

He glanced up at her and flashed her a smile before studying the beer bottle in his hands again. Olivia leaned against the railing of the patio with him.

'I do,' he said.

Olivia's heart skipped a beat and she didn't register the next word leaving her mouth.

'What?'

'Want to talk to you,' Scott said, not fazed by her reaction.

Olivia exhaled, relieved that he didn't seem to notice. She took a sip of her beer, hoping that she could relax a bit more.

'You were great,' she said. 'With the party. And the kids. You looked like a natural.'

'You think so?' He turned to face her, his eyebrow raised.

Olivia nodded. He was standing so close to her and, even after a long day, he still smelled amazing. His eyes glistened with the reflection of the streetlight as they searched her.

'But you don't want to talk about the party, do you?' She sensed he was holding something back.

Scott shook his head slowly, not taking his eyes off her. He reached down and held her hand, nudging her closer to him. Olivia felt her breath quickening. Was he finally going to kiss her again? She wanted him to. If she lifted her chin a little more and leaned up towards him, she could brush her lips against his. She slowly started to stand on her tiptoes to do that when she was interrupted.

'I'm going away for a while.'

Olivia's feet flattened, dropping her the inch or so that she had gained. She leaned back to really study his face, trying to process what she had just heard. She couldn't get any words out. Instead, she just kept looking at him.

'Olivia?' Scott tugged on her hand again. 'Did you hear what I said?'

She searched his eyes with hers. Why couldn't she say anything? It shouldn't be a big deal—they're not exactly together. She managed a nod.

'Well?'

'Why?'

Scott released her hand and leaned against the railing again, still facing her.

'I'm going back to Australia to see my family. It's my dad's birthday and I booked the trip months ago.'

Olivia stayed silent for a moment. He booked the trip months ago and is only telling her now?

'I leave on Tuesday,' he continued when she didn't reply.

Three days before he leaves? She shouldn't be surprised though. Why should he share his plans with her? She could feel tears welling up, but she knew she shouldn't be feeling that way.

'When will you be back?' she whispered.

Scott shook his head, studying the beer bottle for a moment before looking up at her. His eyes seemed to have the same sadness that she felt.

'I don't know.'

Olivia wiped her eyes. She couldn't let herself feel like this. She didn't even know if he *would* return. He didn't have a job to come back to. He had no ties keeping him here. What if he missed living in Australia and he doesn't realise it until he's back with his family? She couldn't expect that he would rush back to Paris just to be with her. It wouldn't be fair of her to ask that of him. But she wanted to. She wanted to tell him to stay, that she would miss him too much. But he had a one-way flight to Australia with no idea when he would come back. *If* he came back.

***

Scott could feel a tugging on his heart while he watched her processing what he had just said. He wanted to pull her into his arms and tell her not to worry. In that moment, he wanted to stay with her and forget about going back to Australia, but he couldn't. His family was relying on him to be there and he had no excuse not to go. He had no work commitments. Nothing was holding him here. Except for Olivia.

He didn't know how long he would be gone for, but he knew that he would miss her every second that he was away. Would she wait for him? It wouldn't be fair of him to ask her to. But he wanted her so much more than he was ready to admit and seeing her sad like this just made him feel like his heart was being pulled out of his chest.

She still hadn't said anything, and it made him nervous. Was she trying to make herself let him go? He didn't want her to do that. He felt like he wouldn't be able to live without her. She had pushed her way into his life and transformed into the air that he needed to breathe.

He reached out to hold her hand again, but she took a step back, looking out over the clear lawn that was covered with jumping castles and tables earlier in the day.

'Olivia,' he whispered.

Before he could say more, they heard a shriek from inside moments before Vanessa and Chad burst through the door.

'I got the promotion!' Vanessa yelled, rushing to hug Olivia.

Right in front of Scott's eyes, the patio was filled with congratulations and excitement. All traces of his conversation with Olivia seemed to have already been forgotten, but he couldn't leave Paris without knowing how she felt about it.

***

Scott sat in his car, gripping the steering wheel as hard as he could. After Vanessa's announcement, they talked as a group for a while before he drove Olivia home. He had to talk to her more about his coming visit to Australia, but she kept off-topic for the whole drive back to her house. When Scott jumped out of the car when they got to her home, she told him not to worry about walking her up. She said that it was late, and she was just going to go straight to bed and didn't want to delay his getting home.

But Scott didn't care what time it was, he needed to talk to her. In the end, he let her walk back to her flat by herself and decided that he would wait until he could see a light turn on in her flat. He figured he could talk to her before the wedding tomorrow. But when he saw the light flick on in her flat, he couldn't bring himself to leave. He tried to talk himself into leaving, but his body refused.

'Damn it!' he said, banging his fist against the steering wheel.

He climbed out of his car and raced into her building, taking the stairs—two at a time—instead of the lift in hopes that he could work out what to say. By the time he got to her door, he still had no idea what he was going to say. He didn't feel calm, only a shortness of breath and a stitch in his side from taking the stairs so quickly. But he didn't hesitate in lifting his fist and banging on the door. He didn't have to wait long for it to open.

'Scott?'

'You didn't say anything!' he said, walking inside before she could invite him in.

He turned to face her as she was closing the door. She looked puzzled, concerned. He paused for a moment, awestruck at the sight in front of him. Olivia was wearing a thin black chemise that was transparent below her breasts. He could see her lacy undies underneath and every curve of her body. She had let her hair down, allowing her golden curls to caress her shoulders.

He turned his head, he couldn't let himself be distracted.

'Nothing!' he continued. 'I told you that I'm going away for God knows how long and you said *nothing*! Not a single word.'

He paused, watching Olivia pull a dressing gown around herself and felt disappointed when the chemise was secured beneath the fleece. He tried to determine what Olivia was thinking. Was she mad? Upset? He thought he could see her eyes glistening, but she refused to look at him. He probably could have made a better entrance. He walked over to her and held her arms, urging her to look at him.

'Olivia?'

'What would you have me say, Scott?' she asked, surprising him with the strength in her voice. 'That I don't want you to go?' She shook her arms free of his hold and walked towards the kitchen. 'That I'm scared that you'll never come back and I'll never see you again?'

He followed her to the kitchen, hoping that she wouldn't start throwing things at him like the last time they fought. The kitchen has more dangerous items than a cushion or a coaster.

'I want you to tell me the truth,' he said.

'I can't!' Olivia said, stopping midstep and turning to face him.

They were inches apart and Scott wanted to close

that gap. But he couldn't. Her eyes were glistening, and a tear started to roll down her cheek. He lifted his hand and brushed it away. She closed her eyes and dropped her head.

'I can't,' she said again, her voice breaking. 'Because it wouldn't be fair of me to say it. I can't tell you to stay or to come back soon. I can't tell you that I would miss you. That I would miss your smile and your touch. Your voice. I can't tell you anything that I want to say because I have no right to.'

Scott watched another tear roll down her cheek and drop to the floor. He watched as it splattered into a little puddle between them.

'You have every right to,' Scott whispered, nudging her chin with his finger.

She shook her head, turning it to the side. He wanted her to look at him, but he didn't want to push her. She was tearing him apart and she didn't know it.

'I don't,' she whispered. 'And it wouldn't make a difference anyway. You have to go, regardless of what I think. It's your family.'

Scott wanted to tell her that he would stay for her, but he knew that she was right. His family has been looking forward to this trip for months. He couldn't let them down like that. And he couldn't just leave as soon as he got there. They would expect him to stay for a couple of weeks at least.

He could feel a lump in his throat. He tucked a curl of her hair behind her ear and traced the edge of it with his thumb. He allowed his thumb to drop to her chin and traced the length of her neck and across her collarbone. He held her gaze when she finally looked at him and pulled her closer to him.

'I want you to say it,' he whispered.

She shook her head.

'I want it to make a difference,' he said.

She lifted her chin, her eyes sincere. He closed the small gap between them, pressing his lips against hers, pulling her body closer to his. She lifted her arms and wrapped them around his neck, pressing deeper into the kiss, allowing her mouth to open so that he could taste her sweet breath. It drove him wild. He wanted her. He needed her. Her tongue traced his lip and he reciprocated every tease. He picked her up and sat her on the kitchen bench without breaking the kiss. He tugged at the strap keeping the dressing gown in place, finally pulling it free. Olivia shrugged out of the dressing gown and wrapped her legs around his hips. He pulled her closer, kissing her deeper and running his hands over her shoulders and across her back.

She dropped her arms from around his neck and started unbuttoning his shirt, tracing her fingers over his chest and grasping his muscles, leaving a trace of fire everywhere she touched. He shrugged out of his shirt as soon as the buttons were undone and wrapped his arms around her again. He could feel the warmth of her body underneath her chemise radiating against his chest. He could feel her desire matching his. He broke the kiss only to trace her neck with his lips, leaving a trail of soft kisses. She tilted her head to the side, exposing more skin for his kisses. She raked her fingers along his back, pulling him closer while he kissed her collarbone.

He kissed another trail across to her shoulder, nudging the thin strap of her chemise off her shoulder with his lips. Then he followed the trail back to her chin and continued onto the other side until both straps were off her shoulders and the chemise was sitting loosely against her breasts. He kissed her again, allowing his tongue to tease hers. She tugged at the buckle of his belt until it loosened and started working on his pants, breaking the kiss to focus on the obstinate button. Scott continued kissing her neck.

'Olivia,' he whispered against her neck. 'Come with me.'

He stopped kissing her neck to search her eyes. Her hands stopped struggling with the button.

'Scott,' she whispered.

'To Australia.' He cupped her face in his hands. 'Come with me. I have another ticket. I want you there with me. Please, say yes.'

Olivia allowed her hands to drop, her eyes glistening again.

'Scott,' she whispered. 'I can't.'

Chapter 19

Olivia stared out of the window in her flat, tracing the rim of her cup with her finger, knowing too well that her coffee had gone cold. She couldn't help zoning out for so long. She could only think of what happened the night before. Her body ached for Scott's touch again and her thighs burned with desire for what could have been. If only he hadn't asked her to come with him. If only she had said yes.

Though she tried her best to cover it with makeup, her eyes felt heavy from the sleep that didn't come and puffy from the tears that kept her awake. She could still feel the tenderness of his kisses and eagerness of his touch. She traced the line on her neck that still burned with his kisses, allowing her fingers to drop when they touched her collarbone. Her mind could only continue to replay the way their intimacy took a turn.

'What do you mean you can't?' Scott had said.

'I can't come,' she replied, pulling the straps of her chemise back onto her shoulders. 'I have a business to run. I can't just drop everything and go on a holiday. It has to be planned.'

'Just be adventurous,' he begged. 'There's no time left to plan.'

'And whose fault is that?'

Those words still felt bitter on her tongue, despite it being the night before. She hadn't meant to hurt him, but she was caught in the moment. He had planned the trip months ago and only decided to tell her now, mere days before he leaves. That hurt her.

She hardly noticed the tear rolling down her cheek. It felt normal to be there after the night she had. Fighting with Scott wasn't how she wanted the last days before he left to go. But she didn't know where they stood now. They had a moment of togetherness that was blown by her refusal to go to Australia with him.

She wasn't even sure if he would still go to the wedding with her.

***

Scott took the stairs slowly, trying to sort out his thoughts and his feelings before he got to her floor. It had been another sleepless night but, this time, it was because of the images that flashed before his eyes every time he closed them. He never thought that his offer would have backfired like it did. He thought it would be romantic and a thrill. He wouldn't have made the offer if he didn't want her to come with him.

But he should have known.

He should have known that Olivia would need time to plan. She is a business owner, but she also had Betty to cover when she needed her to. Surely it wouldn't be impossible for her to leave at short notice. If she would just consider it.

His body still ached for her. She still occupied every inch of his mind and his desire drove him wild. Obviously, she felt the same for him. That much was clear. Right up until his offer. Since then, he wasn't so sure. Was she just caught up in the moment? Had it been so long since she'd felt that kind of connection with a man that she longed for it?

He had never been so unsure of a woman's feelings for him. But one thing was certain—he hated fighting with her. He hated arguing with her and he hated not knowing where they stood. He didn't even know if she still wanted him to come to the wedding with her.

His hand froze inches from the door and he looked around him. The hallway was quiet, calm, the complete opposite of how he felt inside. He tapped his hand quietly against the solid wood and waited, but there was no answer. He lifted his hand to knock again, but instead found himself turning away from the door. Before he knew it, he had pressed the button for the lift and was waiting for it to open.

***

Olivia rested her head against the door, trying to compose herself enough to open it. She took multiple deep breaths to steady her voice and pulled the door open before she lost the courage and was surprised to find that she was staring at thin air. She almost closed the door, convinced that she was hearing things, when she heard the ding of the lift. She stepped through the doorway to see him standing at the lift, waiting for the doors to open.

She couldn't urge herself to move towards him. She couldn't even whisper his name. If it wasn't for his last glance in her direction, she was convinced that he would never have even known she was there. The lift dinged again, and the doors closed.

***

Scott registered the lift doors closing, finalising his decision. He couldn't shift his gaze. He didn't know what this would mean for them. She hadn't said anything and neither had he. But it was as though the silence between them said everything that needed to be said.

The hallway was quiet again, but he was no longer the only one standing in it. She was a vision in her elegant deep-blue dress. Her knees peeked out beneath the hem and the bodice was tight around her waist and hugged her breasts. He could see her chest through the lace that caressed her from her collarbone to the top of her breasts. Her golden hair rested against her shoulders in the way that he liked best.

He took a step towards her, and then another, his pace quickening when she took steps of her own. They met in an embrace and he pressed her body against his. It had never felt so nice to be wrapped in her arms. He kissed the top of her head as she buried her face against his chest.

***

'You're here!'

Olivia smiled as the bride-to-be rushed towards her.

'I was starting to worry that you had forgotten,' the flustered bride continued. 'Now that you're here, everything's perfect.'

Olivia apologised for running behind schedule. The one thing she hated most in the world was disappointing her clients. That's why she always promised to be there and made true to her promises. But this morning, she wasn't even feeling like going to the wedding, let alone if she would have actually been able to make it. She scolded herself for feeling so selfish. She was, after all, the florist for the wedding.

'Your day would have been perfect with or

without me, Annie,' Olivia said, presenting the bridal bouquet.

'Well, now it's a dream come true,' Annie smiled, burying her nose in the bouquet. 'These are amazing! I don't know how you do it, but you are incredible.'

'That's what I try to tell her,' Scott answered, poking his head out from behind the car.

He lifted the final box of flowers out of the boot and locked the car before stacking the boxes together. Annie raised an eyebrow at him and smiled mischievously back at Olivia.

'You didn't mention that you were bringing a date,' Annie said.

Olivia blushed, closing the box that she had retrieved the bridal bouquet from.

'He's not my date,' she said, unsure if she was telling the truth. 'But he is my assistant for the day.'

'Don't tell my bridesmaids that, otherwise you won't see him again,' Annie replied, glancing back at Scott. 'But you and your *assistant* should stay for the reception. I have two empty seats that need filling.'

Olivia watched the bride hustling back towards the building to finish getting ready. She always loved providing the flowers for weddings, and especially loved when she could stay. But, for some reason, she didn't quite feel the same as she had at previous weddings. It was starting to seem like she would only ever be the florist and never the bride.

'Maybe one day,' she muttered under her breath then remembered that Scott was there too.

'What was that?' He turned his attention to her.

Olivia broke her gaze from the doors that Annie had just disappeared through and shook her head.

'Oh, the bride-to-be wants us to stay for the reception.' She shrugged, stacking her box onto another before picking them both up.

'Well, as your *assistant* I'll have to do whatever my boss decides,' Scott said, passing her with his own arms filled with boxes. 'But you can't really say no to a bride on her wedding day.'

***

Scott walked steadily to the room at the far end of the hallway. He managed to pick up the box with the boutonnieres for the men and the groom's family and possibly felt too eager to deliver it to them. It wasn't because he wanted to get away from Olivia, but it did annoy him a little that she refused to call him her date. After all, he had previously considered that he was going as her date, even though he had offered to help her with her delivery. But the thought that she hadn't even considered that he was going as anything other than her assistant frustrated him.

They still hadn't talked about what went on last night and the time was only getting closer to him leaving for Australia. He wanted her to come with him, but he didn't want to push her away. But he worried that she wouldn't wait for him to come home. She was way too beautiful for him to expect that of her. Surely another man would swoop in while he was away, and he would be forgotten.

He could feel his grasp on the box tighten as he grew closer to the end of the hall. He knew that she shouldn't be making him feel this way. He could feel himself plunging way too deep way too quickly. But it was as though she had a hold on him that he couldn't get out of. Perhaps the distance would do them some good.

He knocked on the open door as he entered the room to see a nervous groom sitting in the corner and his groomsmen huddled around the refreshments table. The groom looked up and smiled at him as he heard the knock.

'I was wondering when the flowers were getting here,' the groom said, standing to greet Scott. 'I bet Annie is relieved.'

'Annie would be too busy fussing over her hair to notice, Ben,' one of the groomsmen said.

The groom, who was obviously Ben, smiled at his friends and looked back at Scott.

'Well, I know that Annie said Olivia was doing our flowers,' he said. 'But I never thought that Olivia was a man.'

Scott smiled at Ben and placed the box on the nearby side table. He took his time opening the box and finding the groom's boutonniere before replying.

'I'm Scott. Her assistant,' he muttered, handing it to Ben. 'Apparently.'

Ben raised an eyebrow at Scott's reply and turned to face the mirror to pin his boutonniere to his suit.

'That doesn't sound like you want to be her assistant, my friend,' he said, turning back to face

Scott once he was happy with how the boutonniere looked.

The groomsmen burst into laughter at the refreshment table, but they remained oblivious to the discussion that was happening between Ben and Scott. Scott watched the men as their laughter subsided and only looked away when he was convinced they hadn't been laughing at him. He hadn't realised that Ben was still waiting for him to answer. He shook his head.

'You know how it is,' Scott said, picking up the remainder of the boutonnieres to give to the groomsmen.

'I'm getting married, aren't I?' Ben shrugged, smiling.

There was no more that could have been said. Ben's family had come into the room and Scott watched as they all moved around him before he slid out the door and headed back towards the hall. He was forgotten just as he would be when he left for Australia.

***

By the time Olivia got to the main hall, Scott had already set up the flowers along the aisle. The beauty of the hall and decorations took her breath away. She walked slowly down the aisle towards the front of the room, making sure that everything was perfect before the guests arrived.

She had been worried about Scott when she was

caught up helping Annie and her bridesmaids with the final touch-ups. She had spent much more time in the bridal room than she had intended. She still wasn't sure where her and Scott stood, it hadn't been discussed. And she hadn't realised that Scott overheard her say to Annie that he was just her assistant until it was too late.

She came to a halt at the end of the aisle when she found herself standing only a few feet away from Scott. He was now wearing his suit jacket that she hadn't even noticed that he brought with him. He looked neat, handsome. His suit framed his body and sculpted around his strong muscles. And for the very brief moment that he held her gaze with his, she felt like all the effort that he had put into making this room so spectacular was for her, not for the bride and groom.

'I've been wondering when you would show up,' Scott said, stepping closer.

Olivia felt her heart quicken. His smile made her feel a burning inside her chest and she craved to have him closer.

'Scott—'

He interrupted her. 'I made something for you.'

He stepped closer to Olivia until she could almost feel the warmth radiating from his body and the smell of his cologne made her senses tingle. He pulled an elegant wrist corsage from a small box that he had hidden from her sight and slid it over her hand. He allowed his hand to continue holding hers for a moment longer before releasing it. She studied the corsage and was in awe at how beautiful it was and touched by the fact that he had made it for her without her knowing.

'Scott, I—' she said, her words catching in her throat from a threatening tear.

'I know,' he said, allowing his thumb to caress her cheek as he tucked her hair behind her ear. 'I'm sorry I pushed you.'

Their eyes stayed connected for what seemed like an endless amount of time and she could feel his breath against her lips. She was sure that they were about to kiss, and she wouldn't fight it, but the doors swung open and the hall was quickly being filled with the guests.

The wedding was about to start.

Chapter 20

'And now, last but definitely not least, the bride and groom!'

Everyone rose and cheered as Ben and Annie walked into the reception hall and took their seats at the bridal table. The MC announced that food would come out in a rather quick succession to allow time for dancing and celebrating at the end before putting his microphone down to focus on some background music.

Olivia made herself comfortable in her chair, glad to finally be able to sit down. After the beautiful ceremony, Olivia and Scott had been kept busy, running back and forth fixing bouquets and displays then making sure the reception hall was perfect. It left them little time to talk all day and little time to think. Now that they were sitting and able to relax, Olivia slipped her high heels off her feet, immediately feeling circulation return to them.

She recalled the moment she shared with Scott before the ceremony. She still couldn't help but think that he decorated the hall for her, not for the bride and groom. It was a picture she couldn't erase from her mind and, for once, she felt like a bride. Walking down the aisle towards Scott made her feel as though it could happen one day. She hoped that it would. It might even be with Scott. But who would know?

She wasn't sure how anything would work out with his trip to Australia. He might never come back to Paris and she would be back to where she was three weeks ago, before she met him, going on unsuspecting dates with guys who just didn't give a damn about her. She wondered what would have happened with Antoine if she hadn't met Scott. Did the chemistry she felt when she met Scott have anything to do with her reluctance to be close to Antoine? Would she have fallen for Antoine's charms if Scott was never in the picture? The very thought made her shudder.

Her thoughts were interrupted by one of the waiters placing a plate with a delicate mini-quiche and a light salad in front of her. She hadn't realised that she'd been lost in her thoughts for so long, but it seemed that Scott was caught in a small-talk conversation with the lady next to him. In fact, everyone at their table was engrossed in a conversation except for her.

* * *

Scott stared at the plate that just appeared in front of him. He was looking forward to finally being able to talk to Olivia, but she seemed so deep in thought since they sat down. He noticed how she stealthily slipped her high heels off her feet and the delicate way that she massaged them against her legs. He was sure that she thought that no one noticed that she'd taken her shoes off. In fact, he probably was the only one to notice. But with legs like hers, how can a guy keep his eyes off her?

It didn't take him long to work out that they had been placed at the single's table. The way the lady next to him zoned in on him may have had something to do with giving it away. He didn't want to be rude, so he answered her questions while grabbing glimpses of Olivia out of the corner of his eye in hopes that she might start to talk to him in the second-long silences while the lady took a breath. Now that the entrée had come, there was time enough for him to change his focus to Olivia. But he just couldn't tear his eyes away from whatever the hell was on his plate.

'Escargot,' the lady next to him whispered in his ear, startling him as she spoke.

He tried to force a smile to be nice, but she was starting to really freak him out. He looked over at Olivia's plate—a mini-quiche and salad—and wished that he could have that instead. He looked back at his plate, his stomach churning. It mustn't taste that bad, since it was considered a delicacy. But, regardless of how much he tried to convince himself to give it a try, he always believed that snails were slimy creatures found in the garden. The idea of eating one never struck him as appetising.

He leaned over to Olivia.

'Do you want some?' He tried not to look too desperate to offload the slimy mess.

She glanced at his plate and smiled. 'I'm happy with my quiche,' she said.

He refocussed on the plate of snails in front of him. He was sure he could see their bodies still moving and their eyes trailing up towards him. He picked up the small spoon resting on his plate and selected the smallest one, closed his eyes, and put it in his mouth. Just as he anticipated, he could feel the slipperiness of the snail and struggled to swallow it, quickly washing it down with a gulp of wine. He could feel his eyes watering and the slippery snail squirming its way down his throat and into his stomach. He was squirming nearly as much as the snail.

'That good, was it?' Olivia said, giggling.

He hadn't realised that she was watching him experience escargot for the first time. Before he could reply, she halved her quiche and transferred it onto his plate. He could have kissed her for her thoughtfulness—if he wasn't on the verge of vomiting from the escargot.

'I don't see how this is a delicacy,' he said, pushing the snails to the edge of his plate.

'It's an acquired taste, I suppose,' Olivia said. 'I've never liked them though.'

He allowed his face to show the enjoyment he was getting from eating the quiche that she gave him, leaning over to kiss her on the cheek for sharing her food.

'You are a lifesaver, do you know that?' he whispered in her ear, feeling her press against his lips.

That must have done the trick, because the lady on his other side emptied her glass of wine and focussed on the rest of the table, leaving him in peace to focus on the beautiful girl that he wanted to spend all night staring at.

***

Olivia locked Scott's reaction to the escargot safe in her memory. She could never forget that. She couldn't believe that he was actually game enough to try it. He seemed to be one to err on the side of caution when it came to food. How he surprised her.

She could still feel his whisper against her ear, the kiss on her cheek and the warm sensation it sent down her spine. She was relieved that the lady sitting on the other side of him wasn't keeping him occupied anymore. She saw the jealous look on her face when he kissed her cheek—and it made her feel good. But would he always pick her over another woman who shows an interest in him? She could feel her hairs raising, though, when the woman turned her focus on the two of them.

'So, how long have you two been together?' she asked, drawing the attention of the whole table onto them.

She felt Scott shift in his seat, obviously as surprised about the question as she was.

'Well … it's—' Scott stammered, glancing at Olivia, his eyes alarmed.

'Kind of hard to say—'

'We're not really—' he said.

'Together,' Olivia muttered.

'Right,' Scott said, agreeing only hesitantly.

'Not that it would be a bad thing,' Olivia said, feeling somewhat under pressure.

Scott turned to face Olivia completely, searching her eyes with his. She watched the uneasiness drop from his face and be replaced with a smile, a gentleness.

'Right,' he said, his face beaming hopefully.

She didn't know what it was about that awkward admission, but she felt something shift inside her— something that she wasn't sure was there before.

'How do you know Ben and Annie?' one of the other singles said.

'I'm their florist,' Olivia was feeling more at ease with the direction of the conversation.

'And you?' He aimed the question to Scott.

Scott nudged his head towards Olivia. 'I'm her assistant,' he said.

Maybe it was in the playful way he said it that made her smile, or maybe it was because he carefully grasped her hand under the table. She turned her hand to interlace her fingers with his. The brief smile she received from him made her heart melt, but the moment was cut short by the main meal being served—a rotating serving of beef burgundy and *coq au vin*. Once everyone at the table had their meals, the interest in Scott and Olivia passed and everyone returned to their previous conversations.

'As much as I enjoyed doing the flowers with you,' Scott started, low enough for only Olivia to hear. 'I missed actually getting to talk to you. Not to mention it's exhausting—how do you manage to do this all the time?'

Olivia smiled at Scott, she missed talking to him too—especially since they seemed on such rocky ground this morning. She assumed that they were back on good terms before the ceremony, but the lack of being able to talk to him since then frustrated her.

'I guess you really have to be passionate about floristry.' Olivia shrugged. 'But weddings are usually pretty exhausting. Mind you, there's not always an invite to stay for the reception.'

'What else are you passionate about?' Scott asked.

The question took Olivia by surprise—she had never really thought about it. 'I'm not sure,' she replied. 'Floristry takes up most of my time, I don't really have a chance to do much else. But I do enjoy walking. I find it helps when I need to process something. What about you?'

'Much the same,' Scott said, finishing his food, and placing his cutlery on the plate. 'I put in a lot of hours at work so never had time for a hobby. But since I quit, I seem to spend a lot of my time with a certain lovely lady.'

His wink made the butterflies in Olivia's stomach flicker. She had never felt this way with anyone before and it was driving her insane. She felt as though she could talk to him about anything and he always had an answer that made her heart flutter. She wondered if he knew that he had this effect on her. And if she had the same effect on him. She welcomed the fresh glass of wine that the waiter poured when clearing her plate.

***

Scott couldn't help but stare at Olivia's golden hair and her slender shoulders while they waded through the speeches. First the best man, then the maid of honour, then the father of the groom and the father of the bride. He had lost track of who else was giving a speech—there seemed to be so many. Though he registered a new speaker at the end of each toast, he heard none of what was being said.

Olivia had turned in her seat to face the speakers, meaning that he could examine every inch of her shoulders, every purposeful curl of her hair, the curve of her neck. He wished they could be alone and he could trace his fingers along every part of her that his eyes rested on. He even imagined—briefly—Olivia walking down that aisle in a white dress. She would look more stunning than an angel. He could tell that she appreciated the effort he put into making the church hall look like it had been pulled out of a magazine. He just kept telling himself that he was doing it for her and it ended up better than he originally planned.

The speeches were finally done, and the MC announced that dessert was going to be served—*poire belle Helene*—whatever that is. Something about a poached pear and some sort of syrup or custard. He wasn't too sure. The waiters came around again and topped up their wine glasses. He supposed it was to tide them over since they were the second-last table to be served the food.

'I thought those speeches were never going to end,' he whispered to Olivia.

She seemed to have trouble stifling a giggle. 'They've probably already been forgotten,' she whispered back.

'I mean, the important ones, sure,' he smiled. 'But I'm pretty sure that every person in the room doesn't need to give a speech.'

He rested his arm over the back of her chair, revelling in her giggles, her uncontrollable smile, the flash of mischief in her eyes, and the way her body shook with her enjoyment. God, how he wanted her. She finally managed to control her laughter, trying not to draw too much attention. She turned in her chair so that she faced him fully, her knees resting against his leg but her feet still angled under the table. He noticed that her shoes had returned to her feet, he supposed when she took a quick trip to the bathroom.

'What are your thoughts on marriage?' she asked, her eyes gleaming like a child.

He felt his heart skip a beat and his nerves standing on edge. He took a second to process her question. The truth is, he hadn't really thought about it that much—at least, before today. The whole being caught in the wedding scene made him think about it all day. What his wedding would be like, what marriage would be like, what it might be like with Olivia …

'I, ahh—' he stammered, unable to put words into a sentence.

He moved the arm that he was resting on the table towards Olivia, hoping that caressing her cheek would bring the words to his mouth. But instead of being the romantic gesture he dreamed it would be, his arm bumped her wine glass off the table, spilling over her lap. Instinctively, he grabbed his napkin and started dabbing the spill from her lap. Before he registered what was happening, Olivia jumped and tried to stand, faltering in her heels and tipping backwards with her chair. He lunged out of his seat to catch her, unknowingly flinging himself in front of one of the waiters who dropped everything that he was carrying over Scott's back.

He had managed to break Olivia's fall, but as he

held her there, he could feel the slime of warm custard seeping down the back of his neck and, before he knew it, a poached pear slid off his shoulder and landed on Olivia's chest.

***

He was mortified.

Olivia had no idea how they ended up in such a situation and, although she was embarrassed beyond words, she couldn't help but laugh at their joint clumsiness. The horrified look on Scott's face as the pear fell onto her chest was just the icing on the cake. Of course, she was acutely aware of every eye in the room being on them, but she was lost in Scott's eyes. He helped her to her feet, apologising for spilling the wine on her lap. And surprising her by trying to blot the spill. And for the pear. But, to be honest, it had been the most fun she'd had all night.

One of the other waiters brought a pile of napkins over for them to clean themselves off with, which they decided to do outside, away from all the curious eyes.

'Thank you for catching me,' Olivia said once they got outside.

'I'm so sorry, Olivia,' Scott said again. 'I don't know what came over me.'

'Don't apologise!' Olivia laughed, helping Scott wipe the custard from the back of his neck. 'It was the highlight of my night. If I knew that my question would lead to that happening, I would have asked it before the speeches.'

His smile was sincere, making her body tingle all the way down to her toes. Heck, she'd had more action with Scott in the last few days than she's had in a long time. She could feel his eyes following her hand as she wiped her chest with a napkin. She revelled in the sensations that his gaze made her feel.

'Did I get it all?' she teased, poking her chest out a little to get a better view.

She felt powerful, dangerous, with his fascinated look—his eyebrow raised, and satisfaction plastered over every inch of his face. He reminded her of a tiger ready to pounce. Very slowly, he nodded and tore his gaze from her chest to lock eyes with her.

They could hear music playing inside the reception room, a slow song. Scott stepped closer to Olivia, taking the napkin from her hand, and placing it on the raised edge of the garden bed. Their bodies were touching, she was sure that he would be able to feel her heart pounding through her chest. He lifted her right hand, holding it at shoulder height, and allowed his other hand to glide over her hip and come to a rest at the small of her back, pressing her body even closer to his. She rested her left hand on top of his shoulder. Slowly, deliberately, he started to move their bodies as one in a gentle, rhythmic motion, each step in time with the song. Olivia searched his hazel eyes, large with passion and a touch of eagerness. He was focussed solely on her.

'I didn't know you could dance,' she whispered,

trying not to blink so that they could stay in the moment.

'I didn't know you could be such a flirt,' he teased, his cheeky side-grin making her own smile more uncontrollable. 'You have the most beautiful smile.'

Olivia could feel the heat rushing to her cheeks. She wasn't accustomed to such compliments from a handsome man. In fact, innocent, becoming compliments seemed to be a rarity. Still swaying from side to side, he closed the small gap between them, taking her mouth with his, gently at first, then deeper. He loosened his grip on her right hand and wrapped both of his arms around her waist. She held both of her hands around his neck, tangling her fingers in his smooth hair, welcoming his kiss even more. If only this moment could last forever.

Chapter 21

Their kiss deepened. Olivia was more welcoming than she felt she would normally be, but he was so inviting, irresistible. They were no longer standing in the courtyard dancing under the stars. Scott had lain her down beneath a billowing tree. She could feel the cool of the grass seeping through her dress, but it only excited her more, encouraging her to pull him closer to feel his warmth. He obliged, allowing his hand to wander—over her shoulder, down the side of her chest, her waist, tracing the edge of her leg down to her heel and back up again, leaving a trail of fire. His hand hesitated between her thighs, long enough to stare into her eyes, seeking her approval. She nodded.

Olivia's eyes shot open. She wasn't feeling the

cool of the grass underneath her, but the plush warmth of her bed. Her heart was racing, and she tried to catch her breath, her eyes searching the room around her and falling onto a plane ticket waiting on her bedside table. Memories of what really happened the night before flashed through her mind.

Their kiss ended with the song. It was a slow, simple kiss, filled with passion and heat. But he didn't let her go. He kept his arms wrapped around her and she rested her head against his chest.

'I'll miss you,' she whispered into his chest. 'When you're in Australia.'

She felt his hand move to the back of her head, stroking her hair. He kissed her forehead.

'My offer still stands,' he said.

'Scott, I—'

He pulled back just enough to look her in the eyes, cupping her face in his hands.

'Don't say it, please,' he pleaded, searching her eyes with his. He reached into the inside pocket of his suit jacket and pulled out a plane ticket. 'This is yours, if you change your mind. I'll wait for you at the boarding gate until the final boarding call. Olivia—' he paused, tracing his thumb over her lips. 'I want you to come with me. Just think about it. I'll know your answer when the final boarding call is made.'

At some stage during her recollection, Olivia moved to the edge of her bed, holding the plane ticket in her hand and finding herself completely unsure of what she should do. Her decision was obvious to begin with. But she had never had such an opportunity presented to her. She hadn't dated anyone who even considered taking her on trips and, if they did, she would have been firm in her decision to stay. So, why was Scott different? Why was he making her second-guess herself?

She placed the plane ticket back on the bedside table. The plane would be leaving early in the morning—she didn't have long to decide. But it shouldn't be so hard.

***

'I didn't know it was so serious,' Vanessa said.

Olivia shrugged. Vanessa dropped into her florist shop on the way to work. Getting that promotion came with later starts. Olivia just spent the last half hour telling her everything about Scott's proposal— the lead up, the offer, her refusal, and now. Throughout her account, Vanessa sat quietly, hanging onto every word, her eyes growing wider with every detail.

'It's not, really,' Olivia said, dropping a mangled daisy on the workbench that she hadn't realised she had been playing with.

'He wants you to go to Australia with him,' Vanessa said, reaching her hand over to place on Olivia's arm. 'That sounds serious.'

Olivia bit her lip. Was Vanessa right? But how could they be serious if they weren't exactly sure what was going on? She wondered why he asked her to go with him. She would be meeting his family, seeing where he grew up. It might be early days, but would it be the only opportunity they would have?

'What's holding you back, Liv?' Vanessa asked, her face full of concern.

'I'm not sure,' Olivia confessed. 'Work, I guess. There's so much to do. And Mum.'

'You have nothing to worry about with work,' Betty piped in. Olivia hadn't realised that she had been listening to their conversation. 'I would go if Alex asked me.'

Olivia smiled. Of course Betty would go. She was into the whole exciting adventure thing and going all in with a decent man. But Olivia was more cautious and reserved. It was just in her nature. Before she could reply to Betty, her phone started ringing—it was her mother's ward.

She answered, expecting more disappointing news.

'Olivia, hi,' the attendant said. 'Just wanted to let you know that Mrs. Harley is having a good day so far—she's almost back to herself. But we don't know how long she'll be back, so I would suggest coming as soon as you can if you would like to visit.'

She couldn't believe her ears. Her mother had had so few good days lately that she had started losing hope on her having them again. She thanked the attendant and said that she would be right over. Surely this visit would help her decide on going to Australia or not. If her mother was really improving, she wouldn't be able to bring herself to leave. She wouldn't want to miss out on any day where her mother was back.

'It's Mum,' she explained to Vanessa and Betty. 'She's having a good day.'

'Go,' Vanessa said. 'I have to get to work anyway.' She gave Olivia a hug and patted her shoulder. 'You'll make the right decision.'

***

'You did *what*?' Alex said, leaning forward in his chair.

'I asked her to come with me,' Scott said for the third time, wondering if Alex was losing his hearing.

'Why the hell would you do that?' Alex asked.

Scott shrugged. It seemed the right thing to do at the time. He really did want her to come with him and, for some reason, he thought she might say yes. He still did want her to come with him, but he was sure that she'd already made up her mind and she was probably unlikely to change it.

'I like her, Alex,' he said. 'It seemed like a good idea.'

'You've known her for, what, a few weeks?'

Scott nodded.

'You should be glad that she turned it down,' Alex continued. 'Taking her to Australia with you is like taking it to the next level. It's taking it to all kinds of serious. Remember Shaz?'

'It was different with Shaz,' Scott said defensively. 'You know how that turned out.'

R.J. Groves

'And what makes you think Olivia is different?'

Scott stared at the coffee table in Alex's hotel room. He thought that Alex would have been more supportive. He definitely didn't expect him to bring up Shaz and start comparing her with Olivia. It was different—completely different. But how did he really know? Hadn't he thought it was great when things started with Shaz? He shook the doubts from his mind. He had other priorities then. And maybe it was too soon to bring Olivia home to meet his family, but he also wasn't ready to let her go and he shouldn't expect that she would wait for him. He learnt that lesson last time.

'I can't explain it,' Scott said. He couldn't if he tried. 'Haven't you ever met a woman and felt like you needed to be with her?'

'Yes,' Alex said. 'With every woman I've slept with.'

Scott sighed. Alex was being impossible. 'I don't mean like that. I don't feel like I have only known Olivia for a few weeks. It feels like I've known her forever.'

'But you haven't, Scott.'

'I know.'

They sat in silence for a minute, Scott still staring at the coffee table and Alex staring at the ceiling. He knew Alex was right about the timing, but Olivia was definitely not like Shaz. Olivia wouldn't be so easy to let go of.

'It's out of your hands now anyway,' Alex finally said. 'But I get that you don't want to lose her. Why do you think I decided to stay in Paris longer? Betty's been great, but she's not the kind of girl who'll wait for me to travel back and forth between here and Australia. But staying in Paris is very different to taking her home to meet the family.'

Would Olivia be the kind of girl to wait? He couldn't tell. But it wouldn't be fair of him to ask her to if she decided not to go with him. Truth is, he hadn't thought about the fact she would be meeting his family. All he thought about was having her there in Australia with him. He wouldn't have to worry about if she would wait or not. Meeting the family shouldn't be such a big deal, though. If his family were here, he was sure they would have met already.

'I guess you just have to decide if she's worth chasing,' Alex said, shrugging.

Scott already knew the answer to that.

***

'Oh, honey, there you are!' Mrs. Harley said. 'I've been waiting all morning for you. This damned place won't let me go for a walk anywhere except for in the garden.'

Olivia smiled, pulling her into a hug. It felt so good to be held by her mother and see her in good spirits. She never seemed to know who Olivia was most of the time.

'Well, it's a beautiful day to be in the garden,' Olivia admitted, taking a seat on the bench next to her mother.

She could see the attendants nearby, keeping an eye on them, and she could feel the warmth of the sun bouncing off her skin.

'I'm sure you've told me plenty of times, my dear,' her mother said, placing her hand over Olivia's. 'But refresh my memory—how have you been spending your time?'

'I run a florist shop, Mum,' Olivia started.

'Oh, I know about that,' she replied, waving towards the attendants. 'They told me all of that this morning. I want to know if there's a special man in your life that I don't know about.'

Olivia smiled, thankful that the attendants made sure that her mother was up to date when she had a good day. She felt her cheeks flush.

'There is, isn't there?' her mother asked, making her blush further.

'Maybe, a little,' Olivia said, sighing. 'I like him, but we're not exactly anything yet. Or we might be. I don't really know for sure. He helped me with a wedding yesterday and we had a moment, but it's not set in stone. He asked me to go to Australia with him.'

'Australia?' Mrs. Harley said, raising an eyebrow. 'Well that sounds like fun. When do you leave?'

'Tomorrow,' Olivia continued. 'Well, if I decide to go. I refused at first, but I'm not so sure now. It's a risk, really. We might lose what we have if I don't go and he might never come back.'

'I see,' she replied. 'Well, don't let me hold you

back. You need to decide if he's worth the risk on your own. What's he like?'

'He's wonderful, Mum,' Olivia admitted, blushing more. She pulled out her phone, flicked to a picture that she took of her and Scott together at the wedding and showed it to her mother. 'That's him there. It kind of felt like a dream, really. Everything was so perfect.'

Mrs. Harley held Olivia's phone, examining the picture closely. As she handed the phone back, Olivia could tell that the look in her mother's eyes was growing more distant. The smile dropped from her mother's face right before she started staring out at the garden. Olivia took her cue, waving to the attendant nearby who looked just as disappointed as she felt. She rose to her feet and started to leave when she heard her mother's voice talk to her again.

'You should bring Eddie with you next time,' Mrs. Harley said. 'I always did like that boy.'

'Eddie?' Olivia asked, confused by her mother's statement.

Mrs. Harley nodded, pointing towards Olivia's phone. 'The boy in the picture.'

'That's Scott, Mum,' Olivia replied, solemnly. 'I haven't heard from Eddie since I was twelve.'

But it was useless, her mother had recessed back to how she spent most of her time. She looked at the picture of her and Scott, wondering how her mother could think he looked like Eddie. She gave up on ever seeing Eddie again years ago. No doubt he'd forgotten about her as soon as he left. But what

would she do if he ever did show up?
What would happen with Scott?

Chapter 22

'This is the first boarding call for all passengers travelling to Adelaide. Please make your way towards the boarding gate.'

Scott checked his watch when he heard the announcement. It wouldn't be too long before the final boarding call was made. He had already been waiting at the airport for two hours, just in case Olivia would come early. But he was starting to lose hope that she would be coming at all. He hadn't heard from her all day yesterday, not that he tried to contact her either. He figured that he would give her time to make a decision. He hoped that giving her time would have helped change her mind.

He held his phone in his hand, his finger hovering over the call button with Olivia's name on the screen.

Should he ring her? Then he would know what she decided and would have a chance to say goodbye. He moved his finger away from the button. He didn't think he could bear her rejection again. Besides, he was never good at goodbyes.

He heard the second boarding call announcement. He debated boarding the plane now. Every minute longer he spent waiting at the boarding gate made him doubt that she would come even more. When he first arrived at the airport, he was so certain that she was going to be there. He thought that she felt the same connection that he did. He was starting to doubt that too.

'Are you travelling to Adelaide, sir?' the lady standing at the gate asked him.

He glanced at his watch. There was still a little bit of time left. He nodded at the announcer. 'I am,' he said. 'I'm just waiting for someone.'

The announcer nodded, leaving him waiting for Olivia. He could feel himself getting nervous. If she was coming, she was cutting it very fine. He scanned the faces of every person he could see in the airport, hoping that the next person he saw walking towards him would be his goddess. But it never was.

He heard the final boarding call, but he couldn't bring himself to leave so quickly. He'd told her that he would wait until the final boarding call, but one minute more wouldn't hurt. The room around him started to clear, but there was still no sign of Olivia. He felt the announcer touch his arm.

'Sir, I need to ask you to board the plane now,'

she said, her eyes apologetic.

He nodded, handing her his ticket to scan. It looked like he would be going to Australia by himself. He started walking down the long corridor towards the plane when he heard the announcer talking to someone. He turned around, hoping that Olivia would walk through the gate. He watched as a tall businessman walked past him, nodding to Scott as he did. He felt disappointed, starting to follow the businessman to the plane for boarding.

'Scott?'

He turned midstep to see Olivia just behind him, dressed in jeans and a loose-fitting jumper and carrying a bag of her own.

'I didn't see you,' he whispered, reaching out to take her bag for her.

She nodded towards the tall businessman who had just boarded the plane. 'I guess it would have been hard to see me through him. He's very much bigger than I am.'

Scott leaned in, giving Olivia a quick kiss on her tender lips. 'You came,' he said, starting to head towards the plane. He felt her slide her hand into his, wrapping her perfect fingers around his.

'Of course I did.' She smiled, her eyes glowing.

***

Olivia couldn't believe she was actually doing this. She tapped her fingers nervously against her leg as the airhostess ran through the emergency procedure. Should that make her feel more comfortable about flying? She hadn't mentioned to Scott that this would only be her second time flying. From memory, her first time on a plane was when she was a child—and she was just as nervous then as she was now. Or maybe more so now.

She glanced over at Scott sitting next to her. He had already tucked his drink bottle, phone, and book into the pocket at the back of the seat in front of him. He didn't look nervous at all—completely relaxed, in fact. He'd obviously flown a bit before. She looked down at her nervous hands, realising that she'd left her drink bottle on the bench at home. She hadn't even considered bringing a book. Her hands clenched on her thighs when the plane started moving. She felt rigid in her seat.

'First time flying?' Scott had a mischievous grin on his face.

'Second,' Olivia said. 'The last time was when I was a child, but it wasn't very fun.'

She remembered taking a couple of trips to the bathroom to empty her stomach during that two-hour flight. She wasn't sure how she would go with this much bigger, much longer flight. But she knew there was a reason she refused to go to Australia with him at first. She moved her hand to brush away a hair that was niggling at her eye, flinging it back down as the plane started to pick up speed. She could feel Scott's eyes resting on her and could still see his mischievous grin out of the corner of her eye.

She could feel herself pressed in place as though

there was an unseen force gluing her to her chair. She couldn't move, at least she thought she couldn't. It wasn't until she felt the warmth of Scott's hand resting on hers that she was able to turn her head slightly.

'It helps sometimes.' He shrugged.

His grin was replaced with a smile so sincere and so caring that it did make her feel better. She turned her hand to intertwine her fingers with his, realising that she'd had a death grip on his thigh. She could feel the sinking in her stomach as the plane lifted off the ground, but Scott held her gaze with his. It wasn't long before the plane started to level out and Scott released her hand. Part of her was glad that the worst of the take-off was over, but the rest of her was disappointed. She enjoyed holding his hand and feeling safe because of him.

She half-expected that Scott would have started reading his book now that the flight had started. She wondered what she would do for the long flight since she hadn't even thought of bringing something for entertainment. Maybe she could watch some movies on the little computer screen on the back of the chair in front of her.

'What changed your mind?'

She turned her head to face him. He hadn't even touched his book, but was facing her, giving her his undivided attention. Olivia shrugged. What had changed her mind? Could she say that she had decided that he was worth the risk? That she wanted to see where this trip would take them?

'I guess I figured that you were right,' she said. 'Betty agreed to look after the shop and Mum's in good hands, so there wasn't really anything else stopping me.'

'Well, I'm glad you came,' Scott said, his eyes flashing with sincerity.

'Oh,' Olivia continued. 'And I couldn't let you go to Australia without knowing the answer to a question that's been bothering me since the wedding.'

'Which is?' Scott raised an eyebrow, his cheeky grin returned.

'Why the hell did you have another plane ticket?' Olivia asked, turning her body in her seat to face him. 'I mean, you can't just get a ticket for an international flight with no notice. So, who was supposed to go with you?'

'Ahh,' Scott said, his grin broadening. 'You think that you're my second choice?'

'It kind of seems that way.' She'd hoped that he wouldn't have noticed that that was how she was feeling, but she supposed her curiosity got the better of her.

'Okay, I guess you were.' Scott laughed. 'But only because I hadn't met you yet. And I'm glad that I'm going with you instead. It wouldn't be nearly so romantic with Alex.'

'Alex?' Olivia asked, surprised. She had been expecting that it was another girl, not Alex.

Scott nodded. 'We booked the flights months ago,' he explained. 'He was supposed to come to

Paris for a visit and then we were both going to go back to Australia for Dad's birthday.'

'So, what happened?'

'He met Betty.' Scott shrugged. 'And he decided to stay in Paris longer. Unlike me, he wasn't originally planning to return to Paris. So, instead of refunding his ticket, I bought it off him and got the name changed to yours in hopes that you would come with me.'

'What if I didn't come?' she asked.

'Then I'd be out of pocket about a thousand euros.'

'That's an expensive risk,' she whispered.

'I was willing to take it,' he said, smiling.

They sat staring at each other for a moment. If she hadn't been strapped into her seat, she was sure that they would have kissed and may not have been so easy to separate this time. She felt the plane bump with a light bit of turbulence, pushing her other question to the front of her mind. The plane ticket hadn't been the only question that was persistent since the wedding.

'You never answered my question on Sunday,' she said, nervously.

'Which one?' he asked, concern on his face.

It shouldn't be so hard to ask, right? It was just a simple question to see what his views were. So, why was she so nervous?

'About marriage,' she forced out. 'You never said what your views were.'

His brow crinkled. 'I was wondering when that

would come up again,' he said, glancing around before focussing back on her.

Why did it seem to be an awkward topic for him?

'I've never really thought about it, to be honest,' he said hesitantly. 'I mean, I guess it would be an easy decision with the right person.'

Olivia smiled, though she wasn't sure how she felt. She couldn't say that she'd never thought about it. She'd dreamed about marriage since she was a child and being a florist meant that she was always seeing weddings. It was a hard topic to avoid for her.

***

Scott scanned the page in front of him. Olivia had long since fallen asleep, resting her head on his shoulder. He'd had a nap himself, or tried to, and figured he could get some reading done before Olivia woke up. But he'd been reading and re-reading this same damn page since he picked the book up, finding that his eyes were scanning the words. but his mind was elsewhere. On Olivia, in fact.

He knew that he would have to answer her question about marriage at some stage. He just wasn't expecting it to be now. He told her the truth, sort of. He hadn't had much of a reason to think about marriage. He had, once, and that didn't turn out well. But since then, the thought hadn't occurred to him. Until he saw Olivia walking down the aisle towards him before the ceremony started with a look on her face that showed she felt like she was in a fairytale.

Then, he couldn't stop thinking about what it would be like with Olivia, even with his mind trying to persuade him not to get too deep. Did he give Olivia the right answer? He'd always believed that marriage would be an easy decision with the right person, but since the last time, he'd always been cautious, guarded, not wanting it to ever be a thing that's rushed.

He closed the book, giving up on any chance of being able to read it. His senses were very aware of Olivia's head resting on his shoulder. The smell of her shampoo was enticing, and he could see her cute pout from this angle. He'd always known she was beautiful, but he hadn't dreamed that she would be so alluring when she was asleep. He supposed it was a good thing they were surrounded by people. She was getting harder to resist every moment they spent together.

He wondered how Olivia would get along with his family. He knew that they would welcome her with open arms, even though they didn't know she was coming with him. He probably should have told them, he figured. But he didn't want to get their hopes up if she decided not to come. He didn't want to get his hopes up.

***

'It's about time! Mum told me you would be here hours ago.'

Scott smiled at his sister as she stormed over towards him. It had been a long flight, even if he did have a pretty woman for company. But seeing his sister so frustrated was quite refreshing. Their flight, surprisingly, wasn't delayed, but he also wasn't surprised that his mother gave her a time earlier than what he was supposed to arrive. Especially since she was late to pick him up last time.

'It's good to see you too, sis,' he said, pulling her into a hug.

'You were behind her telling me the wrong time, weren't you?' She slapped him on the chest.

'I had nothing to do with it, promise,' he said, his hands in the air. He smiled at Olivia who had just found them after going to the bathroom.

'Is she with you?' his sister asked, slapping him on the arm this time. 'Did we know you were bringing a gorgeous girl home?'

He shook his head, flashing one of his cheeky smiles to his sister. He put his arm around Olivia when she reached them. 'Olivia, this is Elizabeth and—'

'Seriously?' his sister interrupted, scowling at him, then extended her hand to Olivia. 'Liz, please. Don't listen to this bastard.'

'—she's my sister.'

'Unfortunately,' Liz muttered. 'Are you guys hungry? I figured we could stop for lunch on the way home. Here,' she grabbed Olivia's bag, 'let me help with that.'

Scott smiled, relieved that Liz and Olivia seemed

to be getting along well. He even thought that Liz's offer to help Olivia with her bag was nice, albeit out of the ordinary for her to offer to help anyone, until she shoved Olivia's bag into his arms. Liz gave him a defiant smile before looping her arm with Olivia's and started to lead her out of the airport. He picked up his own bags, somehow balancing them all and followed behind, shrugging as Olivia turned to flash him an apologetic look.

It didn't bother him. He would have offered to carry her bag anyway. But he was annoyed that Liz stole that moment from him.

***

Olivia felt bad. She didn't know that Liz was going to make Scott carry her bag. Not that she had much of a choice in the matter since it was practically ripped from her grasp before she could refuse. She couldn't help but smile at the banter happening between brother and sister all the way to the café. But she also got the vibe that Liz wasn't expecting that she would be there. She supposed it was her own fault, since Scott wasn't even sure that she would come. She just hoped that he filled his parents in. Imposing on his family without any warning was not the kind of first impression she wanted to give.

Being in Adelaide was so different to being in Paris. It was a city, but it seemed so much calmer than the hustle and bustle of Paris. She admired the buildings as they drove through the street—it was as though brand new, tall buildings had been built on top of historical, traditional buildings. It fascinated her. And there were churches everywhere. She hadn't seen such a beautiful place before.

Sitting in the back seat of Liz's car, Olivia was able to sit quietly and take it all in. She enjoyed hearing Scott's carefree laugh as he joked with his sister, her refusal to let him drive because he would drive on the wrong side of the road, his teasing. But he hadn't forgotten about her, because every few minutes he would turn to smile at Olivia—the smile that made her heart swell.

It wasn't too long before they got to the café. Olivia and Liz sat down at a table outside while Scott went in to order.

'So.' Liz started her interrogation as soon as Scott was out of sight. 'Scott's told me a lot about you, but I didn't think that you were coming with him.'

He'd been talking about her? She blushed. 'It was a last-minute decision,' Olivia explained. 'I wasn't planning on coming at first. Scott hasn't told me much about his family, is there anything that I should know before I meet your parents?'

Liz shook her head. 'We're pretty easy-going. There's not much to say I suppose.'

'What has he told you about me?' Olivia was curious.

'Only good things,' Liz said, reassuringly. 'But he never said that you were actually together.'

'We're not, really,' Olivia said. Liz raised an eyebrow. 'Well, I don't really know. It's complicated,

I guess.'

'Complicated doesn't sound like Scott,' Liz said, her brow furrowed. 'He usually jumps in head first.'

Olivia's heart skipped a beat. Was Scott not being himself with her? She watched as the expression on Liz's face changed to one suggesting that she'd said something she shouldn't have. But Olivia needed an answer.

'Head first?' she asked. 'Has he been serious with someone before?'

Liz swallowed, glancing up towards the café door. 'I shouldn't have said anything,' she said finally. 'I'm sure he wouldn't have brought you here if he thought things were complicated.'

'Are you talking about me?' Scott took a seat next to Olivia.

'About you, not to you.' Liz teased him, seemingly relieved that he had returned to the table. 'Hey, why haven't you told Olivia anything about your amazing sister?'

Scott shrugged, glancing at Olivia. She thought she saw a flash of concern cross his face before he turned to his sister again. Maybe it was reflecting the worried look on her own face now that her mind was filled with more questions about this mysterious man.

'Well, I didn't want to scare her from coming with me.'

Liz poked her tongue out. 'I thought Alex was supposed to come back with you,' she said. 'Is he all right?'

'He decided to stay.' Scott shrugged. 'He found a girl and decided to give it a chance.'

'Oh,' Liz said, smiling as the waitress brought their coffees over.

Olivia thought that she saw some sadness in Liz's eyes and wondered why. Scott must have noticed it too.

'Why?' he asked, taking a sip of his coffee.

'No reason,' she said, tipping some sugar into her cup. 'Just wondered why he wasn't here.'

Chapter 23

'We're home!' Liz shouted, barging through the door of their parents' place. 'And look what the cat dragged in!'

Scott cringed at Liz's analogy. He knew that she wasn't referring to her bringing him home, but rather him bringing Olivia with him. Maybe it would have been a good idea to give them a heads-up, at least they wouldn't be so surprised when they saw her.

'My darling boy!'

He could hear the excitement in his mother's voice trailing from the kitchen and desperately hoped that she would find Olivia to be a pleasant surprise. He could smell the rich aroma of lamb stew wafting through the house and hoped that she made plenty—as she usually did—to make feeding an extra mouth simple enough. He figured he could always sacrifice his meal for Olivia if he needed to, but he hoped it wouldn't come to that.

He smiled at Olivia, hoping to calm her nerves. Truth is, he felt just as nervous as she looked.

'Quick, Rob, our boy is home!' his mother yelled, turning into the hallway. 'Oh, and a girl,' she said, surprised to see a blonde-haired beauty standing next to him. 'Rob, he brought a girl!'

'Quit your harping, woman, I'm right behind you,' his dad mumbled, squeezing past his mother to greet them. 'Well, it's about time you brought a pretty lady home, Scott. Your mother was starting to think she'd never get any grandkids.'

'Shush yourself, Rob, we don't want to scare her.' His mother jumped in, hugging Scott and taking hold of Olivia's hands. 'What's your name, honey?'

'I'm Olivia. It's so nice to meet you, Mr. and Mrs. Henders,' Olivia said, a broad smile across her face.

'Oh, none of that, honey, it's Suzie and Rob. We're not formal around here.'

'Let them in, Suze, they must be tired and hungry,' Rob said, shaking Olivia's hand and patting Scott on the back.

Scott watched as his mother grabbed Olivia by the hand and led her towards the kitchen, telling her to make herself at home and mentioning something about how Scott should have told her that he was bringing a pretty girl home so that she could have worn something nicer. He smiled at how well Olivia seemed to fit in already and bit his lip when he realised that her butt looked exceptionally good in those jeans, even after a long, tiring flight. He was relieved that his family had, so far, been accommodating—he'd hoped they would.

'I bet you need a beer,' Rob said, nudging Scott's arm.

That he could agree on. He knew that there was an interrogation brewing that could happen at any time.

***

'That smells incredible.' Olivia took a seat at the table where Suzie told her to sit. 'Are you sure I can't help with anything?'

'You just sit there, honey, everything's been done already,' Suzie said, pulling some plates onto the kitchen bench. 'It's lamb stew—Scott's favourite. He'd be upset if I didn't make it for his welcome home.'

Olivia smiled at the comment. She couldn't imagine Scott being upset if his favourite meal wasn't cooked. She supposed there was a lot she didn't know about him.

'I worried about Scott when he moved to Paris.' Suzie continued dishing up some rice onto the plates. 'He was so ambitious and determined to start a new life there I thought I'd never see him again. But the good boy always makes an effort to come home and keep in touch. He's changed so much since he came to live with us.'

'Are you talking about me, Mum?' Scott said, walking into the kitchen. 'Mmm, smells good!'

He gave his mother a quick kiss on her cheek before coming over to sit next to Olivia. She smiled at him, wondering where he'd been. Catching up with Liz and Rob, she supposed. But what did Suzie mean by Scott coming to live with them? Did she mean to say since he left for Paris? And did she really have hopes on grandkids so soon?

'Mum makes the best lamb stew you've ever had,' Scott said, squeezing just above her knee with his hand.

'I don't think I've ever had lamb stew before,' Olivia admitted, enjoying his touch. Maybe more so since it was out of sight of anyone.

'Just as well,' Scott said, his eyes flashing. 'Once you try Mum's, any other lamb stew becomes sub-par.'

'Don't be silly, Scott, it's not that good,' Suzie said. Olivia could see a blush on her cheeks from the compliment.

'She has a secret ingredient,'

'Yes, tinned tomatoes,' Suzie said.

'It's a family recipe,' Scott teased, winking at Olivia.

He seemed to be enjoying spending time with his family. He did seem more relaxed around them, as though he really were home. She smiled at how he effortlessly teased them, receiving only friendly banter in return. In fact, she felt at home being here with him and his family. Since her mother's car accident, she'd lost any family connection she'd had. Though, the dynamic in her family was never like this. She wished it could have been.

'Can I smell stew?' Liz entered the room with Rob.

'Do you have to ask?' Rob's eyes lit up at the plates being filled.

Liz ignored her dad, walking over to Suzie to peer into the pot of stew. 'Mmm,' she said. 'With marrowbone?'

'Only the best for my kids,' Suzie said, nudging Liz out of the kitchen.

Rob came over to the table, taking a seat next to Scott at the head of the table. He popped the lids off a few beers, passing one to Scott and one to Olivia. She thanked him for the drink and was relieved to have a beer. She wondered if Scott negotiated for one for her since he had first hand experience at how messy wine can be.

***

It wasn't long before they were all sitting down at the table eating dinner. Scott couldn't remember tasting anything better than his mother's lamb stew. He hadn't even realised how much he missed it—or how much he missed his family. Technology made it easy enough to keep in contact with them, but there's nothing like seeing them in the flesh.

Scott enjoyed watching how his family included Olivia in their conversations, explaining to her everything that she looked unsure on. It was nice to see that she would be able to fit into his family so easily—she was already starting to stir them up a little. He hadn't been too sure about how they would react to him bringing a woman home. He'd only ever done it once before, but that was never to actually stay at their place.

His mother even announced that she was glad Olivia was here, that she was such a delight, refreshing even. Liz seemed to warm up to her as soon as she mentioned she owned a florist shop. He supposed it was because Liz worked as an events planner—they had something in common. His dad just seemed to take most of it in, telling the odd story every now and then. He couldn't help but smile at Olivia's interest in his dad's work—retired, but restores woodwork. He wondered if it was something that she was genuinely interested in or if she was just good at keeping conversation going.

'You know, I don't know why that boy didn't tell us you were coming,' Suzie said to Olivia. 'You would be welcome anytime.'

'I suppose it's my fault,' Olivia admitted. 'I decided to come at the last minute.'

'You weren't planning to come?' Rob asked, flashing a questioning look to Scott.

'I had a few things to sort out first with the shop and my Mum.'

'Isn't she well?' Suzie looked concerned.

Olivia explained about her mother's accident a few years back and how she has suffered from dementia since. He remembered when Olivia told him about it—how she seemed to struggle with her mother's condition. He watched now as his family took in the news and noticed Olivia's eyes glassing over. It made him want to hold her close even more to comfort her. He noticed his mother's eyes glassing over—her mother had had dementia too, though from age not injury.

'But she's in good hands,' Olivia finished. 'The centre is doing everything they can to help her.'

'Oh, honey,' Suzie said.

Scott could tell that she wanted to take Olivia into her arms and give her the biggest hug she could muster. He could also tell that she was trying her best to refrain from doing so. The table went silent for a moment, the only movement being Liz clearing the dirty dishes from the table.

'Olivia supplied the flowers for a wedding on the weekend, Mum,' Scott said, trying to ease the silence around the table. 'You should have seen it—it was incredible.'

He was relieved to notice the colour return to Olivia's cheeks and the smile return to his mother's face. He couldn't have his family tiptoeing around Olivia.

'I have pictures,' Olivia added, pulling her phone out of her pocket, and starting to flick through the pictures to show his family. 'Actually, Scott helped me with all of these. He even made me a gorgeous corsage to wear for the wedding.'

'Did he now?' Liz asked, glancing up at Scott.

Scott cringed to think of how his sister would use that information. He hadn't thought that through before he mentioned the wedding.

'That was somewhere before I spilt a glass of wine on her dress,' he added.

'Always the gentleman,' Liz teased.

Damn it.

He still wouldn't have taken that night back, even if he potentially ruined Olivia's dress. The only way his night could have been better would have been if he got to help her take it off.

***

Scott was a genius. Olivia figured that he must have noticed the change in atmosphere after she mentioned her mother. She hadn't expected that she would have to explain what happened when she mentioned that she had things to take care of. She was hoping that Scott would be able to think of a change of topic, especially since she was at a lack of topics to change to.

And he did. Bringing up the wedding brought the perfect change of atmosphere. His family showed more interest in seeing the pictures than she had imagined they would. She supposed it must be a novelty—surely Scott hadn't brought many florists home to meet his family before. She wondered who he had brought home, though she tried to shake it from her mind. Suzie seemed over the moon to see the wedding pictures, especially the one of her and

Scott. Rob even told her that she had quite the talent. Or maybe it was to Scott. She wasn't quite sure. But she loved how Scott's family teased each other. But she could still see the love they all shared.

Showing off the pictures of the wedding led to dessert—a sticky date pudding—and more light-hearted conversations. The evening seemed to go so quickly, and Olivia was feeling the tiredness from their flight. Though, it seemed that everyone's eyes were drooping, Suzie being the first to say that it was time for bed. Olivia helped Scott get their bags from Liz's car, surprised at how quickly his family had dispersed in the time it took them to do so.

'So, they seem to love you.' Scott teased her, leading Olivia down the hallway to her room.

'Your family is amazing,' she replied. 'I wish mine were like them.'

Scott stopped to smile at her before opening the door to the bedroom. She could get used to that smile. In fact, she was starting to feel like she already was. She followed him into the bedroom with her bags, scanning the room around them, her eyes resting on the comfortable looking double bed in the middle. She hadn't realised how tired she really was until now. She felt as though she would almost have to crawl to the bed.

'You can put your bags over here,' Scott said.

She looked over to where Scott was indicating, surprised to see that he was standing with no shirt on and was already rummaging through his bags, eventually pulling out his pyjama shorts.

'I'll give you a few minutes to change,' he continued, taking his shorts out of the room with him.

Olivia dug through her bags, finding her negligée right at the bottom and quickly changed into it. She scanned the room again, wondering what Scott was meaning by giving her time to change. But she didn't have much time to think. Scott walked back into the room, tapping lightly on the door as he did. She covered herself with her arms, becoming increasingly aware of how little her negligée covered. Scott paused next to her, putting his jeans in his bag and allowing his eyes to look her over.

'Do you sleep in that?' he asked, his eyes teasing.

Olivia nodded, wondering why she couldn't find her words. He raised an eyebrow, looking her over once more before nodding and heading towards the bed.

'Nice,' he said, pulling the covers back.

'Umm, Scott.' She finally managed to speak as he sat on the edge of the bed—the only bed.

'Is something wrong?' He was probably wondering why she was still standing near her bag covering as much of herself with her arms as she could.

'Where am I supposed to sleep?' She felt more childish than she should.

His mouth dropped open a little, then he glanced at the empty side of the bed next to him and back to her. 'There's room for two,' he said, shrugging.

Olivia couldn't bring herself to say anything else.

She hadn't shared a bed with a man in a long time and she felt as though she were a virgin again—confused and nervous. In fact, she was worried her legs would shake so much she wouldn't be able to walk over to the bed. She glanced at the bedroom door. It definitely wouldn't be appropriate for her to sleep on the couch in her negligée. She glanced back at Scott, taking in his bare chest, hoping that she hadn't taken too long to decide what she would do.

She took a slow step towards the bed, still keeping her arms tight around her. By the time she had moved a few steps, Scott picked up the pillow from the side of the bed he was sitting on and took the spare blanket from the end of the bed.

'I can sleep on the floor if that would put you at ease,' he said, laying the blanket on the floor beside the bed.

Olivia climbed into the bed, pulling the blankets right up so that only her head was poking out.

'Wouldn't the couch be more comfortable?' she asked nervously.

Scott lay down on the floor, pulling the blanket around him and making himself as comfortable as he could.

'Not on a leather couch,' he said. 'Goodnight, Olivia.'

'Goodnight, Scott,' she replied, though she was starting to feel like it wouldn't be so easy to fall asleep now, despite being incredibly tired.

Her eyes were still wide open as she lay in the bed on her back, afraid to move in case it made a sound. It wasn't exactly the most comfortable position for her, but then, Scott wouldn't exactly be comfortable on the floor. Her mind finally caught up with her and she started to wonder why she was so uneasy about sharing a bed with Scott.

She did like him, after all. A lot. And it's not as though he was naked—he had his pyjama shorts on. And he would have been just as tired as she was. Surely, he wouldn't have been expecting something to happen while they were in the bed together. They would have only been sleeping. In the bed. Together. That's it. Him in his shorts with his incredibly bare and attractive chest and her in her incredibly skimpy negligée.

Olivia wasn't sure how long she spent debating with herself about the fairness of Scott sleeping on the floor and her sleeping in the bed when there was clearly enough room for the two of them—and with room between them, if they both slept on the edge of the bed with their backs to each other. After all, she shouldn't expect him to sleep on the floor for their whole trip. She decided that he could sleep in the bed. It was only fair. After all, it was *his* bed. As quietly as she could, she leaned over the edge of the bed so that she could see him.

'Scott?' she asked before she could change her mind. 'Are you awake?'

But the only response she got was heavy breathing—that of a deep sleep.

Chapter 24

Scott closed the door behind him. Having spent the night on the floor, he wasn't feeling like too much of a sleep in. He couldn't say the same for Olivia though—she was still caught in a deep sleep. He wondered why she seemed so uncomfortable last night about the one bed issue. He hadn't thought about it himself until he took her into the room, and then he was looking forward to sharing the bed with her. He didn't have his hopes up about doing anything with her, but he wouldn't have turned her down if she had other plans.

But he also didn't want her to be uncomfortable—which she seemed to be with the idea of sharing the bed. He hoped it was just because it had been a long day and not that she was

genuinely nervous about being in a bed with him.
She hadn't seemed so reluctant when they were
kissing after the twins' party. Though, that never lead
to anything else. He would promise to be good,
though, if it meant not having to sleep on the floor
for the whole trip. But it would be a hard promise to
keep.

He considered waking her, but she had seemed
pretty tired. Not to mention that she looked too
enticing with her bare leg over the top of the blanket
and her back uncovered. Having the pleasure of
waking her up would have been too much. Besides,
leaving her sleeping would give him some time to
spend with his family and hopefully gauge how they
felt about her.

It seemed that Liz had already gone to work, and
his mother's car was out. He checked through the
house for his dad, eventually finding him in the shed
working on restoring a boat. He knocked on the shed
door.

'Need a hand?' he asked, walking over to run his
hands along the boat.

'I was wondering when you were going to roll out
of bed,' Rob said, handing a sander to Scott. 'Figured
you wouldn't want to help your old man anymore
now that you were bedding a pretty lady.'

'What, and let you take all the credit for restoring
this beauty yourself?' he teased, sanding a rough bit
back. 'What was wrong with it anyway?'

'It was never finished,' Rob shrugged. 'It's been
handed down for generations, each generation

putting their own touch to it. The guy who has it now doesn't have time to finish it and wants to actually use it.'

'And has plenty of money to spend?' Scott asked. Building a boat takes a long time to do—he imagined that the guy must be paying his dad well to get it done.

Rob nodded. 'Boats are funny things, Scott,' he started. 'If you do something to one side, you'll have to do it to the other to make sure it doesn't affect the way it floats. Do something wrong and you've stuffed it up. It needs to be treated with care and a tender touch—much like a woman.'

He accompanied the last statement with a nudge against Scott's arm. He knew that boats weren't as fragile as his dad made it out to be, but he could see where he was coming from.

'So, what's so special about Olivia?' Rob asked. 'I mean, there must be a reason why you brought her home so soon. You only started talking about her in the last few weeks.'

Scott dusted the sander with his hand. 'There's just something about her,' he shrugged. 'It feels like I've known her forever and there's been a chemistry between us since we met. I saw her at a café, she left her book on the table when she left, and I followed her to give it back. She looked like she was at a crossroads, standing in front of the café looking furious but unsure of where to go. I must have startled her when I called out, because she turned to face me and tripped.'

'And you caught her,' Rob said.

Scott nodded. Of course, it wasn't too hard to catch her when she fell against him. 'It was like being electrocuted when we touched. I just knew that I wanted to know who this girl was and see more of her.'

'Sounds exactly like how I felt when I met Suze,' Rob said. 'When did she agree to be with you?'

'Well, that's the thing,' Scott started.

***

Olivia's eyes still felt heavy, but she couldn't believe she had slept so late, especially since she hadn't slept in since she started the florist shop. Going from the clock on the bedside table, it was past lunch time. She blamed it on jetlag—serves her right for daring to do something adventurous. Scott wasn't on the floor anymore and he'd placed the pillow and blanket back onto the bed. No one would be able to tell that he hadn't slept on the bed.

She changed her clothes and made the bed, making sure it all looked as neat as she could manage, and went in search of Scott. She still wondered what Suzie meant by Scott coming to live with them. For some reason, she gathered that Suzie hadn't muddled her words, but she would rather hear it from Scott than anyone else. She bumped into Suzie putting groceries away in the kitchen.

'Afternoon, honey,' Suzie said, smiling. 'I didn't wake you, did I?'

'Not at all,' Olivia said. 'I wasn't planning to sleep in so long though, I'm usually an early riser.'

'Jetlag will do that,' Suzie said, stuffing the plastic bags into a pouch. 'It must hit us girls the worst. The last time we went to visit Scott in Paris, I slept for most of the trip. Rob only slept in a little later on the first day then went back to normal. Do you want a coffee, honey?'

'Thanks, but I think I might try some fresh air first,' Olivia replied. 'Have you seen Scott anywhere?'

She felt a little childish asking where Scott was—like a schoolgirl with a crush. But Suzie just smiled as though she thought it were sweet.

'I saw him in the shed with Rob earlier,' she said. 'I think they were working on the boat.'

Olivia thanked her and headed out to the shed to find him. Fresh air seemed to be a good idea, especially since she started feeling better in the short walk between the house and the shed. Maybe she could convince Scott to go with her. As she walked along the side of the shed towards the door, she could hear Scott talking with his dad. It sounded like they were in a rather deep conversation. Olivia turned before she got to the door, deciding that she didn't want to interrupt. Besides, maybe a walk alone would help her sort out her thoughts. But something stopped her in her tracks.

'So, you're not actually together?' she heard Rob say.

'Well, not really,' Scott said. 'I mean, we clearly like each other. But every time it feels like we're getting somewhere, it just gets put on hold our something comes up. It's complicated, I guess.'

'Nothing is ever that complicated, Scott,' Rob said. 'It either is, or it isn't. You're sharing a bed, right? So, that says something.'

There was silence from Scott.

'Don't tell me you slept on the floor,' Rob continued. There was more silence. 'Well, we don't have to tell your mother about that. But why did you want her to come home with you if you're not together?'

'I didn't want to lose her,' Scott said.

Olivia pulled herself away from her spot near the shed, deciding that she would need to take that walk by herself. She hadn't meant to eavesdrop, but she also wasn't expecting that they would be talking about her and the relationship she had with Scott. But then, that should probably be expected since she did sort of turn up unannounced. It seemed that they were on the same page about it being complicated, but what Rob said was sticking in her mind.

Nothing is ever that complicated ... it either is, or it isn't.

So, which was it?

***

He hadn't seen Olivia all day. After talking to his dad and helping him with the boat, he went inside to check on her, but she wasn't in the bedroom. His mother said that she was looking for Scott earlier and that she sent her out to the shed. She'd mentioned something about getting some fresh air. He wondered if she had decided to go for a walk by herself when she found out that he was in the shed with his dad. That would be the likely thing she would have done, right? Otherwise she would have come in to the shed with them. Unless she overheard them talking.

Scott flipped the steaks on the barbecue. He had planned on going out to look for her, but his mother wanted him to start the barbecue and his dad said that it would be pointless if she came back before dinner and they had to wait for Scott to return. They had a point. Besides, he wouldn't know where to look for her. He placed the sausages on the barbecue, piercing them with a knife as he went.

He hoped that she hadn't managed to get herself lost. Of course, she shouldn't be too far away if she was on foot. If she kept walking, she would eventually find the house. Besides, if she managed to find her way in Paris, she would be able to find her way around here. But he still couldn't help but worry about her. He would have liked to have gone on a walk with her to spend some alone time together. Especially since she seemed out of sorts last night. He hoped it was just because she was tired from the flight.

He turned the sausages and pushed the steaks to the side to keep them warm. He watched as Liz's car pulled into the driveway and she got out. He was relieved that Olivia climbed out of the car as well.

'Look who I found wandering the streets,' Liz said as she passed him to go inside the house.

He smiled as Olivia stopped next to him. 'Did you get lost?' he asked.

'A little,' she said, smiling back. 'I finally found the right street though and Liz picked me up when she was driving past.'

'You should have told me you were going for a walk,' he said, turning the barbecue off and putting the sausages and steaks on a plate to bring inside. 'I would have come with you.'

'I needed some time to think anyway,' she replied, shrugging. 'Besides, I didn't want to interrupt you and your dad.'

He followed her towards the house, wondering what she meant. Was she regretting having come to Australia with him? What did she need to think about? Had she overheard him talking with his dad?

***

She did need some time to think. Especially after what she overheard of Scott and Rob's conversation. She needed time to sort out what she was feeling. But really, she only spent a short part of her walk thinking before realising that she hadn't taken much notice of where she was walking and had no idea where she was. She spent the rest of her walk trying to find the street that the house was on. It turned out to be a rather long street, so she was glad when Liz drove by and offered to give her a lift.

Despite having time to think, she probably would have made more progress if Scott did come with her. At least then she might have found some answers to her questions instead of having the time to think about them without any answers.

It either is, or it isn't.

Rob's words still played on her mind. She wondered what Scott had decided. Was he sure they were together or was he still as equally confused as she was? But it wasn't the only thing that weighed on her mind. Suzie's comment about Scott coming to live with them still confused her—especially since he had the same surname as Rob and Suzie. It really opened her eyes that she might not know as much about Scott as she thought.

She was starting to wonder if coming to Australia with a man she had only known for a few weeks was a good idea after all. But she had been so sure and excited that it would be all right when she decided to come. And she didn't think that she was blinded by the fact she wouldn't know Scott as well as she hoped—maybe she expected that she wouldn't. But to have a comment like that sprung on her just sent her mind on a rollercoaster.

Then again, seeing Scott's eyes light up when he saw her near the barbecue reminded her of why she did decide to come.

'Oh, there you are, honey,' Suzie said when Olivia and Scott walked into the kitchen. 'I was wondering where you went. Is everything all right?'

Olivia glanced back at Scott who was also

focussed on her, his eyes expressing the same concern that Suzie voiced. She nodded, smiling to ease their concern.

'Everything's fine,' she said. 'I just got a little lost until Liz found me.'

She hoped that that would suffice. It seemed to settle Suzie though, since she started ushering everyone to the table for dinner. But Scott's eyes lingered on her and she knew that he wasn't entirely convinced. Even so, he let his hand slide underneath the table when his family was caught in a heated discussion throughout dinner to give her thigh a gentle squeeze just above her knee. She would be lying if she said she didn't like it.

Olivia felt bad for sleeping in so late and making herself scarce throughout the day, so she offered to clear the table so that Scott's family could continue their discussion. She wasn't surprised that Scott said he would help and ushered his family into the lounge room. She started filling the sink with hot water to wash the dishes, relieved that his family's discussion kept conversation off her over dinner. She could hear Scott's family still talking in the lounge room. Whatever they were talking about was obviously a passionate topic for them, though Olivia hadn't taken much notice on what, exactly, the topic was—she had been too focussed on her own scattered thoughts and Scott's hand on her knee.

She picked up a plate and dipped it in the hot soapy water and started scrubbing it, but almost dropped it when she felt strong warm arms snake around her waist from behind her. She looked down at the hands linked across her stomach and felt Scott press her body back against his. She closed her eyes to take in the warmth of his lips against her neck and felt him turning her to face him. She obliged, lifting her chin to meet his lips with hers in what she felt was the most tender kiss they had ever shared. She felt his hands drop to cup her bottom while he pressed her even closer against him.

'Scott,' she whispered, breaking the kiss. 'What if your parents see?'

He pulled back enough to search her eyes and shrugged. 'They won't mind,' he said, guiding a stray hair behind her ear and caressing his thumb over her cheek. God, she loved it when he did that. 'I'm sure they think we do more than kiss, anyway,' he added with a cheeky grin.

Olivia felt her cheeks grow hot and turned back towards the sink to hide her blush. He wrapped his arms around her waist again and held her close. She enjoyed the warmth of his body against hers and could get used to that fluttery feeling that he made her feel every time he touched her.

'I know it's not fine,' he whispered, leaning his head against hers. 'What's on your mind?'

Olivia hesitated. Surely, she couldn't tell him everything that's on her mind right now. But maybe he could answer the one question that bothered her most.

'Just something that your mum said.'

'What did she say?' He loosened his arms from

her waist and moved next to her so that he could face her.

'She said that you've changed since you came to live with them,' Olivia said hesitantly, focussing on the plate she had in the sink. 'I figured that she meant for it to sound different, but it still made me wonder what she meant.'

'Oh,' he said, pausing for a moment. 'She meant it how it sounds.'

Olivia stopped scrubbing the plate and looked up at Scott. His eyes were sincere. 'I don't understand,' she whispered.

'Rob and Suzie aren't my birth parents,' he explained. 'They adopted me when I was fourteen. I was passed through more foster families than I could count in the year before they took me in. They made me feel like I was home more than I had ever felt before. And they treated me well, so I didn't play up with them.'

'Scott, I didn't know,' she said, wanting to reach out to him.

He shrugged. 'I don't talk about it,' he said. 'As far as I'm concerned, they've always been my family.'

Olivia blinked back a tear, struggling to find any words to say. But their discussion was cut short by Liz walking into the kitchen.

'Mum and Dad want to play a game of cards,' she said, a smile on her face. 'Want to join in?'

Olivia glanced up at Scott, the sadness in his eyes replaced with the cheeky look that had grown on her. She smiled at him, wondering if it was a family tradition.

'Go ahead,' she said, urging him to join his family. 'I'm pretty tired, so I think I'll just finish up out here and go to bed.'

'Are you sure?' he asked, letting his fingers brush gently against her arm.

She nodded, aware of the hairs standing upright where he just touched. He leaned towards her, pressing a tender kiss on her cheek before following his sister into the lounge room.

Somehow, finding out what Suzie meant by her comment had made her more at ease with the other questions that bothered her. At least now she was more certain of how she felt about Scott and understood why he hadn't told her about being adopted until now. Besides, how could he tell her everything when they had only known each other for a few weeks?

Chapter 25

'Are you ready?'

Olivia stared at herself in the bathroom mirror. She shouldn't be nervous. It was just lunch. With Scott. Alone. She'd been alone with him plenty of times and hadn't felt nervous at all. In fact, she'd been alone with him in a more precarious situation than eating food in a public place. So, why the hell was every cell in her body racing?

Sure, it may have had something to do with the fact that he told her to wear a pretty dress because he wanted to take her out for lunch. Okay, he may have called it a date. And it would really be their first actual proper date. But it's not as though she decided to come to Australia with him without expecting that there would be some kind of intimacy with him. Like a date. Or a kiss. Or more.

She touched her lips where she could still taste him from their kiss the night before. Was it normal that she thought he was addictive? Or that she wanted so much more of him? She was glad to have the dishes to distract her after their kiss, but she still lay awake in bed for a while trying to calm her senses. She hoped that it might have been a quick card game with his family, but it seemed like hours before she eventually fell asleep and, when she woke up, the blanket and the pillow were neatly folded and placed on the bed again.

She knew that he had slept on the floor again, even though she moved the blanket onto the side table in the corner of the room in hopes that he might have slept in the bed. But then, she still hadn't told him that he could. Maybe she was subconsciously trying to stay awake until he came into their room. And maybe spraying a little bit of her perfume on her neck before bed wasn't an accident. There was always tonight. She could feel her cheeks warming at the thought.

She would be lying if she said that she wasn't looking forward to their date. Especially since she tried on all three of the dresses that she brought to Australia with her to see which one would be best for their first date. The first one was too formal for a lunch date and the second she figured she could wear to Rob's birthday party tomorrow. She settled on the third—a blue floral dress that was light enough to be comfortable and suitable enough for anywhere they might go for lunch. She left her hair out, though made sure her curls sat just right.

'Olivia?' She heard Scott's voice again and realised that she hadn't responded to his question.

She took a big breath and adjusted her dress a little, making sure that she showed just a little more cleavage than she normally did, and opened the bathroom door to find Scott standing nearby, dressed in dark jeans and a short-sleeved buttoned shirt. She smiled when his gaze dropped to her breasts before he tore his eyes away to study her face.

'Is it too much?' she asked, doing a teasing twirl in front of him so that he could take it all in.

When her twirl brought her back to facing Scott, he caught her in his arms, meeting her lips with his. What a perfect way to start a date.

***

She was killing him. Slowly and agonisingly. He wondered if she knew how much she tortured him. He had figured that she would be breathtakingly beautiful in anything that she wore for their date. But *that dress*. The very dress that he first saw her walking down the street in. The one that had him convinced that he had seen a goddess and compelled him to consistently have inappropriate dreams and thoughts about her. That damned dress that made him want to have her right here and now.

He deepened the kiss, pulling her closer and

feeling the trace of her fingers as she wrapped her hands behind his neck. God, she made it hard to resist her. He could feel his desire pulsing throughout his body and the smell of her perfume tantalised him just as it had when he saw her sleeping last night. Even as he stroked her hair back from her face and planted a soft kiss on her cheek while she slept, it still took an incredible amount of effort to tear himself away from her and set up his bed on the floor. He briefly considered just sliding into the bed next to her, but he figured that sleeping on the floor let him keep some amount of control over himself.

With all of the strength that he could muster, he broke the kiss, fighting his urge to be closer to her. If he didn't, they wouldn't make their date. The way that her large, sky-blue eyes blinked up at him and her pursed lips didn't make it any easier.

'I'll take that to mean that you like it,' she whispered, catching her breath.

'Hmm?' he asked, tucking a stubborn curl behind her ear.

'The dress,' she said, raising a perfectly shaped eyebrow.

He nodded. 'It would look better at the end of my bed,' he said.

Her eyes widened, gazing up at him, as his mind processed what his mouth just said. Had he said that out loud? *Damn it.*

'We should go,' he said, tearing himself away from her and leading the way out of the house, hoping that she was following.

He kicked himself for not having more control. This was supposed to be their first proper date. And so far, he'd done everything out of order. *That damned dress*.

***

The drive to the café was filled with silence. Olivia was sure that he must have felt as nervous as she did, especially after his comment on her dress. She smoothed the dress over her thighs, proud of the fact that it seemed to be having the affect that she hoped it would. Briefly, she felt that their kiss had eased her nerves, but the silence in the car seemed to bring them back again. When the car stopped out front of the café, he turned in his seat to face her.

'What I said before,' he started. 'I meant to say that you look completely irresistible.'

Olivia blushed. He furrowed his brow as if recalling what he said.

'Incredibly beautiful.'

'Thanks,' she said, smiling. Maybe she should wear this dress more often.

He smiled back, looking a little relieved, before turning to his door and climbing out of the car. She lifted her hand to open her own door, but paused when he held up a hand and skirted around the front of the car, opened her door for her and reached out a hand to help her out. She took it, feeling as if she was getting special treatment.

Once she was out of the car, he closed the door

but didn't release her hand. Instead, he guided his fingers between hers and led her towards the café. She couldn't help but notice how perfectly their hands fit together. He released her hand only to open the café door for her. As she was about to walk through the door, a woman walked out. She stepped to the side to let her past, but the woman came to a stop between her and Scott.

'Oh, Scott!' the woman said. 'I didn't know you were back.'

'Ahh,' Scott said, hesitantly, glancing over at Olivia. 'Only been back a couple of days.'

Who was this woman? And why did Scott look so uncomfortable talking to her? Olivia felt uncomfortable herself, since the woman had her back to her the whole time.

'Well, I have the day off today,' the woman continued, stepping a little closer—too close—to Scott to allow someone else to walk through the door. 'If you're not busy—'

Scott interrupted, nodding towards Olivia. 'Actually, we have plans.'

The woman turned to see where Scott was indicating, and her brow crinkled. She looked Olivia up and down, making her feel incredibly uncomfortable under her scrutinising gaze, and turned back to Scott.

'Oh,' she said. 'Well, I guess I'll see you tomorrow, then.'

'What?' Scott said, his body rigid.

'At Rob's party,' the woman said, matter-of-factly. 'Ted's taking me. Anyway, have fun with—' She turned to face Olivia again, this time her face questioning.

'Olivia,' she said, stretching her hand out.

'Shaz,' the woman said, staring at Olivia's outstretched hand but not taking it. She turned back towards Scott. 'See you tomorrow, Scott.'

Scott didn't hesitate in guiding Olivia into the café as soon as Shaz left, but Olivia could still tell that his body was rigid, and he was uneasy. He had seemed like he was looking forward to going on a date with her before, but since they bumped into Shaz, his mind seemed to be elsewhere. Maybe her dress had lost its charm. He led her to a booth and waited for her to slide in before he took a seat opposite her.

'Who's Shaz?'

'She's no one,' Scott shrugged. 'I used to know her before moving to Paris.'

'Used to?' Olivia pressed on, confused.

'Nothing special,' he said, picking up the menu.

'If it was nothing special,' she said. 'How come you didn't introduce us?'

Scott put the menu down and reached across the table to hold her hand with his. 'For starters, you're better off not knowing her,' he said. 'And I wanted to get back to our date.'

Olivia managed a smile, hoping that it looked sincerer than she felt. She convinced herself to let it go, but she could tell that there was more to Shaz than Scott was telling her. She wondered what it was—or even if she wanted to know.

***

Failure. The date was a failure. And it had started so well! Trust Shaz to ruin it for him. She always had. He could tell that Olivia had more questions—ones he wasn't ready to answer. And the whole Shaz thing brought a rift between them that he didn't want there—especially on their first proper date. He wasn't lying when he said that Olivia would be better off not knowing her—he wished he never had. But that's not entirely the reason why he didn't introduce them. After all, he'd never planned on introducing Olivia to his ex-girlfriend.

He'd had so much planned for their date. They were going to have lunch, then go for a walk. There was a nice park nearby where he hoped they could kiss again and he could give her a flower—a picked one, since no florist was as good as hers. It was going to be a perfect date. But then Shaz ruined it. By the time they finished lunch, he figured they should just go home. The date was probably beyond saving anyway.

They drove home in silence—a more uncomfortable silence than they had endured when they drove to the café. He followed Olivia towards the front door, but stopped at the edge of the veranda. She turned to face him, her eyes questioning.

'Is something wrong?' she asked.

He shook his head. 'I think I'm going to go for a

walk,' he said, backing away. 'But you go on ahead. I'll be home later.'

He didn't turn back to look at Olivia, but he could feel her eyes following him as he walked away.

***

Olivia watched until Scott was out of sight, confused and concerned. He had been distant through their whole date, and the topic of Shaz was clearly one he wanted to avoid. But if they were going to have a chance at having any kind of relationship, she didn't want to have to avoid talking about things. She would just have to talk to him when he got home. She went inside, hoping to get to the bedroom without being seen. But bumped into Liz on the way through.

'Oh, you're back!' Liz said, excited. 'I thought you would be gone for longer.'

'What do you mean?' Olivia was confused. She hadn't known how long they were supposed to be gone for.

'Scott was saying he had the whole afternoon planned,' Liz said, hesitantly. 'But maybe I heard wrong. Where is he anyway?'

'He went for a walk,' Olivia said, shrugging. 'I guess the date didn't go as planned.'

'Uh-oh. What happened?' Liz asked, concern on her face.

Olivia considered not telling Liz at first, but she was worried about Scott and maybe Liz would know something that would put her at ease until she could talk to him again. She sighed, deciding that it would be for the best.

'We bumped into a woman named Shaz.' Olivia saw the colour drain from Liz's face and decided to continue. 'And Scott seemed really uncomfortable and avoided talking about her when she left. I don't know. I might be a bit paranoid, but did anything happen between them?'

Liz looked almost as uncomfortable about the discussion as Scott had on their date. 'It's not really my place to say,' she said. 'But they sort of had something going on a long time ago. Like, years ago. Way before he met you. You have nothing to worry about, if that's what you're asking. It's history now.'

Liz gave her a pat on the shoulder and went to another room before Olivia could ask another question. She wished that Liz had put her mind at ease, but she hadn't. She wondered what had happened between Scott and Shaz to make Scott so awkward on their date. Surely it couldn't have been so simple. What was the something that Liz was talking about?

***

'Where the hell have you been?'

Liz's voice was firm, loud against his impending headache. He hoped that he hadn't made too much noise coming through the front door. In fact, he hadn't expected that anyone would still be awake at this hour. It seemed that Liz was the only one. She dragged him into the lounge room, making his head spin at the sudden movement.

'Scott, I asked you a question,' she said, leaning closer so they wouldn't be heard. Her face was disgusted when he lifted his gaze to look her in the eye. 'Have you been drinking?'

'A little,' he managed to slur out.

A little was an understatement. He had meant to only have one drink while he tried to work out how he can make it up to Olivia. The second came when he started to think about the questions that she would definitely have for him. The next one was out of anger that, out of everyone he knew that they could have bumped into, it had to be Shaz. Before long, he'd lost count of things that he was drinking about and found his way home with more difficulty than he anticipated.

It was out of character for him to drink like that and he maybe wouldn't have had so much if he knew that he wouldn't feel drunk in any way until the frigid air hit him when he decided to go home. He was relieved that it was Liz that greeted him instead of Olivia. He was certain that Olivia wouldn't be pleased. He could deal with Liz.

He eased himself further down into the couch, only being disturbed when Liz came back into the lounge room with a coffee and handed it to him. When had she left the room?

'Drink,' she demanded. 'I need to talk to you and I can't do it until you're sober.'

'I'm fine, Liz,' he said, taking the coffee.

'Well, you sure as hell don't look it,' she said, scowling.

'Why the hell is Shaz going to be at Dad's party?'

'What do you mean?'

'She said that she's going with Ted,' he continued. 'Why would you say that she could come?'

'I swear I had no idea,' she said, her face shocked. 'I invited Ted because he's our cousin. He didn't say anything about wanting to bring anyone—especially Shaz. Why would he be bringing her anyway?'

'Well, they're obviously a thing,' he retorted, feeling the scold down his throat when he took a big gulp of his coffee. 'When did that happen?'

Liz shook her head. 'This is the first I'm hearing about it, Scott. But you need to tell Olivia about what happened between you and Shaz and you need to tell her soon to fix whatever the hell went wrong on your date.'

'What?'

'Don't act dumb,' she continued. 'I know you had the whole day planned and she was home way too quick to have had a good time. She's worried about you. You have to tell her.'

'I can't, Liz,' he said, his mind clearer. 'We're rocky as is, it'll only make it worse.'

'No,' Liz said. 'Her hearing about it from someone else will make it worse.'

'Are you saying that you'll tell her if I don't?' He leaned forward on his seat.

She sat tall. 'I've already lied for your ass tonight,' she said. 'If she asks again, I'm not going to lie a second time.'

'Liz—' He felt his body heating up.

'But,' she interrupted, putting her index finger in the air. 'I'm not the one you should be worried about. There is a party tomorrow and Shaz will be there. And everyone else that will be there knows your history with her. As far as I can see, you have a very limited time to tell her before someone else does. You do the maths. I'm going to bed.'

He threw his head back against the couch. She was right. He had to tell her. Otherwise, he had to work out how to stop her from hearing it from anyone else.

Chapter 26

Scott could hear the echo of his family's voices travelling from the kitchen to the lounge room. He rubbed his eyes, his head already throbbing, hoping that the glare of sunlight coming through the window wouldn't be so sickeningly bright and cringing when he forced his eyes open. He could feel his stomach churning when he sat up. He didn't know the first thing about curing a hangover, but he figured some painkillers, coffee and dry toast would probably have the most favourable effect.

He couldn't remember falling asleep on the couch, but he was sure that Olivia would have noticed that he didn't sleep in their room. He could hear his parents and Liz talking in the kitchen—no Olivia—planning his dad's party. The smell of baked goods wafted towards him, unsettling his stomach even more. Today was the party. And partying was the last thing he felt like doing. He rose to his feet and headed slowly to the kitchen, bracing himself for whatever his family would throw at him.

'Look who's back in the land of the living,' Rob said, raising his cup of coffee towards Scott.

'Barely,' Liz piped in, the ring in her voice pulsing through Scott's sore head. 'You look like hell.'

He tried to think of something clever to say back to Liz, but he was so focussed on getting to the coffee and painkillers that his mum had already placed on the edge of the bench for him. He managed a grunt and a wave in her general direction. He savoured the gulp of coffee that helped him swallow the painkillers, already feeling his throbbing brain easing. He went over to his mum and gave her a kiss on her cheek.

'Sorry, Mum,' he said, knowing that it would be best to apologise to her first.

She scowled up at him, took the almost-full cup from his hands and poured the coffee down the sink. He cringed as he watched the liquid gold disappear for good. She was pissed.

'You promised to help me,' she started. 'And however you're feeling, I'm going to hold you to that. So, whatever is going on between you and Olivia, work it out.'

She turned back towards her mixing bowl, stirring vigorously. There was no point in arguing with her— she would win. After all, he *did* promise to help her.

He just didn't expect that he would feel like his head was about to explode when it came time to help. He gave up on hoping for another coffee, so headed to his room to get changed.

He opened the door slowly, urging his head to stop thumping, and was greeted by the sight of Olivia dressed in a white floral dress. Well, partially dressed. He took in the sight of her bare back, covered only by the lacey back of her bra as she battled with the zipper. He closed the door, startling Olivia.

'Oh, you scared me,' she said, smiling, acting as though there wasn't a rift between them.

He stepped closer towards her. 'Do you need help?' he asked.

She nodded, turning her back towards him again. He brushed her hair to the side, exposing the nape of her neck, and allowed his fingers to trace her spine until he got to the stuck zipper. He thought he could see her fine hairs standing on edge where his fingers touched and hesitated for a moment. Her skin was so perfect—so smooth, so flawless. He would much rather be taking the dress off her and kissing every inch of her body. But his family was waiting for him and he wouldn't want to rush pleasing the goddess standing in front of him.

He committed the sight of her bare back to memory and reluctantly tugged at the zipper until it complied. Liz's suggestion ran through his mind. He had to tell Olivia what happened between him and Shaz, and he was quickly running out of time.

'Olivia,' he said, turning her to face him, allowing his hands to drape down her arms until he could interlock his fingers with hers. 'About yesterday—'

He was cut off by the press of her luscious lips against his. She tasted minty, sweet, addictive. He wanted more. He tightened his grip on her hands in an effort to restrain himself. God, if that zipper wasn't done up, he would have had the dress off her by now. She broke away from the kiss, slowly, and tore a hand away from his to cup his cheek, daring him to look into her eyes.

'We will talk about it,' she whispered, searching his eyes. 'Later. But for now, we need to help with the party.'

She didn't wait for a reply before she tore away from him and left the room. His head wasn't the only part of him throbbing.

***

Olivia leaned against the closed door, taking a few deep breaths to compose herself. She knew that Scott hadn't even made it into their room last night. She woke up during the night and went to the bathroom, wondering where he was or if he'd made it home. He had. She found him asleep on the couch, fully clothed, reeking of alcohol. She didn't get much sleep after that.

Of course, she'd spent most of the night wondering how she should confront him. And she would have liked to have it over with sooner rather than later. But the party would be soon, and she'd promised Suzie to help as much as she could. She was furious that he left and didn't come home until late. And she was concerned about why bumping into Shaz had that effect on him. And she wanted answers.

So, why the hell did she kiss him?

Because of that damned look he had. She could see the apology in his eyes, the resolve to open up to her. She felt the tenderness of his touch and could feel his breath against her bare skin, his hesitation to pull the zipper up. It weakened her. And she got scared. Scared that he would tell her something she didn't want to hear. Scared that the truth about what happened between him and Shaz would be worse than her frustrated mind had concocted. Scared that she wouldn't be able to fake it at the party if it was.

So, she kissed him and told him that they could talk about it later—after the party when no one would know or see them together. She just had to make it through the party.

***

'This is Olivia—Scott's special lady. Isn't it wonderful?'

Olivia flashed her best smile to the older women as Suzie introduced her to yet another group of people she had never met or heard of before. She didn't want to hint that it may not be as wonderful as Suzie made it out to be. Between helping with the party and being dragged around for introductions exactly the same as this one, she hadn't even been able to speak to Scott since their first guests started arriving. Which may or may not have been a good thing.

She still didn't want to talk about yesterday until after the party, but it was hard to avoid it. It was as though they couldn't talk about anything not related to the party until the issue had been addressed. And she hated it. She could see him—see his smile—and loved that, no matter what he was doing, he was always looking at her whenever she spared a glance in his direction.

She wondered if he knew that his mother was introducing her to all of their family friends as his special lady. Or that she would have to come up with answers to all the tricky questions that they would ask. She felt like more of a specimen being shown off than just being introduced so that people would know who she was. She spared another glance towards Scott. He was watching her, though he seemed to be caught in a conversation himself.

She shouldn't expect that he would be able to move through the party with her, doing the introductions himself. After all, he knew everyone at the party and hadn't been home for a while. It was only natural that everyone would want to talk to him.

'Oh, she's gorgeous. Look at that hair! You can see why our Scott likes her,' one of the three ladies said to the others.

'Maybe a bit on the skinny side,' the plumper lady said, jabbing a finger at Olivia's waist. 'But she'll fill out when the babies come.'

'They mustn't be too far away. How old are you, honey?' The third one took her turn.

Olivia raised an eyebrow at the three ladies, trying to be as polite as possible. 'Umm, twenty-seven,' she said, trying again to catch eye contact with Scott in hopes he might save her.

'Twenty-seven?' the third lady said. 'I'd already had four kids by the time I was your age.'

'Two sets of twins don't count as four pregnancies,' the first lady said.

'So?' the third lady added her opinion. 'They were all in school by the time I was twenty-seven.'

'Well, they all start later nowadays,' the plumper lady said before turning to Olivia. 'So, where is it?'

All three of the ladies went silent, staring at Olivia in anticipation. She was starting to feel a bit intimidated and unsure of what to say. 'Excuse me?'

'The ring, honey! Show us the ring!' the plumper lady said, starting to look a bit red in the face.

'Oh,' Olivia said, blushing. 'There is none.'

'He proposed without a ring?' the first lady asked, each of their eyes widening.

'We're not engaged,' Olivia explained. 'You must have us confused with someone else.'

'No, we don't,' the third lady replied. 'We didn't think that Scott would have brought you home if you weren't committed to each other. Bringing a pretty lady home just to show off. Who's to say you won't run off like that other one?'

Olivia's mouth gaped open before she quickly closed it again. That other one? Were they talking about Shaz? She would be lying if she said that she wasn't offended at the lady's comment. As if right on cue, Liz came over and tugged on Olivia's arm.

'Sorry to steal her away from you, ladies,' Liz said with all her charm. 'But I really need Olivia's help with something.'

Liz guided Olivia away from the ladies. Olivia could have hugged her for saving her. 'Thank you so much, Liz. You're a lifesaver,' she said. 'What do you need help with?'

'Oh, I don't,' Liz replied. 'You just looked like you needed saving. They're horrible ladies. Always making you feel like you're not good enough.'

Olivia smiled at Liz, wondering what conversations she had endured with the ladies. She thought she saw Liz's cheeks redden slightly before she shook it off and turned back to Olivia.

'You should go find Scott,' Liz said. 'They won't bother you if you're with him.'

It sounded like a good enough plan to Olivia, so she set out to find him. She caught his eye from the other side of the yard. He was talking to a man who looked about Rob's age and even looked uncannily like Rob. Scott waved at Olivia, so she started heading towards him, only being interrupted by another lady grabbing onto her arm.

'Olivia! I was hoping I would see you.'

Olivia turned to the woman, feeling her skin

prickle when she saw Shaz standing in front of her. Her short brown hair was framing her face and her smile looked too put on. Olivia could feel annoyance building inside her chest. Of course it would be Shaz coming between her and Scott again. And after all her efforts of avoiding her throughout the party, she was so focussed on getting away from the ladies and getting to Scott that she hadn't realised that she would be walking right past her.

'Isn't it awkward not knowing anyone at a party?' Shaz laughed.

'You don't know anyone here?' Olivia asked.

'Oh, I do,' Shaz replied, shrugging. 'But under much different circumstances. I don't think they're jumping over the moon to see me here.'

'I don't understand,' Olivia said. 'Are you friends with Scott?'

'I wouldn't say we're friends, exactly. He didn't tell you?' Shaz asked, her eyes flashing a look of triumph. 'We dated for a few years but, when it started to get serious, he freaked out.'

Olivia felt a pang in her chest. So, they *had* been together. And it wasn't just a fling—it had been serious. But how serious was it? Why had Scott been avoiding the topic instead of telling her what happened?

'What happened?' Olivia managed out, unsure if she wanted to know the answer.

Shaz shrugged. 'He just disappeared one day and wasn't the same when he got back. He was gone for months and didn't bother to call or anything. All he said when he came back was that he was moving to Paris.'

'Where did he go for so long?' Olivia asked, hoping that it wouldn't be a habit of Scott's.

'Turns out he went to Leeds. God knows what for,' Shaz said, her voice drenched in sarcasm. 'But I'm glad he's found someone to settle down with. Have you set a date yet?'

'What?'

'For the wedding?'

Why was everyone asking her that? Olivia shook her head. 'We're not engaged,' she explained.

'Oh,' Shaz said, raising an eyebrow. 'Maybe he hasn't gotten over his commitment issues, after all.'

***

Scott ended his conversation with his uncle once he saw Olivia beelining towards him. As much as he enjoyed catching up with everyone, he felt bored with the conversations, wishing that he could introduce Olivia to everyone himself. He'd seen his mother leading Olivia through the crowds and was glad that Liz retrieved her from the three ladies—the gossips of their suburb. He wondered what crazy assumptions they managed to come up with.

He started heading towards the middle of the yard where he hoped to meet Olivia halfway, slowing down to scan the crowd for her. Where was she? He had only just seen her heading towards him and she looked like she was on a mission to reach him. He

stopped dead when he finally laid his eyes on her—
and who she was talking to. He felt his nerves rattling
his body, desperately hoping that Shaz wouldn't be
telling her about what happened between them.
Judging by the triumphant look on Shaz's face and
Olivia looking like she'd just been stabbed in the
chest, he had a pretty good idea.

Damn it.

He rushed over to them, determined to pull Olivia
away from whatever their conversation was and
assess how much damage had been done. When he
reached them, he put his arm around Olivia and
planted a kiss on her cheek, refusing to acknowledge
Shaz.

'There you are, love. I've been looking
everywhere for you,' he said, only turning to
acknowledge Shaz when she coughed. 'Oh, sorry to
interrupt.' He was not sorry at all. 'But I need to steal
Olivia for a while.'

Not waiting for a reply from either of them, he
grabbed Olivia by the hand and led her to the edge of
the crowd. He could feel that her body was tense.
Whatever it was that Shaz said, he had to fix it. He
had to tell her the truth—and it couldn't wait until
after the party. He led her to the street, out of sight
of anyone from the party, and felt Olivia tug her
hand free of his. He turned to face her. She had
come to a halt and her arms were crossed over her
stomach.

'Is it true?' she asked. 'Did you and Shaz date?'

He felt anger at Shaz boiling at his surface for

making his fears a reality. He swallowed, nodding slowly.

'How serious?' she continued, her voice barely above a whisper.

He hated that Liz was right. He should have told her straight after bumping into Shaz. He probably should have told her before they bumped into Shaz. Damn her for being right.

'We were engaged,' he said, bracing himself for a storm.

But it didn't come. He could see her eyes glistening with unshed tears and saw her swallow a few times, not saying a word. She looked like she was more than uncomfortable with the news. He took a step towards her, stopping when she returned his advance with a step backwards.

'Olivia,' he started, his body aching to take her in his arms.

'But?' she urged, shaking her head.

'But it wasn't right,' he said, rushing towards her, and holding her shoulders. He felt her body tense beneath his hands. 'Believe me, Olivia. There was so much pressure to take the next step. From her. From everyone. But I wasn't ready. Not with her.' He traced her arms with his fingers and held her hands. 'It wasn't right.'

'So you ran,' she whispered, her hands limp against his.

'I took time.'

'You didn't tell her.'

'I couldn't,' he replied, knowing that it wasn't a

good enough excuse.

'Why did you go to Leeds?' Olivia asked, looking up at him, her eyes demanding an answer.

He felt his body flushing with heat. 'She had no right to tell you that,' he said through his teeth.

'Answer me, Scott,' Olivia said, pulling her hands out of his tightening grip.

'I can't.'

'Why not?'

'It had nothing to do with her, Olivia,' he said, running his fingers through his hair. 'And nothing happened.'

'But you were gone for months,' she said. 'Surely *something* happened.'

'Nothing that matters.'

'Then why won't you tell me?' she pleaded, her eyes glistening again.

He lifted a hand to cup her cheek. He wanted to tell her. He wanted to tell her everything. But now sure as hell wasn't the right time and place.

'I don't want it to come between us,' he said.

He felt her cheek tighten and saw her tears threatening to spill.

'It's too late for that,' she said, her voice shaky.

'Olivia—'

She shook her head, taking a few steps back before turning to walk away from him. She didn't go back to the party. She kept walking down the street. And as much as he wanted to follow after her, he couldn't urge his feet to move. He was more focussed on something else.

He could feel his anger and frustration racing to the surface of his skin. Shaz had no right to tell Olivia anything. He waited until Olivia was out of sight before marching back towards the party, his fists clenched. He scanned the crowd for the short-haired brunette that caused all the trouble in the first place, finding her without too much effort. He stormed up to her and stood in front of her.

'Oh, hi Scott,' Shaz said.

'You need to leave,' he said, his jaw tense.

'Excuse me?'

'You've already caused more trouble than you're worth.'

His cousin, Ted, came over, putting an arm around Shaz. 'Is there a problem, Scott?' he said.

'Just your girlfriend putting her mouth where it doesn't belong,' he said, exchanging his glare from Shaz to Ted. 'And what the hell made you think that it would be all right to bring her?'

He felt a tug on his arm as Liz stepped in front of him. 'Scott,' she said, her voice steady. 'You're making a scene.'

He glanced around them, realizing that Liz was right. He hadn't noticed until now that he had been yelling. Sure enough, they had become the spectacle of the party. Exactly what he hadn't wanted to be. He felt Liz tugging on his arm again, trying to lead him away from the crowd. He obliged, but not without finishing what he started. He leaned close to Shaz and made sure that his voice was only a little above a whisper.

'Stay the hell away from us.'

***

'What was that?' Liz yelled, closing the door behind them.

'I don't want to talk about it,' Scott said, leaning against the back of the couch. He had too much he had to work out, like how to fix things with Olivia.

'Well, I don't care.' Liz crossed her arms. 'I told you that you should have told her what happened before someone else did.'

'And where were you? You said that you would help make sure she didn't get cornered by Shaz.'

'I already rescued her from the three stooges,' Liz said defensively. 'But that doesn't excuse you almost starting a fight in the middle of a party.'

'You wouldn't understand,' he said, staring at the whites of his knuckles against the back of the couch.

'Then explain it to me!'

'I love her, Liz,' he retorted, spinning around to face his sister. 'And I watched her walk away from me, pissed, because of Shaz's big mouth. I tried to tell her this morning, damn it. And we agreed to talk after the party. And now—'

He paused, studying Liz's expression. She had her arms crossed, though she looked more relaxed. Her eyebrow was raised, and her lips were turned to a smirk.

'What?' he asked.

She raised her other eyebrow, still quiet. He

furrowed his brow, trying to recall what he said to make Liz's demeanour change so quickly. Then it hit him.

   I love her.

Chapter 27

Olivia tramped through the rain. It had long since gotten dark. In fact, it grew dark shortly after she left the party. She walked for a while—though not too far so she wouldn't get lost again—stopping in the park up the road where she could still see all the cars parked in front of Rob and Suzie's place. When she finally managed to cool down, she waited until the party was over so that she wouldn't have to answer as many questions. But when she saw that last car drive away, she found herself not quite ready to go back.

She still felt the frustration boiling underneath her skin. She was angry that she had to learn what happened between Scott and Shaz from the lady herself. She was frustrated that she never even considered that Scott may have been in a serious relationship before they met. She was confused as to why everyone thought that they were engaged just because she came to Australia with him. She was hurt that he didn't open up about his trip to Leeds and said that it didn't matter. It was obviously bad enough to come between him and Shaz, so why wouldn't he tell her now? And she was annoyed that she would have to put on a brave face to go inside the house and would probably have to talk to all of his family before she got a chance to clear the air with him.

Did she make a mistake when she agreed to come to Australia? Was it foolish of her to do such an outrageous thing so soon? She had been so sure. Her thoughts flashed back to their second meeting when he found her alone in the park and how they got caught in the rain. She remembered thinking that he meant that she shouldn't be alone in a park because she's a girl.

I was going to say that it's because you're so damn beautiful.

She still remembered it so clearly and it still brought a smile to her face.

I would respect your wishes.

She remembered wishing that this handsome stranger would kiss her then. But with or without a kiss to remember him by, he had implanted himself in her mind for every day to follow. He had, somehow, managed to break down her guard and gave her someone else to care about—someone to care about her. She half-expected that he would have found her again in this park but, when she checked, he wasn't following her. She suspected that he wouldn't just be able to leave the party like she did. But it didn't stop her from having a little hope that he might.

Maybe she cared about him more than he cared about her. The rain poured a bit harder as she neared the house, shivering from the cold and the wet and regretting having left without getting a jacket. But then, she wasn't exactly thinking clearly. Or thinking at all. Wasn't she supposed to fight for someone she loves instead of running away?

Love. Now that's a strong word. But she shouldn't be feeling it, right? She always thought that you grew to love someone—that it takes time. The thought of falling for someone so quickly never seemed to her as a rational or sane thing to do. But then, Scott had made her feel something she'd never felt before. He made her feel safe with every touch. He made her feel beautiful just by the way he looked at her. And he never gave up on her—never gave up on a chance to be closer to her. He had already challenged everything she'd grown to expect in a man, showing her that nice, caring guys do exist. It didn't surprise her that she fell for him.

She hesitated at the door, listening to hear any movement, and opened it slowly. All of the lights except for the lamp in the lounge room were off. How long had it been since the party finished? Suzie rose from the couch and met her at the door, handing her a towel to dry herself off. She hadn't realised how completely drenched she was until now.

'You and Scott need to not make a habit of being gone for so long,' she said, leading her to the kitchen.

'I'm sorry, Suzie,' Olivia said, truly meaning it. She didn't want to be in her bad books. 'I needed to clear my head. I didn't realise that it was so late.'

Suzie filled a mug with heated milk and chocolate powder and placed it on the table for Olivia, taking a seat opposite her. 'You've been crying,' she said.

Had she? Olivia lifted her hand to her eyes—they were puffy, and her cheeks burned with heat. 'I was frustrated,' she explained, still wondering when she had been crying.

Suzie reached a hand across the table and placed it over Olivia's. 'Don't give up on him, honey,' she started. 'My Scott takes a while to open up to people, but he will. Just give him some time.'

'I just don't understand why he didn't tell me about Shaz,' Olivia said, feeling unshed tears catching in her throat.

'Have you told him about your ex-boyfriends?'

Olivia blinked. He knew about Antoine, but that was probably because he was around when that all happened. Would she have told him about Antoine if it was over before they met? She definitely hadn't told him about all the other jerks she'd been with. Suzie's face was mellow, caring, concerned. Everything a mother would be. She stared into her hot chocolate and shook her head slightly.

'I know that he cares about you, honey.' Suzie's voice was soothing. 'He wouldn't have brought you home if he didn't. And besides, I've seen how he looks at you. A mother knows when she's no longer the most important woman in her son's life.'

Olivia wondered how that would feel. Would she ever have a son to experience that feeling? She wondered if he would look like Scott. She looked up at Suzie, studying her face. This woman could see right through her and she knew it.

'Shaz wasn't right for him,' Suzie said, lending her a sweet smile. 'But I can see that he has hopes that you are. I would agree if he asked me. Don't let things from the past come between you.'

Suzie left Olivia at the table to finish her drink. She could feel the drink warming her from the inside out and felt much more settled by the time she was headed back to their room. She wondered if she was right for him—if he was right for her. But she knew that she had hopes too. She snuck through the bedroom door as quietly as she could. Scott had left the bedside lamp dimmed for her. He was asleep on the floor, curled under the blanket, his expression peaceful. She wondered if it took him long to fall asleep.

She tiptoed to the side of the bed, allowing the towel to fall to the ground. She could feel the cool of her drenched clothes clinging to her body as she reached her arm behind her. She looked forward to curling under the blankets and warming up. She just had to get past this damn zipper.

***

Scott watched as the towel fell from Olivia's shoulders onto the ground. Her curls hung in loose, wet clumps that made him want to run his fingers through them. She delicately balanced on one foot to remove one high heel, then switched to remove the other, returning her arm to behind her back to reach for the zipper—just out of reach. He didn't know that he'd made the conscious decision to help her, but before he knew it, he was on his feet and standing behind her.

He lifted his hand and guided hers away from the zipper. She jolted as though she'd been shocked, turning quickly to face him, her body inches from his.

'I thought you were asleep,' she said, her face softening to find that it was him.

He stroked a wet curl away from her eye, tracing the red tinge in her cheek with his thumb. 'I couldn't,' he said, his voice low. 'Not without you here.'

Her eyes were large, round, a deeper blue than usual, her lips relaxed in a way that made him want to kiss them. He turned her gently so that her back was towards him and brushed her hair to the side. He tugged at the zipper, nudging it undone. The rain had definitely made it harder to undo than it was to do up. He grinned as the zipper ended at the small of her back.

Instead of stepping aside to let her change, he

ran his hands up her back, moving his thumbs in a slow, massaging motion up to the base of her neck. He could feel her body relaxing beneath his hands. Her skin was cool from the wet clothes. He wanted to warm her. He slid his hands onto her shoulders and down her arms, guiding the dress off her body. He wondered if it would have fallen off with ease if it hadn't been wet. But for now, it clung to her soft hips, only extending his enjoyment of taking her clothes off.

He moved his hands back up her arms, across her shoulders and down her back, massaging as he went, until he got to her hips. He pushed the dress over her hips, feeling a rumble at the base of his throat to see her matching lace underwear clinging to her bottom, and watched as it joined the towel on the ground. She stepped out of the dress and he nudged it to the side with his foot, his hands on her hips stopping her from turning around.

He wanted her. He needed her. He wanted to lay her on the bed and have his way with her, rough, fast. But she deserved better than that. She deserved passion, love, pleasure. And those can't be rushed. Even if she was impossible to resist. He tugged her a little closer to him, feeling the cool of her skin against his bare chest, and started to kiss the side of her neck.

***

Slow, gentle, deliberate kisses. Each one in a slightly

different spot. She could feel the warmth of his bare chest—a tactical move to not wear a shirt to bed—penetrating through the cold coating the rain left on her damp skin and mingling with the warmth that she felt in her own body. She could feel the firmness in his grip on her hips, his thumbs still moving over the small of her back.

His kisses began just below her right ear, forming a trail of warmth and heat down her neck and across her shoulder. He nudged the strap of her bra further off her shoulder with each tender kiss. He lifted his lips just off her body and followed the trail back up to her ear. She was sure he didn't let them touch her, but she could feel the warmth of his breath following the trail of kisses that he left. He started again just below her left ear, mirroring the same thing he did on the other side. She could feel a tremble through her legs and felt him move only slightly backwards, beginning a new trail of kisses down her spine and sliding his hands up until they met with his lips at the join of her bra.

He traced the clip with his fingertips before flicking it undone, returning his hands to her hips and continuing to kiss down her spine. Her bra fell to the ground, but she didn't feel embarrassed. She felt free. Ready. Her breasts peaked from the attention he was giving her body. She craved him. She wanted him more than she wanted anything in her life.

His kisses stopped at the small of her back where his thumbs lingered. He slid his thumbs slowly beneath the top of her underwear, pushing them down a couple of inches, before returning his thumbs to over her underwear. He ran his hands over her bottom, squeezing a little, and down the length of her legs—down the outside, up the inside. She felt another tremble when his hands reached the inside of her thighs. How long would she be able to keep standing? His hands left her body mid-thigh, returning to the small of her back and massaging up her spine again.

God, his touch.

He turned her slowly to face him, taking in her bareness. He traced her clavicle with his fingers and moved his warm, strong hands down to cup her breasts, teasing her peaks with his thumbs. He would be the end of her, she knew it. She placed her hands on his forearms, running them up his arms, squeezing his biceps as she felt him flex. She linked her hands behind his neck, seeking his darkened, desire-filled eyes. She could see his pulse pounding in the side of his neck and moved to kiss it. She felt him groan while she gave his neck the same attention he gave hers. He moved his hands back down to her hips to pull her harder against him and sought her lips with his.

He tasted sweet, addictive. She wanted more. She tightened her arms around him, standing on the tips of her toes to savour his taste. He parted her lips with his tongue, searching every part of her mouth. She was more than willing to comply. He moved his hands from her hips to her thighs, lifting her until she could wrap them around his waist and pressed her against the wall, still kissing her deeply, thoroughly. He broke the kiss only to leave another trail down the front of her neck.

She leaned her head against the wall, arching herself to give him the freedom to move. His lips kissed down to the notch where her clavicles joined and traced the mound of her breast until he found the peak with his mouth. She felt every muscle in her body shuddering from the ecstasy he made her feel. She couldn't hold herself much longer. He moved his sucking across to the other side. She bit her lip, tasting blood. He released her from the torture, returning to devour her mouth with his.

She could feel every muscle in his body tense as he kissed her more passionately, quicker. Desperate. He broke the kiss, his lips only just out of reach, his breath mingling with hers, his eyes seeking an answer.

'Olivia,' he moaned.

She took in the way he said her name, the way he made her feel full with just the way he touched her, spoke to her, looked at her. She smiled, nodding.

'Yes,' she whispered, knowing what he was asking.

She felt a rumble at the base of his neck as he took her lips with his again, pulling her from the wall and carrying her to the bed. He laid her gently on the side of the bed, refusing to move his lips from hers. She felt for his waist, finding the top of his pants and pushing them down to join her clothes on the floor. He started kissing down her neck, following her cleavage down to her belly button, pushing her underwear down with his thumbs and running his hands back up her thighs. This time, one hand going further than it had before.

He kept kissing her stomach, glancing up towards her. *God, his eyes.* She saw a smile curling on his lips as he moved his fingers rhythmically. He was torturing her. She wanted him. She needed him. She wrapped her legs around him, pulling him back up to kiss him and felt his fingers replaced with something larger, firmer. There was no resistance. She took him fully, tracing the strong, pulsing muscles in his back with her fingers, his name a whisper on her lips.

'Scott.'

I love you.

***

'You really told her to leave?'

Scott stared into the gorgeous blue eyes looking up at him. His body still throbbing from their passion. He had his arm around Olivia's naked body, drawing patterns on her back with his fingers, while she lay against his chest, her fingertips tracing his muscles.

'She didn't have a right to say anything,' he said. 'She shouldn't have even been at the party.'

Olivia hesitated for a moment, moving to rest her chin on his chest to look at him. 'Will you tell me what happened?'

He kissed her forehead, conscious of her foot sliding up and down his leg. 'It started as a bit of fun,' he began. 'Just going on a few dates, enjoying each other's company. I guess it filled a void for both of us. There was so much pressure to propose to her, so I did. But there was something missing.'

'What was missing?' Olivia asked, hanging onto every word he said.

'Love,' he said, stroking her golden hair. 'We were never in love, and it made me question the whole marriage thing with her. So, I took some time and went to Leeds, my hometown, for a few months to gather my thoughts and when I came back, she didn't believe me that nothing happened, so I ended it. Turns out that she'd been cheating on me for months anyway. But it didn't matter, because I'd already decided that it wasn't right with her and planned to go to Paris.'

'What did you do in Leeds, Scott?' she asked, tentatively.

He brushed his fingers across her soft cheeks, knowing that he had to tell her. And would it really hurt? It's not like what he planned had turned to fruition. 'I remembered a promise I made to a friend when I was a kid,' he began. 'A promise I wouldn't have been able to keep if I was with Shaz. So, I went back to Leeds to see if she was still there.'

'And she wasn't?'

Scott shook his head. It seemed she was more willing to listen after their love-making than she had been earlier.

'Just as well,' Olivia continued, resting her head back against his shoulder to continue studying his chest. 'If she was, maybe you wouldn't have come to Paris and we wouldn't be together now.'

Scott knew she was right. If his childhood friend had been in Leeds, he definitely wouldn't have gone to Paris when he did. He wouldn't have had a reason to. But he was sure as hell glad that he did.

'Scott?' Olivia asked, propping her chin on his chest again.

'Mmm?'

'How did you end up in foster care?'

He looked into her eyes, so sincere, caring. How had he ever been able to keep anything from her?

'My father was abusive,' he began, his fingertips continuing to draw on her back. 'And when my mum finally built up the courage to leave him, we did. We lived with my uncle in London for almost a year, but she took it all pretty badly. She overdosed, and I found her when I got back from school. She was already cold.' He wiped a tear from Olivia's eyes.

'I'm sorry, Scott,' she whispered.

'Me too,' he said. 'I stayed with my uncle for a few months after that, but then he said that he and his wife couldn't look after me. So, he put me in foster care where I hopped between houses until Rob and Suzie took me in. After they adopted me, we moved here.'

'And the rest is history?' she said, smiling.

'The rest is history.' He nodded gently. He could feel her body relaxing against his.

'You know,' she continued. 'I grew up in Leeds.'

He leaned in and kissed her tenderly, sweetly.

Not as deep and desperate as they had before, but he could still feel the spark.

'Well, I'm surprised we never met,' he said, breaking the kiss. 'I wouldn't forget you if we did.'

Chapter 28

It was lunch time by the time they emerged from their room, Olivia having a shower and Scott searching for something to eat. She guessed that a night of love-making and then again in the morning would do that to you. Her body felt exhausted but fulfilled at the same time. And she felt closer to Scott than she ever imagined she could feel with anyone.

At first, she was worried his family would be suspicious of them sleeping in so late, but Scott assured her that no one was home. He said that they were regular churchgoers and had never missed a Sunday at church for as long as he could remember. So, she let herself indulge in all that was Scott.

She smiled as she stepped out of the shower and wrapped the towel around her, glancing at herself in the mirror. Was it possible that everywhere on her body that he touched had a glow? Maybe she was on a high from the incredible night she spent with Scott. Or maybe she was delusional. But she felt freaking awesome.

Shaz wasn't a threat anymore and her questions were answered—well, most of them anyway. She'd managed to come up with one more while she was in the shower. Maybe she was overthinking it, but there was something about his Leeds story that just didn't seem to add up. It seemed almost too coincidental. It made her suspicious.

She pulled her jeans and a shirt on and went out to the kitchen, determined to ask him for more details and hoping that he would still be open about it to her like he was last night. She needed him to be open with her all the time, not just in those moments after sex. Especially since she'd fallen for him—and fallen hard.

***

Scott slid the fried eggs onto the two plates in front of him and garnished the plate with a sprig of parsley. He wasn't the best cook, but he was determined to make Olivia the best bacon-and-eggs breakfast she'd ever had in his life. He knew it would be the best he's ever had. After all, he will be eating it with the most beautiful woman he'd ever laid eyes on. The same woman he'd spent the night making love to—the morning session was just an added bonus—and the same woman that he'd fallen in love with. There were a lot of unknowns in his life at the moment, but he had never been so sure of anything as he was over this.

He was head over heels in love with Olivia Harley. And it would kill him if she didn't feel the same way about him.

His heart flipped at the smile she gave him as she sat down at the table. He kissed her tenderly as he placed her meal in front of her, then sat down opposite her with his meal. She giggled when she looked at the plate to see two googly egg-eyes, a bacon mouth and a parsley nose.

'A smiley face? Really?' she said through her giggles.

'It's happy to see you,' he said, shrugging, trying to tame his own smile. 'Besides, I can't have you eating sad eggs. That's just rude.'

'*Touché*,' she said, stabbing her fork into the yellow of one of the eggs and watching the yolk ooze onto the plate.

'Oh, now, that's just cruel,' Scott said, provoking another laugh from the goddess opposite him.

Yes, he could get used to having her with him, hearing her laugh and feeling the warmth that it spread through his body. And the way she just devoured that piece of bacon—he'd be lucky to get through breakfast without taking her back to his bed.

'Can I ask you something?'

'Anything,' he replied, fighting the urge to lean over the table and kiss away that spot of egg yolk on the corner of her mouth.

'It's about Leeds,' she said, licking the egg yolk away. 'Who was she?'

'Who?' he asked, snapping his focus from her lips. She would want an honest answer, and he'd have to focus to give it to her.

'The girl in Leeds,' she said. 'You never said who she was. Or what you went back to see her about.'

'Oh,' he said. *Really* focus. 'She was just a childhood friend—' *who held my heart until now.* 'I missed her after I moved away—' *pined for her.* 'I even wrote lots of letters to her and later found out that they were never sent—' *just as well.* 'Before I left, I promised to take her somewhere—' *to Paris.* 'And I went back to do that, but she wasn't there. I knew things weren't right with Shaz and I needed a new beginning, so I moved to Paris—' *to find her.* 'Which turned out to be the best decision I ever made because I met you.' *Phew, that was close.*

She squinted at him and he hoped that she couldn't read between the lines. Then, she shook her head and laughed awkwardly. He felt his skin prick.

'I'm going to be honest with you,' she said, putting her fork down on the plate. 'I don't think she was just a childhood friend.'

He swallowed, putting his own fork down. How was he going to talk his way out of this one?

'See, I had a childhood friend once,' she continued. 'And I was sure that I was in love with him.' She put her hands in the air, palms facing him. 'I was twelve—a kid. So, of course I thought that.'

She picked up her fork again and took another bite of her breakfast.

Twelve.

'I thought I would never see him again when he moved away, but he promised that we would.'

'Where?' He didn't even register the word leaving his mouth.

'Paris,' she said, matter-of-factly.

Paris.

'Like a fool,' she continued. 'I waited for him, hoping that, just maybe he would return to Leeds and I would see him again. I—' she pointed to her chest, '—let myself believe that, even though I never heard from him since his parting words. And then, like an even bigger fool, I moved to Paris.'

No.

'And waited for him. But he never came.'

Was he sweating? How long had his breath been caught in his throat for?

'What was his name?'

'Why?' She looked shocked at his question, before her eyes glinted. 'You're not *threatened* by him, are you?'

'Olivia.'

She sighed. 'His name was Eddie Jameson.'

Surely not.

'You are joking, right?'

She frowned. 'I've never been more serious.'

It couldn't be—

'Livvy,' he said.

Her eyes softened. 'You know, the only person

other than him who has ever called me that is Emmy.'

It had to be.

'That was me.'

Her fork clattered to her plate as she stood abruptly, frowning. 'You're making fun of me.'

He was on his feet and standing in front of her, holding her arms before he knew what he was doing.

'I'm not,' he said. '*I* am Eddie Jameson.'

'But, your last name—'

'Rob and Suzie adopted me, remember?' he said.

'But, Scott—'

'Is my middle name.'

***

He was telling the truth. He had to be. Surely, he wasn't just making it up. He was from Leeds, so was she. His story added up. But it was too much for her mind to figure out. She hadn't meant it to come this far, she just knew there was more to the story than he was letting on. She hadn't meant to tell him about Eddie, but it had all been pouring out of her mouth before she could stop.

'No,' she heard herself say, shaking her arms free of his hold.

'What?' he said, reaching for her. She stepped back. 'Olivia, *you* are who I went to Leeds to find. I moved to Paris to find *you*.'

'You knew.'

He shook his head. 'No, I didn't.'

'*My* name has never changed.'

'It was *fifteen years* ago, Liv,' he said. 'I knew you as Livvy, not Olivia.'

'It didn't strike you as the same?'

'You've never realised that 'Harley' is a popular surname?'

Was she crying? She could feel her body shaking. Though, from what? She'd just realised that she found Eddie, her childhood friend, who she had been daydreaming about until the day she met Scott. She'd resigned to the fact that he was long gone and had found herself falling for Scott—the same person! And slept with him, nonetheless. And he didn't have even the slightest suspicion?

'Woah, did we just walk in on something?' Liz said.

They both looked towards Suzie, Rob and Liz standing in the doorway, looking almost as confused as she felt. She had to get out of there. She had to clear her head.

'Excuse me,' she muttered, sliding past the Henders family and through the front door.

'Liv, wait!'

She squeezed her eyes shut—why did hearing his voice hurt?—and closed the door behind her.

***

He watched the door close. What the hell was going on? They just discovered that they had been waiting for each other this whole time and she walks out? He tried to follow after her, but Rob held onto his arm.

'Scott, we need to talk,' Rob said.

'I can't,' he said, trying to shake off his vice-like grip. 'I have to go after her.'

'No,' Liz said. 'I will check on her. You'll probably just make it worse.'

He watched Liz go through the door after her and turned to Rob.

'Remember what I said about the boat?' Rob asked. Scott nodded. 'Well, what did you do to make it tip?'

'She's the one, Dad,' he said, running his hand through his hair in exasperation. 'She's the one I went to Leeds to look for.'

'Your childhood friend?' Suzie asked, tears welling in her eyes.

'Yes,' he said, turning his gaze to her. 'The one I've been in love with my entire life. The one I made the promise to. We just discovered that we were childhood friends and, now, I think she's second-guessing us.'

'Oh, honey,' Suzie said, the tears pouring.

'Take a seat, Scott,' Rob said, nudging him towards the dining table. 'She just needs time. Let Liz talk to her. She'll come around.'

'I hope so,' he said.

His body felt numb. She *had* to come around. He could feel his heart breaking more every second that she was gone.

***

'Olivia, wait!'

She slowed her pace for Liz to catch up, somewhat relieved that it wasn't Scott—Eddie. What would she call him now? Maybe Liz could help her make some sense out of it all.

'Olivia, what happened?' she asked, falling into step.

'He didn't tell you?'

Liz raised an eyebrow. 'It's not like he had time,' she said. 'He wanted me to come straight after you.'

Olivia stood up straighter. Didn't he realise that she just needed some time to figure the whole thing out? 'Well, he shouldn't have,' she found herself saying. 'I'm fine.'

Liz rolled her eyes. 'Okay, I lied,' she said. 'He didn't send me—I told him I would check on you.' She shrugged. 'It was either me or him and I figured you didn't look like you wanted to talk to him.'

Olivia looked at her, her frustration subsiding, and forced out a smile. Had she really been so much of an open book for Liz to know what she was thinking just by walking in on her discussion with Scott? She wondered if Liz had been in a similar situation—that would explain how she knows how she felt. But then, she couldn't really imagine that anyone else would have just slept with their childhood friend—and crush—without realising it.

They fell into step and started walking around the block together in silence. What had come over her back inside? Surely, she should be happy that Scott and Eddie were the same person, right? She'd waited so long and held up her hopes that Eddie would find her. She did her part, after all. She stayed in the two places that he would be able to find her.

Her mind flashed back to the conversation she had with her mother the day before she left for Australia. Her mother had known—she said that Eddie was *the boy in the picture*. She'd brushed it off, convinced that her mother was just confused. But she should have seen it before—they had had moments that made her think back on Eddie. The way that Scott said *It's Paris!* the night they had a hotdog together. He acted differently at the twins' party when she briefly mentioned a childhood friend. She was sure that there were more moments. She just had to connect the dots. So, why was it such a surprise now?

'It's fine if you don't want to talk about it,' Liz said. 'But maybe I can help clear up any concerns you have.'

They kept walking, Olivia debating *what* she should tell Liz, not *if*.

'Besides,' Liz continued. 'If you don't tell me, I'll just have to get it out of Scott later and *that* would be cutting into his time with you. Either way, I will find out what happened.'

'Isn't that a bit nosy?' Olivia said before she could stop herself.

'I'm a nosy person,' Liz said, shrugging. Olivia was glad that she didn't seem offended—she hadn't meant for it to sound how it did.

Olivia sighed. 'Have you ever fallen in love with someone, *then* discovered that he was your best friend when you were a child?'

'Can't say that I have,' Liz said. 'Wait, *that's* what this is about?'

Olivia nodded. Liz studied Olivia's face, then raised both of her eyebrows as her mouth dropped open.

'Oh, you're her, aren't you?'

Olivia furrowed her brow. Did Liz know?

'You're from Leeds, right?' Olivia nodded. 'So, you're the girl he went back to find. I can't believe I didn't recognise you from the picture.'

Wait, what?

'You know that he went back to Leeds to find me?' Olivia asked. 'And what picture?'

Liz smiled. '*I* was the one who encouraged him to go back to Leeds. I never liked Shaz, so I guess I was clutching straws,' she said, shrugging. 'He had this picture of him and a blonde-haired girl named Livvy that he carried with him everywhere when he came to live with us. He always said that he would find her one day.' Her shoulders dropped as she smiled at Olivia. 'I can't believe that the girl in the picture is *you*! You know, he probably still has that picture— you should ask him about it.'

'So, it shouldn't be awkward between me and him, then?'

'Why should it?' Liz said, shrugging with a side-grin. 'You're obviously meant to be together. That's fate if ever I saw it. Or God bringing the two of you together—whichever your beliefs are.'

She couldn't deny that it was fate. But she was also convinced that there had to be another hand at work to bring them together. After all, would she have still fallen for Scott if she had known that he was Eddie this whole time? Or would she have only been fixated on the boy he used to be instead of the incredible man that he had become?

Liz was right. Why should it be awkward between them? They were always meant to be. But there was one more thing she had to know.

'So, do I call him Eddie now?'

Liz laughed. 'Honey, he hasn't been called Eddie since my parents adopted him. He chose to be called Scott then and, I'd say, he would still rather Scott.'

***

'Hey, asshole!' Liz yelled, walking through the front door. 'Your girlfriend is waiting for you outside.'

Scott jumped to his feet and raced to the door. He let Liz's insult glide over. He'd get her for it later, when he thanked her for helping him. But, right now, Olivia was his priority. He pushed through the door and saw Olivia leaning against the big tree in the yard—the same one he remembered climbing and daydreaming about her as a kid. God, she was a vision. He walked towards her.

'Hey, handsome,' she said, smiling.

He felt a wave of relief wash over him. She obviously wasn't mad at him still, that was a start. He took her in his arms and pressed his mouth to hers. For a moment, time stood still. He would hold onto her and never let her go. Watching her walk out that door, wondering if what they had just started was already over, it broke his heart. For the first time since his mother died, he felt truly helpless. But now, this kiss was pulling all the pieces of his heart back together. Reluctantly, he broke the kiss and brought his hands up to cup her face between them, stroking her cheeks with his thumbs, and stared into her eyes.

Something had changed in them. He could see that she was ready. That whatever the hell Liz talked to her about had helped. She was his.

'Liv,' he said, his heart flipping when she fluttered her eyes down then back up towards him. 'Watching you walk out that door—'

'Scott,' she whispered.

'I thought you were leaving—'

'I'm sorry.'

'I didn't think you wouldn't be as happy as I am that we found each other,' he continued.

'I am.'

'I have worked too damn hard to find you and to be with you, Liv,' he said. 'I'm never letting you go.'

'I don't want you to,' she said, reaching her hand up to touch his cheek. 'Scott, I love you. I always have.'

He swallowed. Was his body threatening to cry? Surely not. He hadn't cried since he watched Livvy disappear in the distance as his mother drove them to his uncle's. Even when his mother died, he didn't cry—he only felt numb and confused.

'I love you, too, Olivia Harley,' he said, pulling her into another time-stopping kiss.

She was the one to break the kiss this time, leaning back to study his face. If it were up to him, he would never stop kissing her. He kept his arms around her.

'Can I ask you something?'

He smiled, nodding. She could ask him whatever her heart desired and he would tell her anything. He would give her the world if he could.

'Liz said something about a picture you had when you came to live with them.'

His smile grew wider. He knew what she was asking, it was another promise that he'd made her. He fished his wallet out of his pocket and pulled the worn picture out of it, handing it to her, watching as her eyes started to water.

'You kept it,' she said, her voice catching.

'I promised I would,' he said, wrapping his arms around her again. 'I've carried it with me everywhere. Do you still have yours?'

She nodded. 'It's in my purse.'

He nudged her chin up with his hand and kissed her tenderly again. He could never lose her. And he knew that, one day soon, he would make her his bride.

The Irish Maiden

Turn over for a sneak peek at
the next in the series by

R.J. Groves

Prologue

'So, there really is only one thing left to say,' Alex said, concluding his best-man speech. He looked towards Scott and Olivia. 'Scott, farewell buddy. It was nice knowing you.' He paused, the crowd erupting in laughter, before leaning back towards the microphone. 'But seriously, I wish you all the best in your new life with your beautiful bride.' He held up his glass. 'To the bride and groom!'

Everyone chorused his toast as he moved towards the bar, the DJ calling up the bride and groom for their first dance. He ordered a shot of whiskey, neat, and felt his pocket for the papers he'd been carrying around. He may be at his best friend's wedding and may have just given the best and funniest best-man speech that anyone here would have ever heard in their lives, but partying was far from what he really wanted to do. Especially with Betty, his recent ex, sitting on the opposite side of the room with the guy she left him for.

The bartender placed the whiskey in front of him and he downed it in one go, pulling a face at the burn it left as it travelled down his throat. He knew there was a reason he never drank whiskey.

'That was some speech.'

And then, there was Liz. He ordered another and turned to face Elizabeth Henders—Scott's sister and the girl he secretly dated for a few months before moving to Paris. She was as beautiful as ever. And completely off limits since, when he tried to come clean about their relationship, Scott said that he would kill him if he ever got involved with his sister. It was just as well, anyway. Liz deserved way better than him.

'Hello, Liz,' he said. 'It's been a while.'

'It didn't have to be.'

'You know why I couldn't call, Liz.'

Because he would have changed his mind.

She nodded. It had been a mutual decision. Scott and his parents had been like family to Alex. He couldn't lose his best friend and certainly couldn't allow himself to come between Liz and Scott. It was for the best. And he was sure that he took it harder than she did.

'Are you ready to join the bride and groom on the dancefloor?' she asked, her tone light.

He smiled at her, picking up the refilled glass of

whiskey. 'I think the real question is: are you?'

The grin he'd grown familiar with over the years crossed her face and he knew that they could go back to the friendship they'd once had, after all. Her eyes dropped to the glass he held. 'I thought you don't drink whiskey,' she said.

'I don't,' he replied, downing the amber liquid again.

She laughed as he took her hand and led her to the dancefloor. They fell into step, dancing around Scott and Olivia, Chad and Vanessa doing the same. As they turned, he caught a glimpse of Betty kissing her date. He swallowed the lump in his throat and tore his gaze away from them. What he'd had with Liz was fun, and Betty may have been a rebound at first, but what he'd had with her was special. And she threw it away for another man.

'Is that her?' Liz asked, trying to see what he was looking at.

He looked at her questioningly. 'How do you—'

'Oliva told me,' she replied. 'She said that she wouldn't have invited her if she hadn't been doing the flowers. She wasn't supposed to bring a date, though. I'm sorry it didn't work out for you, Alex.'

The song changed and more people joined them on the dancefloor. He shook his head. 'It doesn't matter,' he said. 'I'll never have to see her again.'

She pulled back, searching his eyes. 'Why is that?'

'Because, this time tomorrow, I'll be standing in front of my new home in Ireland.'

She didn't seem to understand, so he led her off

the dancefloor, pulled out the papers from his pocket and showed them to her.

'Kinsale?' she said, her eyes scanning the papers.

'In good ol' County Cork,' he said, smiling. She laughed.

'County Cork?' she said. 'I can't imagine you living anywhere outside of a city.'

'Well, prepare to be amazed,' he said, feeling a temporary moment of relief at the light-heartedness in which they could joke.

'So, what does this all mean?' she asked, handing the papers back to him.

'It means that I'm the new owner of an inn, *The Irish Maiden*, courtesy of my deceased great uncle.'

'Your *great uncle*?'

He shrugged. 'He married my grandmother's sister. They never had children and I'm apparently the only relative he had that's still alive.'

'Does Scott know?'

He nodded. 'I told him and Olivia last night.'

'Well, Mr Carter,' she said in her best Irish accent, her grin slightly higher on her left side, but her eyes saddened. 'I hope you find happiness in Ireland.'

So did he, but he wasn't getting his hopes up.

At least it would be a distraction.

Books by R. J. Groves

The Bridal Shop series
Save the Date
Be My Valentine
Say You'll Be Mine

Jilted Brides series
Finding a Bride
Written in the Sand

Cities of the World series
In Paris
The Irish Maiden

Set Ups series
The Set Up

Mail Order Brides series
The Calm in the Storm
The Warmth in the Winter
The Song in the Silence

Standalones
Writing You
Two Babies Too Many
Second Chance
The Boyfriend Application
Sweeter Things
Home Bound
Stay With Me
Her First Noel
When Dreams Come True
To Fall For You

Thank you for reading! I hope you enjoyed this story as much as I did writing it.

R. J. xx

www.ingramcontent.com/pod-product-compliance
Lightning Source LLC
Chambersburg PA
CBHW050007120726
47903CB00006B/1673